DESCENT INTO THE HALLWAY OF MADNESS

By Anthony Di Angelo

Written By: Anthony Di Angelo

a.diangelo1983@gmail.com

First Edition

Disclaimer: This is a work of fiction. Names, characters, places and incidents are the product of the author's imagination or are used fictitiously. Any resemblance to actual events or locales or persons, living or dead, is entirely coincidental.

This book is dedicated to my grandmother who passed her many creative talents down to her children and grandchildren. I miss you every day.

CHAPTER ONE

Detective Jonathan Davis entered his meager apartment and cleaned up his living space. It was how he unwound after a particularly trying case. As he tidied, he contemplated his life choices and replayed his many mistakes. He opened a window and noticed the heat of the California afternoon had given way to a gentle cool breeze. John stood at the window and took a deep breath of the perfumed air. How he loved the scent of distant rain, carried into his apartment on gusts of wind.

He loved his work, but the pursuance of the most heinous of criminals had become routine. More bodies zipped into bags. More evidence tagged and collected. Spending day after day amidst the dark and disturbing deeds of these animals had made John somewhat callous. He blamed the job for ruining his marriage. Ever since the divorce two years ago, he'd felt utterly lost. He craved almost ceaseless action because he couldn't stand the silence of solitude.

After being home for nearly an hour, John thought it best to venture out. He didn't want to dirty his pristine home, so he went to a small tavern nearby to enjoy a burger and a beer. He walked through a cloud of cigarette smoke as he entered the establishment. He immediately felt sick to stomach. How could anyone enjoy such a filthy habit as smoking? This was probably the only vice he had never indulged in.

After he ate his dinner, John wasn't ready to return home. It was far too quiet and lonely. He felt the familiar urge for passion. If nothing else, he could distract himself from his torment of the destruction of his personal life. He swiped through the contacts on his smartphone until he highlighted the intended name. There was always a sense of regret when he called this number and John hated that he was too weak not to call. It was a release that he needed.

After a brief conversation, John hung up the phone. He left the tavern, got in his car and dropped his phone into the glove compartment. As he drove across town to a seedy part of the city, he tried not to think about what he was about to do. The sun set as he drove, and light rain dotted his windshield. When he arrived at the dank, sleazy, pay-by-the-hour motel, he paused, then got out of the car. As a cop, he knew very well that this motel acted as a brothel. He also hated to admit that he was what could be considered a regular.

When he entered his usual room, he was hit with the stink of sweat and desperation. He didn't care. Release was close at hand in the form of a young woman who lay back on the bed. Within a few minutes, the stained walls echoed the moans and screams of passion in perfect synchronicity with the headboard's pace of thumping against the cracked drywall. John's pupils widened as his heart rate steadily increased. His breathing became heavier and heavier as he came closer to reaching climax. As had happened many times before, the strength and vigor of his erection faded. John wrapped his vice-like right hand around the young woman's slender throat and squeezed.

The powerful thrusts of John's hips sped up, his right hand still around the young woman's neck. His grip tightened as he reached climax. John let out a loud moan of pleasure which sounded more like the growl of an animal. He thrust into the woman several more times to extend his pleasure. Then let himself relax. He released his grip from the nearly unconscious woman's neck. She coughed and gasped for the air she desperately needed.

The young woman was a prostitute named Alexis with whom John had a regular standing appointment for nearly a year. She struggled from underneath his heavily muscled body. Her hands had been handcuffed to the headboard and the metal had torn into her skin from the strain.

Blood trickled down Alexis's wrists and forearms. Her chest continued to heave as she tried to catch her breath. She coughed from the pressure exerted on her throat. Black streams of mascara were carried by her tears and rolled down her cheeks as she looked up at John in terror.

Once John caught his breath, he lifted himself off of Alexis. He looked down at the naked woman still bound to the small bed. He admired the way the sweat dripped down the curves of her body. The room was bathed in scarlet red neon from the cheap motel's sign just outside the window. The bright red light captured her curves perfectly as she lay there helpless. John grabbed the towel and wiped himself dry before sitting back down on the mattress.

"J-John." Alexis stammered, trying to mask the fear in her voice. "Unlock me now."

Alexis's voice startled John. He was entranced in thought. "Sorry." He reached for the keys to the handcuffs which were in the pocket of his pants now sprawled on the floor. He paused as he went to unlock her as he noticed the blood dripping down her arms.

"Oh my god," John exclaimed, "I didn't realize. I guess I got carried away there. I'm sorry Al. You okay?" He unlocked both arms and tried to get a look at her wounds. Alexis was quick to pull herself free and rise from the bed.

"Look," Alexis said as she wrapped a robe around her body and covered herself. "This is the last time I'm gonna see you, John."

John removed the handcuffs from the headboard and slowly got dressed. John thought about what had happened between them. He would almost always forget their sessions almost immediately. Being a divorced police detective, John felt guilty of giving into the loneliness of his life to pay for sex with a prostitute. The shame he felt always kicked in and he would erase what he had done from his mind so he would not feel dirty.

"Why?" John asked after he took a moment to think about what had just happened. "I thought you were okay with the roleplay, you never complained before."

"Just please put the cash on the bed and leave. Okay?" Alexis pleaded as she walked towards the bathroom to splash some cool water on her face. She cleaned her tear-smudged make up and winced as she ran the cuts on her wrists under the cool water. Her eyes continued to monitor the mirror to make sure her client left as she requested.

Embarrassed by the shame of what had happened, John finished dressing. He slipped his feet into his loafers and then put on his shirt. He returned his pistol to its holster and slid his arms into his jacket. A quick scan of the small room confirmed he had retrieved everything. He reached into the inner-jacket pocket, he removed a wad of cash and counted out three, one-hundred-dollar bills and tossed them onto the still sweat-soaked sheets of the mattress.

"I'm sorry." John responded as he motioned towards the door. He turned to look at Alexis's face in the bathroom mirror. "What's the problem? What changed? This has always been fine with you."

"Lately, you've been different." Alexis said, she turned to face him while still holding a towel on her bleeding wrist.

"Different ... different how?"

"More aggressive. You know I don't have a problem with it being rough. Usually, I like it. But the last few times you've taken it way too far. Look at my fucking wrists John. Look at my neck," Alexis shouted angrily. She bent her head back and extended her neck to show the dark red handprint that now marked her throat.

"I'm so sorry. I don't know what came over me, Al. I promise it'll never happen again. Next time will be different, I swear." John dropped his eyes down to the floor. He was mortified at how rough he had gotten with her.

"There won't be a next time." She responded sternly. "I've told you the last few times you need to tone it down and it keeps getting worse. We're done here. Goodbye John."

Shame and disgust overcame him as John stared at her wounds in disbelief. His face was hot with embarrassment and he could feel his jaw tremble. "Okay," he said softly. "Here's your money. I'm so sorry." He removed several more bills and added them to Alexis's usual fee as a way of apologizing. He took one last, long and lingering look at the terrified young woman before he left the room.

The rain was falling harder as John made his way to his car. The evening's events played over and over in his mind. He could not make himself remember the sex he just had with Alexis and thus could not recall why she was so upset. What had happened to give her that look of absolute fear? She never had that look before, so what was different this time? His mind raced as the rain fell stronger.

Since his divorce John had begun to explore his darker sexual fantasies. With his wife, the sex was always soft and gentle. They rarely explored different positions and he could get excited simply with the thought of being with her. Now, he could only become excited when simulating rape. The thrill of being so forceful and making his partner submit to his will made him so hot and powerful. Alexis had played the part of a helpless victim perfectly.

When John made it to his car, he started the engine and kept thinking of that look on her face. She looked at him as if he was some sort of freak. The humiliation of what had just transpired filled him with intense disgust. He turned the mirror away from his gaze, he did not want to see his reflection. The shame of the event made him feel dirty and sleazy. Something he often felt after being with Alexis, but this time was even worse.

The sound of the pelting raindrops hitting the metal and glass seemed to mesmerize John as he sat in his car staring back at Alexis's door. His hands were wrapped tight around the steering wheel. His lip quivered, and his eyes welled up with tears as he kept picturing that look of judgment on her face and hearing the spurning sound in her voice over and over in his ears. The devastation of what he had done tormented John. How could he have taken things this far? He felt no better than the long list of scumbags he had arrested over the years.

The buzzing of a cell phone interrupted his tormenting thoughts. The jingling ringtone echoed its annoying melody as he scrambled to remove the device, he had left in the glove compartment. The device's face was illuminating the dark interior of the car as it continued to ring. When John looked down to see who was calling him, he noticed several missed calls from a number he did not recognize with no voicemail. He unlocked the screen and dialed the number.

The phone rang several times then went dead. Frustrated, John hit redial and waited as it went dead again. He considered calling into the station to have the desk clerk rundown the number's address. He waited for a moment bringing up the internet on his smartphone and trying to run his own search yielding no results. He tried once more and was finally successful.

"Hello?" the whispery voice asked.

"This is Detective John Davis. Someone at this number has tried to call me several times."

"I have information on a killer," the voice responded.

John quickly found a notepad and pen to take notes. "Okay. Go ahead."

"Not over the phone," the voice demanded, "meet me at the old abandoned apartment buildings near the industrial district and bring my usual fee."

The call ended and John returned his phone and notepad to his pocket. He recognized the voice, despite the attempt to hide the identity with the whisper. The voice belonged to one of John's confidential informants who called himself, Tricks. John had employed the snitch when he worked in the narcotics division. For a small score, Tricks would give up his own mother. John had received many good leads from this individual's information. All he needed was a small hit of heroine for payment.

John knew where to get the drugs. He once worked as a narcotics officer for over five years. There were small-time dealers he kept in business in exchange for information leading to the arrest of higher profile criminals. The practice seemed too redundant. No matter how many dealers were locked up another one would pop up to take over the clientele. This feeling of pointlessness had plagued John for years now. He had certainly lost the sense of duty he once had when he graduated from the academy so long ago.

Armed with the newly acquired payment of a small plastic bag of heroine, John drove to where he was to meet his informant. He was never scared to venture into these dark parts of the city. He had done battle with the evil doers who dwelled there and had always found a way to be victorious. With his pistol on his hip and a back-up revolver strapped to his ankle, his twelve-gauge shotgun, and his switchblade, he considered himself more fearful than any street hood or murderer he would come across.

The rain had finally stopped. The streets glistened with the amber glow from the surrounding streetlights. The streets in front of the abandoned apartment buildings were eerily quiet and free of cars or people. John parked his unmarked police sedan across the street from where he was to meet his informant. He checked his ammunition and prepared himself.

He went to the trunk and put on his bulletproof vest. He removed his flashlight and extra magazines for his pistol.

"John," the familiar whispery voice called out from the shadows.

"You want your shit, Tricksy? Then get out here and tell me what you know," John responded without turning around.

A slender man exited the shadows and walked over towards John. The man wore a torn track suit that looked dirty and smelled as if it hadn't been washed in years. The skin on the man's hands were blackened with dirt and filth. His face donned a long wiry goatee that had pieces of garbage and the remnants of food stuck to it. The beanie sitting atop the man's head kept his long hair behind his ears. The man was cautious as he approached John, careful to not be seen.

"Jesus," John exclaimed, "ever hear of a shower?"

"You have my stuff?" Tricks asked and ignored John's comment.

"I do," John said, "you'll get it depending on what you have for me. What is so important that you bring me out here in the middle of the night?"

"Do you remember Lucas Durante?" the man asked.

The name immediately caught John's attention. Lucas Durante was a killer who John had been trying to catch ever since he first joined the homicide unit. Durante would target transient young women and brutally rape them for days, sometimes weeks before finally killing them. Over the years John had pieced together evidence which suggested Lucas Durante was the killer but had nothing concrete. There was a witness who described Durante perfectly and could place him at the scene of a body dump but before the police could arrest him, he vanished.

Those cases had long since gone cold. Since the victims were mostly unidentified runaways, the pressure to solve their murders was minimal. This case had stuck with John for years. If he could finally capture Durante, he could maybe recapture that same passion and love for the job he once had when he was a young officer. The families of the victims could finally get peace. John could continue his polished reputation as the department's best homicide detective.

"Of course, I remember him but that was years ago. He is long gone and has been for a very long time." John tried to hide his excitement. The information was coming from a drug addict after all.

"He *was* long gone, but he's back," Tricks replied.

"How do you know this? How do you know Durante? How do you know I was looking for him?" John masked his expression with anger and switched to his more threatening posture in order to get his informant to talk.

"I've been selling to this guy for a while now. He gives me free dope if I bring him girls from the train and bus station. He looked familiar but I didn't think about it. He had some good dope," Tricks Explained.

"Ok, so what makes you think this man is Lucas Durante?" John asked.

"I found this in my place, I collect them." Tricks reached into his track jacket and removed an old newspaper with ripped edges and heavily stained wrinkled pages. The cover had the picture of Lucas Durante with an article asking for the public's assistance in finding the man. The article was dated nine years prior, near the time that Durante had disappeared.

"This is the man you bring girls to?" John asked. He stared down at the picture of the killer he had been chasing for nearly a decade.

"The guy I know looks a little older … a little heavier but I'm positive its him," Tricks insisted. "Now hand over my dope."

"Not so fast," John said as he handed back the old newspaper. "Which building is he in?"

Tricks pointed at the large, dark building directly across the street.

John ordered the dirty man to remain near the car and threatened to withhold his payment if he didn't obey. He wanted to check and make sure this was a good lead before giving the man his drugs. John closed his trunk and locked the car. He made his way swiftly across the street. There was a chain link fence which barricaded the abandoned complex. There were sections that had been cut through and remained open. John found a big enough opening and slipped through. He crept up to the door at the side of the building.

John pried open the door as quietly as he could manage. He clicked on his flashlight and drew his pistol. Tricks had said Durante was held up in an apartment at the far end of the hall on the fourth floor. John slowly climbed stairs listening for any sign of movement. The decrepit stairs creaked with each step he took. Draft winds whistled in the distance. There was a sound of water dripping on the decaying floor through the many holes in the ceiling from the rain. John continued ascending the stairs.

The fourth-floor access door was closed and difficult to push open and remain silent. John crept slowly down the narrow hallway. The windows facing the courtyard were all boarded up. There were lines of amber light that peeked through from the streetlamps and lit up the trails of dust particles which floated in the air. John made his way along the hall. The doors to the surrounding apartments were either removed or open and John was careful to check each room to prevent being ambushed.

The nervous excitement was building in John's stomach as he continued onward. Suddenly there were faint sounds of coughing which emanated from the room at the end of the hall. John was at the door. He could hear more coughing and shuffling from inside. He tried the doorknob, but it was locked. He bit the handle of his flashlight to give himself light. He holstered his pistol to free both his hands, then removed a small pouch from the pocket on his bulletproof vest. It was a lock pick kit. John inserted the small tools into the lock's opening and slowly manipulated the tumblers until he felt it unlock.

John returned the small tools to his vest then armed himself once more with his pistol. He cautiously entered the room. There were gas lanterns around the room providing a dim glow of light. The living room area had the remnants of old furniture. There was women's underwear scattered on the floor amidst dust and garbage. In the kitchen there was a camping stove and a cooler on the countertop. Dirty dishes and opened cans of food and drinks were scattered on the floor covered in dirt and cigarette butts. Glass bottles of various brands of beer and other liquors had been scattered everywhere.

The windows had been completely covered with no visual to the outside. John ventured further into the apartment towards the bedroom. The bathroom had buckets instead of a toilet. The first bedroom was small and had a dirty mattress on the floor. Padding had been secured onto the walls and chains nailed into the floorboards. Someone must've been kept prisoner here and the room had been soundproofed. Polaroid pictures were strewn about the mattress and floor which depicted pornographic scenes with multiple women.

John was alerted by the sound of someone coughing inside the bedroom at the end of the hall behind the final door. He prepared himself and took a deep breath. He stepped into a hard kick to the door directly beneath its handle. The door jam broke into splinters as the door flung open and slammed into the wall. John quickly entered the room with his gun drawn. There was a man laying on the floor surrounded by more polaroid stills. There was an array of sexual devices hanging around the room.

"Police," John shouted at the man on the floor, "show me your hands."

The man was startled by John's loud entry and quickly sat up. He seemed disoriented and confused as he looked around the dark room. He kept shielding his eyes from the brilliant bright light of John's flashlight. John repeated his order and the man did not respond. He appeared to have no idea of what was going on.

"Get on your knees. Put your hands on-top of your head and interlock your fingers. Now," John demanded. His booming voice echoed throughout the dark building.

The man seemed to comply but appeared frightened. His body shook and trembled as he struggled to get onto his knees. John removed his handcuffs and motioned to put them on the man's wrist. He paused for a moment as he saw Alexis's blood still covering the shiny surface. He was quick to return the cuffs to his belt and instead grabbed the plastic zip-tie restraints attached to his vest.

Before John could secure the man's wrist, the suspect used his legs and vaulted off the floor. The back of the man slammed into John and knocked him off balance. The man managed to grab John as he stumbled and drove his head into the wall and knocked him to the floor. John dropped his gun and flashlight from the force. The suspect picked up the pistol and made his escape. John quickly forced himself to recover and gave chase. He removed the small revolver he kept in his ankle holster.

John made it to the door of the apartment. Two gunshots from his stolen pistol were fired and narrowly missed John's head. The suspect ran the same way John had earlier entered the building. John kicked open the door next to the suspect's apartment leading to the second stairway and quickly descended. He took two stairs at a time to make it to the ground floor before the suspect could get away. His mind was still somewhat foggy from the hit against the wall and he struggled to focus as he exited the building.

Several more shots were fired at John in an attempt to keep him from exiting the building and continue his pursuit. The fleeing man made a quick dash for John's car and was blindly shooting the pistol to scare John from chasing. He emptied the remaining rounds of the pistol's magazine as he neared the parked sedan. Almost at the car, his hand stretched out to open the handle. The door was locked. He quickly cocked back his arm to smash the window.

Unfortunately for the suspect, John was a marksman with his pistol. He already exited the building and had taken aim. The first shot hit the suspect's left elbow as he raised his hand to smash the car's window with the pistol's handle. The bullet struck bone as it smashed through the flesh. The strike caused the suspect to drop the weapon. The second shot hit the man behind his right knee. The bullet destroyed the joint and brought the suspect to the ground.

John walked towards the man carefully with his pistol still at the ready. Despite his injuries, the suspect still struggled to escape. He grabbed the pistol off the ground and spun around to take another shot at his pursuer. He had forgotten that he had already spent his ammunition. John fired a third shot aimed at the suspect's shoulder. The man spun around to take his shot at John. The bullet intended for his shoulder struck him in the throat. He gasped and choked and clasped at the wound his throat.

Blood quickly pooled around the man who writhed in pain and panic. John unlocked his car and grabbed his radio from its home on the dashboard. He called in an officer involved shooting. He gave his location and requested immediate medical assistance. He ignored the dispatcher's request for further information as he had to act quickly if he was to keep his suspect alive. He tore a large piece of material from the suspect's jacket and held it tight against the wound on the man's neck to try and stop the bleeding.

In all the excitement John had nearly forgotten about Tricks, his informant still waiting at the car. John wanted to keep his snitch confidential, so he told him to grab his payment of dope from the trunk of his car and leave. Tricks used John's keys to pop the trunk then searched for the plastic bag he so longed for. He found his chemical treasure then disappeared into the shadows from whence he came.

All alone, John looked at the man's face and studied his features. It was certainly Lucas Durante. The man responsible for the deaths of numerous young girls. The man struggled and fought to stay alive and John had the thought of removing his hands from the wound. He could let the monster bleed out. He could spare the taxpayers a lot of money for a trial. Why risk letting some defense attorney getting him off with insanity or some other slippery lawyer tactic? If any man deserved to die it was certainly that man, *Lucas Durante.*

The ambulance arrived within minutes and rushed Lucas Durante to the hospital. The crime scene investigative officers showed-up shortly afterwards and collected their evidence. John cleaned off the blood on his hands and waited to go back into the apartment where he had nearly been killed. The forensic team went through the small space and collected the samples. Fibres and fluids were tagged and logged and placed into plastic bags and carried away in boxes.

John was finally told he could go back into the apartment. The small gas lanterns had been replaced with the halogen work lights of the crime scene team which lit up the killer's dark deeds in profound white light. John walked from room to room looking for clues. He had this thought as he worked that he had been doing this job for too long. There was something strangely familiar about this place and it almost felt as if he had been there before. He ignored the thought and kept searching.

The search had gone on for hours. Countless pieces of evidence had been catalogued and John was about to leave to write up his report. He motioned to leave the bedroom when something caught his eye. There was a rack which held the various sexual torture devices used on the killer's victims that had been removed for evidence. With the rack gone, the wall behind it was left exposed. The entire room had been covered in a dark red wallpaper that had a distinct and intricate pattern. Behind the rack of tools there was a large, squared-shaped piece of wallpaper where the pattern appeared to be upside down.

John removed his knife and used the short blade to pry the piece of wallpapered dry wall. It was put in place as a cover. There was a small locked chest hidden within the wall. John carefully removed it and called a member of the forensic team to scan the box for fingerprints. It had been wiped clean. John asked if anyone had found a small key that might fit in the lock with no such luck. He put his knife back to work and managed to open the lid with little difficulty.

Along with a member of the forensic team, John carefully removed the items from the cabinet and inventoried them. There were various colors of bundled hair and pieces of women's jewelry. There were stacks of polaroid pictures like the ones John had discovered when he first entered apartment. There was also a box filled with a collection of computer memory sticks or flash drives that hopefully belonged to a video camera found in the bedroom earlier. This disturbing collection was likely the killer's trophies.

It was still dark in the early hours of morning when John finally left the crime scene. He drove back to the station with a sense of completion and fulfilment. He had finally caught the killer he had first stumbled onto in his first year as a homicide detective. As he drove back to police headquarters, he reminisced of when he first received his detective shield remembering how proud his wife was of him. Blood had blushed his cheeks as he pictured her smile and her picturesque beauty. He didn't want to admit how much he missed her.

It was nearly a half hour's drive back to the station, but John had veered off course and found himself parked outside his ex-wife's house. She had moved on since the divorce two years earlier and now lived with a doctor from the hospital where she worked as an administrator. He would often find himself parked outside her house with a hope to catch a glimpse of her. He would imagine their life together. How it was. How it should have been. He left before his presence could be noticed.

John returned to the police station and went to the locker room to take a shower. He could still smell Alexis's cheap perfume on his clothes. He didn't want to ruin this feeling of victory with last night's humiliation. He always kept spare clothes in his locker at work for when he worked long nights or in case of a dirty crime scene. A practice he had started when he worked for the narcotics squad. Now that he was showered and in clean clothes, he felt ready to write up his report.

The stationhouse was still quiet. There were few departments still working but all the commanding officers, office staff, and day shift officers were still off shift as it was only four in the morning. John made himself a pot of coffee and enjoyed a cup of it at his desk. He turned on his computer, brought up the required screen, and typed in his information. He recounted the events of what had happened hours before with precise clarity, trying to capture every detail. Several hours and three cups of coffee later, he had nearly finished the paperwork.

The fluorescent lights came on as the morning staff arrived for the day's work. John had been working in the dark and must have fallen asleep at his desk. He gave his report a final read and selected the option to print it out. He sat at his desk waiting for the printer to finish its task. He greeted several of his fellow officers as they started their day. Was it that he was tired from being up all night? Or perhaps remembering his ex-wife made him think of the other woman that was missing from his life. His partner, Selena. John's gaze was fixed on his partner's desk, as it often had since she left, and wondered how she was doing with her troubles.

John walked over and looked at the pictures she kept on her desk. Selena Lopez was his protégé and had become an amazing detective in the short time since achieving the rank. She had been placed on administrative leave since the tragic death of her daughter almost two years ago. She had attempted to return to work months earlier, but it was obvious she wasn't ready. John smiled as he saw the picture of them both at the department's baseball game months before her daughter's death. He sat on the dusty desktop and thought of her. He hadn't spoken to her in such a long time. She refused to return any of his calls or emails. He hoped she was getting better.

* * *

Detective Selena Lopez sat at the bar watching everyone around her enjoy their evening. The small nightclub was crowded with people dancing along to the music blasting from the DJ's speakers. The dancefloor was mixed with men and women grinding along to the rhythm of the bass. Sweaty bodies rubbing against one another as alcohol and drugs fueled their sexual energy and made them seek a connection. She looked over the young males for someone to help keep her mind off her sorrows.

After the consumption of more than her share of drinks, Selena stumbled as she walked on her high-heeled boots. She held herself up at the bar trying to get the bartender's attention for a refill. She had already been turned down and denied service at three other bars that evening. She was having difficulty standing straight and her temper was flaring at the refusal of her request for another drink. The patient bartender tried his best to reason with her. The young man recognized her and had a sense there was something wrong. This was not Selena's first time in the club. She had been frequenting the local bars for some time and it almost always escalated to having her thrown out.

A young college student had overheard the slurred yelling from the other side of the bar. He was quick to notice a beautiful drunken woman fighting with the bartender. Since his only goal for the evening was finding a girl to go home with, one so drunk would be his best bet. He approached Selena as she was about to strike the bartender. He grabbed her fist and slid his freshly poured shot of tequila in her hand. She took the small shot glass and swallowed the golden liquid in one fluid motion.

"Look," the young man said loud enough to be heard over the music, "you're going to get tossed out. Why don't we get out of here?"

Selena threw the shot glass at the bartender and wrapped her arms around her new friend's neck and yelled, "let's go handsome."

He helped Selena into a cab outside the club. She attacked him with a fury of passionate kissing. The driver of the Lugar De Paz City Cab inquired where they wanted to go, Selena gave her address. For the twenty-minute drive she tantalized the young man with her tongue in his mouth and her hands on his body. She had all but removed her shirt leaving her blouse completely unbuttoned and her lace bra and bountiful cleavage fully exposed. She slid off her moistened panties and dropped them into the young man's lap.

The driver tried his best to keep his eyes on the road and off the scene of passionate foreplay in his backseat. They arrived at the given address and Selena exited the cab and stumbled up to the door of a small house. The young man scrambled to give the driver the required fee and get out of the car. By the time he reached the front door, Selena had already opened it and was standing in the living room area removing her remaining clothes.

The young man quickly shut the door behind him and ran towards his next conquest. Selena had removed everything and stood before him completely nude. He wasted no time and lunged towards her. Their mouths met again. They wrestled each other's tongues. His hands grabbed her firm legs. They slid up from her muscular thighs up to her round, firm buttocks. He gave it a playful smack before picking her up and slamming her back onto the couch.

Selena yelped in heat and once on her back she took control and forced his head down to her chest then between her legs. He reciprocated and drove her wild with the force of his tongue on her. He had had enough teasing and tore off his pants. Quick to apply a condom, he slid inside her and thrusted with so much power it slid the couch across the hardwood floor. Their combined screams and moans filled the empty house. In her excitement she took control and forced him onto the floor to straddle him.

The pair of strangers continued their hot, passionate sex for the next hour. They enjoyed each other's bodies until they climaxed again and again. When they had finally concluded their escapades, they fell asleep on the area rug in the middle of the floor. Selena had fallen asleep in the young man's arms and he fell asleep stroking her thick, black hair. They remained in that very same position for several hours.

The alcohol wore off and Selena woke up on the floor. Without any idea of who was lying next to her, Selena felt a sense of panic. Sore and completely naked, she found her shirt and quickly put it on. She kicked the young man still who was still snoring, fast asleep on her rug. She found her panties and put them on as the young man eventually woke up. She tossed him his clothes and looked for the skirt she wore the night before and her purse. The young man barely had the chance to dress before she demanded he leave.

"What the hell is your problem?" he yelled as she pushed him out the door.

"Look, last night was fun but it was a mistake. Please leave," Selena demanded.

"Hey, I'm sorry it happened like that but come on, talk to me. What's your name at least?" he asked as he stood shirtless on the porch with his pants still unbuttoned.

"Detective Selena Lopez, Lugar De Paz homicide, now fuck off," she yelled then slammed the door and swiftly locked it.

Selena walked over to the couch and sat down to piece together her hungover memory. She struggled to replay the events of the night before in her mind. All she could retain were flashes of her latest drunken outburst at the bartender combined with images of sex with another unknown younger man. The recollection left her filled with embarrassment. She found her phone and looked at the pictures, something she would do for several hours a day. She searched for the pictures of her family when her daughter was still alive. She looked down at the small screen which displayed the smiling faces of her ex-husband and late daughter. She remembered her daughter's birthday when they had taken the picture.

The grief, combined with the extremely potent hangover, overcame her. Selena tossed the phone across the room not wanting to remember anymore. She reached into the small table beside the couch and removed her service pistol. Tears poured from her eyes and she was sobbing heavily and calling out her daughter's name to the emptiness of her house. She unlocked the safety mechanism and slid the pistol's muzzle into her mouth to the back of her throat. Her tear glazed eyes stared upon the family picture on the fireplace mantle. She closed her eyes. With a trembling hand, she pulled the trigger.

There was only the metallic sound of a loud click. The pistol's slide stuck open as the chamber was not loaded. Selena removed the pistol from her mouth and dropped in on the floor. Her sobbing got heavier as she lay on the hard floor. She had descended into a dark world of grief. She abused any pleasure, either chemical or physical to keep from living with the pain of losing her daughter and soon after, being left by her husband. The tragedy had left her a broken woman.

* * *

A shadow lurks about the city in the blackness of the night. The dark veil of night is a predator's favourite time. Slithering from shadow to shadow as they stalk their prey. Lying in wait for the right time and place for the perfect ambush. Lurking in the darkest recesses of their surroundings with their intended victims unaware of the impending attack. In the animal kingdom, this is an act of survival. In the world of man, this is a killer's perfected method of satiating a devious thirst for bloodshed.

There are many men and women who have killed and would kill again for various reasons. Self-defense, profit, to keep secrets hidden and protect themselves. They might kill for revenge for some tragic event that had happened to them or someone they care about. But the most dangerous are those who kill for the joy of inflicting pain. The killers who stalk fellow humans for sport. For one serial killer, it had been a long time since this evil game was last played and the monster desired to return from such a long hiatus.

This killer had been hidden away for some time and remained under the protection of a carefully constructed cover life created to hide the truth. The powerful urge, however, had returned. The terrible itch hadn't been scratched for too long. The disgusting addiction could never be overcome or cured. The facade of being an upstanding citizen could no longer suppress the monster dwelling within. The *normal life* mirage had kept this killer feeling as if those animal needs had broken free and the need to kill had dissolved. The desire to take human life returned.

Recently, this killer-in-hiding was driving home from work, where everyone had been fooled into believing the fake persona of a good person. As this predator drove home, instinct took over and the car veered off course. The normal route home was in the opposite direction. The vehicle drove on as if controlled by automatic pilot … as if motivated by some unseen entity.

The car drove by a brightly lit building, illuminated by flashing tubes of neon. The massive sign depicted an exotic dancer sliding up and down a dancer's pole. The dark urge took charge and directed the car to park in an unlit parking lot not far from the striptease establishment. The car was carefully hidden from view of onlookers or cameras. The predator's instinct knew to protect the cover life and put on a hooded sweatshirt to hide the face from sight.

The loud music and pounding bass could be heard from outside the club. There was a large line-up of patrons waiting to enter but were being corralled by the two behemoths guarding the front entrance. Returning to the prowl, this predator knew it was best to remain invisible and cleverly slipped into the side door undetected. Years of perfecting the ability to remain unseen allowed this killer to move like a phantom.

Once inside the club, the hunt had begun. The search for *that special someone* for the grand return to the game had begun. Not just anyone, there were specific prerequisites ... a checklist of attributes the killer would follow for the intended kill. The chosen victim must be a female in her early twenties. The first victim in the cycle of kills always had blonde hair and was usually a prostitute. This killer despised sex workers and took a certain pride when one more was reduced from the herd. Plus, they were less likely to be reported missing.

The club, *Night Moves*, was a popular establishment. On Friday and Saturday nights the space inside stayed filled with both men and women. It was a strip club showcasing female dancers, but the customer base was mixed with men and women alike. The massive crowds came for the music, the large dance floor and cheap drinks. The wise-cracking local DJ also drew a large crowd of his many followers. The gorgeous exotic dancers danced in hanging cages around the club when not dancing in the spotlight on stage.

With heightened senses at the ready, the killer maneuvered through the gathering of sweaty, gyrating bodies grinding together to the rhythm of the popular DJ's track list. The killer's predatory eyes scanned the crowd while breezing from one dark corner to the next as everyone partied. The thrill of the hunt returned and honed this killer's senses as the search for the perfect victim continued. None of these drunken, drugged, and sweaty fools knew the danger lurking; that one of them was now being picked for slaughter.

Time passed slowly and the killer's eyes combed the crowd with much dismay. The hopes of escaping from the shackles of a *normal life* and returning to the thrill of killing had become deflated as the search thus far yielded no worthwhile results. There was no one matching the checklist for the prey. Frustrated, the killer was about to leave when those animal eyes spotted the long, flowing, blonde hair on a young woman now exiting the private backroom where the dancers changed clothes and put on makeup in preparation for their performances.

Her light hair swayed capturing the blinking lights off the dance floor. Her beauty turned heads. The intentions could be read on all the men's faces as she sauntered by. Men with girlfriends were sneaking glances at the beauty as she glided through the crowd. Woman stared too with daggers in their eyes. All were jealous of the dancer's profound beauty.

The young female took a seat at the bar and chatted with the males around her. She was tantalizing potential clients with a private dance. Although there were many offers, she kept negotiating for a higher price. She was sizing up the customers to see which ones had the largest bank account. The way she carried herself and controlled her admirers, the beautiful lady appeared to have been doing this type of negotiation for quite some time. Finally, she chose one of the men and led him by the hand to the V.I.P. room.

Within seconds, the killer slyly removed his cell phone and snapped pictures of the young woman's face before she exited to perform her private dance. The prey had been chosen and the attack method had begun. Now, it was time to conduct more research. Heightened with excitement, the predator exited the club and waited out of view in a dark corner of the parking lot. With eyes focused like a hawk, the slayer leered down like a bird of prey from its perch looking for a field mouse.

The hours passed and finally the crowds poured out of the club. There was a line of taxis and Uber drivers picking up their drunken fares. Many of the patron's cars had been left behind in the parking lot. The predator remained hidden in position with an unflinching gaze fixed on the club. A collection of burnt out cigarette butts had formed outside the car window. The blue smoke encircled the prowler's head with a freshly lit smoke held firmly between pursed lips. A golden *Zippo* lighter twirled between the anxious fingers of its left hand.

When the lights finally went out, the two large guards walked several scantily clad young ladies to their cars and watched them drive away. The chosen blonde was one of the last to exit the building. She got into her European sports car and sped off into the night. Unfortunately, not before the killer snapped photos of her license plate.

It was easy for the predator to catch up to the dark-colored sports car. The killer stayed several car lengths behind to remain undetected. Many years of experience made this killer an expert in these twisted methods and was fluent in the ways of stalking. Using the cover job as a way of perfecting the dark craft without anyone being aware.

The young woman parked her car in a parking structure across from a rather expensive apartment building. The would-be attacker crept in and located her parking stall and was able to discern which apartment was hers. The night's research had provided adequate intel. The killer left the area to finally head home.

With the victim chosen, the killer now spent the next several days looking into the young woman's lifestyle. The killer's day job aided in the research as the kill was being planned and prepared. Still, the cycle needed one more element that had yet to be attained. While the killer had painstakingly chosen the intended young woman who fit the criteria, there was something else the checklist demanded … a detective.

This killer had operated this way for years. With each cycle of kills there was the need to taunt the male or female who would be heading the investigation. A detective had to be chosen and with the same precise detail used to profile the victim. The killer would research the gumshoe and thus begin the game of cat-and-mouse that had been ongoing for years.

Perhaps, this killer enjoyed the possibility of being caught more than the kill itself. Perhaps the killer wanted to be stopped. Either way, the killer needed to find a worthy adversary before proceeding with the return to the game.

For nearly two weeks the killer had spent long hours watching the young dancer live her life. Her routine had been memorized and the killer had even sampled her private show. Pictures of the young dancer adorned the walls of the killer's secret hideaway, where the dark deeds were to be committed and where the collection of trophies were kept. Still, the game was unable to begin without the challenge of a detective. Fate intervened in the delivery of the city's most popular newspaper, *The Lugar De Paz Gazette.*

The killer prepared to start another boring day of the cover life. The newspaper provided the last requirement to start the game. On the front page was a photo of a handsome detective having successfully captured another feared killer. The man was heralded as a hero. The article mentioned how this detective was the pride of the Lugar De Paz police department and had brought many bad men and women to justice. The city honored the detective for his bravery and courage and painted the picture of him being somewhat of a superhero.

The thrill of the hunt had supercharged the urge to kill. The predatory senses all tingled with excitement like a drug addict about to pump poison into their veins or a drunk about to down another bottle. The killer had found a worthy adversary. It would be an epic duel … an ultimate challenge to overcome. If this man was the city's hero, he would have to prove it to catch this villain. The killer set out a plan to stalk his next pursuer while admiring the man's frontpage photo and studied the name intently. Detective Johnathan Davis.

CHAPTER TWO

The small briefing room attached to the homicide division was filled with detectives and fellow officers awaiting the day's orders from their commander. John stood in the back sipping the coffee he had poured moments earlier. He listened to the combined chatter of the men and women engaged in their conversations.

John had always felt somewhat socially separate from everyone. Not that he didn't enjoy being around people, he simply found the activity of gossip and small talk pointless and chose to remain removed to enjoy his coffee with the peace of his own thoughts.

The Deputy Chief entered the room with homicide's Captain Thomas McGee directly behind. The room fell silent as the two men walked to the front. The captain had a stack of files in his hands and wrote stats and facts onto the large whiteboard behind the podium at the front of the room. He clipped a picture of Lucas Durante at the top of the board then turned around to face his audience.

"Good morning everyone," Captain McGee announced, "let's get started. First, I would like to congratulate Detective John Davis on his apprehension of

Lucas Durante. This has been a long time coming and we finally got this son-of-a-bitch."

The crowd roared with applause. The people nearest John patted his shoulders and shared in the captain's enthusiasm. John remained still and reciprocated with his usual quiet smile of appreciation. He hated being put on the spot and wanted to get on with the meeting. He waited for the room to return to silence and he focused his attention back on the captain who had moved on to discuss the latest homicide cases to hit the active list.

"We have several new cases open as of this morning everyone," the captain continued. "There was an apparent murder/suicide uptown, looks like a squabble between husband and wife. There was a case of road rage in early morning traffic, a man was shot to death for cutting someone off. We also have a dead escort or stripper located near her place of work. I have issued everyone today's assignments; the new cases have been assigned so check the board. Let's be safe out there everyone. John, come see me in my office please."

John nodded with his compliance. He went to the board and saw he had been assigned the escort body dump. He knew that area well. It was near a gentleman's club called, Night Moves. The same club where he had met Alexis. John was already considering the case as good as solved since he had a good working relationship with the club's owner and knew most of the women who worked there. He left the briefing room to accompany his captain in his office as requested.

The small office's walls were littered with the framed achievements of the honorable Captain McGee, a thirty-year veteran of the police force. He was considered a living legend, having captured some of the most infamous criminals and breaking up some powerful street gangs. John admired the history staring down at him from the hooks on the walls. He hoped he might one day have the same legacy.

"Take a seat," the captain said, interrupting John's viewing. "I read your report on Durante's capture. I still don't understand why you went all the way out there without notifying anyone. You mention a confidential informant without including his name. Who is he?'

"My informant's name is Tricks," John explained, "he is a snitch I bailed out back in narcotics. He is a little heroin-fueled rat. Don't get me wrong, he has given a lot of good leads over the years, but he has also wasted my time a great deal. I only use him when absolutely necessary."

"How did he recognize Lucas Durante after all this time?" the captain asked.

"Tricks told me that he had been exchanging girls for dope. According to Tricks, Durante recently showed up in town. He hasn't been here long," John said. "Tricks said there was something about Durante that scared him. After bringing him a few girls, Tricks would never see them again. He recognized Durante's face as being familiar and checked his collection of old newspaper clippings and found an article on Durante's escape. Once Tricks made the connection, he called me."

"So, you went out there all alone?" Captain McGee asked with a disapproving tone.

"Like I said captain, half the time Tricks' information ends up being bullshit. I thought he was stoned and wasn't expecting to find anything out there," John explained trying to win favor back with the captain. "Besides, I wouldn't be out there alone if I had my partner. How is Detective Lopez anyway?"

"Still struggling apparently, but I'm hoping to bring her back soon," the captain replied. "Next time you're called out in the middle of the night to abandoned buildings in a bad area, call for back-up. I won't stand for any rogue activity, understand?"

"Yes sir." John replied.

"Mr. Durante is currently in a coma, so we have to wait to pursue charges, but the evidence found in his possession is piling up. Make sure you follow up with forensics and keep me apprised on their findings," the captain ordered as he flipped through another file folder.

"Of course, sir," John responded watching the captain intently. The man would always shuffle paperwork in this manner when he wanted to discuss something sensitive or uncomfortable. John sensed the captain had more to say.

"Are you still keeping up your appointments with Dr Morrison?" the captain asked still flipping through papers pretending to read them.

"I am sir, she is helping quite a bit. Helps me keep things in perspective," John answered. Dr Morrison was his psychiatrist whom the captain ordered John to see after his divorce led him down a dark path like the one his partner was currently traveling down.

"Good, keep that up," the captain said meeting John's gaze with a slight smile. "One last thing John. I'm giving you the Night Moves call girl case because I know you have your connection to the owner and his family. Don't let your association with them or your social life impede the investigation. Close the door behind you please."

The door closed behind John and he made his way to his desk. John wasn't impressed with his captain's comment. Everyone had always suspected John of being on the take when he was working in narcotics. He always had extravagant things and extra cash and would often be seen with the owner of Night Moves who was the grandson of a well-known crime boss. John would always challenge the allegations though they were partly true.

John left the station with the files of his new case and drove to his favorite coffee shop to brief himself on his next investigation. He knew it was too early to pay a visit to Night Moves, since it was still morning, and no one would be there. He still had nearly two hours to kill before his appointment with Dr Morrison and he wanted to get out of the station for a while. Too many people within such close quarters made it difficult for him to concentrate on his cases. He often would retreat to where he could think. It was his process.

The small coffee shop was decorated in the style of a fifties themed, nostalgia diner. There was a large counter with chrome-rimmed bar stools, large booths with the tables equally chrome-rimmed. The open concept to the kitchen filled the small space with the delicious and fresh food being prepared in back. John proffered this place to any of the corporate coffee chains for the friendly service and quite frankly the better-quality coffee and food.

The booth at the far end of the restaurant had the largest window that overlooked the busy street. This was John's usual booth. The staff all knew John by name due to his frequenting the establishment several times a week for over a decade. The waitresses would often flirt with John or the owner would come out and have a pleasant conversation. It was a friendly atmosphere and John was glad that most of the other cops didn't come there. They had all gravitated to their lattes and cappuccinos of the big chain stores and John felt all the luckier for it. He enjoyed having this place all to himself.

The usual order of eggs benedict with soft-poached eggs and extra hollandaise was placed in and John was already pouring his second cup of coffee as he read the pages of the forensics report. He took a moment and looked around the room surrounded by the black and white pictures of old-time stars of music and movies. The faces of Marilyn Monroe, Elvis, James Dean, Steve McQueen, and Natalie Wood all watching him with their eternal smiles. Then John noticed the picture of Anna-Maria Lopez, the late daughter of his partner Selena.

John had brought his partner Selena to the coffee shop many times. She enjoyed the place as much as John and they would always discuss cases here or celebrate the success of another one closed. When Selena's daughter was looking for part-time work, John had suggested she apply at the coffee shop where Selena could keep an eye on her, and the teen could earn some money of her own. The staff welcomed her in, and it wasn't long before she was working there full-time. Now the picture of her haunting beauty adorned the walls next to countless other young faces of those who had long since died.

Not wanting to dwell on personal tragedy, John returned his focus to the pages of his new case. He read over the report of how the body had been discovered and waited for his breakfast. He finished his meal and several more cups of coffee until it was close to his appointment with Dr Morrison. He left the comfort of his usual diner and got into his car. What pain would be brought to the surface today? John wondered as he started his car and drove towards the medical center.

The usual secretary, a young and plucky college student, checked John in upon his arrival at Dr Morrison's office and asked him to wait in the waiting area. John was early as usual and pretended to read one of the magazines while he waited for Dr Morrison to see him. He was the only one in the small waiting area, which made John feel more at ease. He hated being seen at the office of a therapist. He hated the thought of people seeing him as a freak or thinking there was something wrong with him.

After waiting nearly thirty minutes, the perky receptionist instructed John to go into the office to see the doctor. John entered the dark office and motioned to greet the doctor in his usual manner, but she was on the phone. He sat in his usual chair and found himself admiring the doctor. She was a classy and strikingly beautiful woman in her early forties, who had maintained her youth and stunning figure very well. John often found himself wondering if this was why he continued to see her on a regular basis since he believed he honestly did not require therapy.

The beautiful doctor ended her phone call and sat across from John. She seductively crossed her long legs and placed her notepad in her lap to take notes of their latest session. John struggled to keep his eyes from admiring her shapely, pantyhose covered legs and instead focused his attention on what appeared to be a newly acquired painting that the doctor had hung behind her desk. She hadn't noticed his leering gaze.

"Hello John, how are things this week?" Dr Morrison inquired as she looked up from the yellow pages of her legal pad.

"Good," John answered, nodding, still trying not to stare at her legs but make eye contact. "Great in fact. Last night I actually captured a perp I've been after since first joining homicide."

"Congratulations. Good for you," Dr Morrison said with the approving tone of a kindergarten teacher praising a child for completing a finger painting. "How did that make you feel?"

"Accomplished. Good. Until after I wrapped things up at the crime scene, before making my way back to the station, I wound up outside my ex-wife's house staring. I sat out there hoping to catch a glimpse of her," John answered watching the doctor's slender hands scribbling down notes.

"You're still seeking her approval. Anytime you've stumbled, you return to her to set things right. Anytime you've succeeded, you return to her to share the success in hopes of changing her opinion of you. As we've discussed many times, you can't keep torturing yourself or her by intruding on her life like this," Dr Morrison said sternly.

"I know, but I didn't intrude, I simply parked on the road and watched the house. I wasn't there long. Just sat there a moment remembering how things were. That's all," John said, defending his actions.

"And if she happened to see you, she would complain to Captain McGee again and he would order you be put on leave. Is that what you want?" Dr Morrison added.

"No." John barked back.

"Okay. Good. So how is everything else? You mentioned in previous sessions that you've been seeing someone recently, how's that going?" Dr Morrison asked in her soft, whispery voice. She looked up from her notes and caught John eyeing up her legs. He was quick to stop.

"Not so good. We broke up right before I received the tip about my suspect." John answered, his face turning red for having been caught looking at the doctor. She pretended not to notice.

"That's too bad, what happened?" Dr Morrison asked.

"We were fooling around and…" John paused, he didn't share with the doctor that he was seeing a prostitute and certainly didn't want to share last night's embarrassing encounter. He decided to lie, "well, she became too aggressive for my liking. This has happened a lot recently and I just had enough. I also suspect she has been seeing other men, so I decided to end things."

"I'm sorry to hear that. Better to find out these things early on than after things become too serious wouldn't you agree?" she said, her voice shifted to her more comforting tone.

The appointment continued in its usual manner. John answered the doctor's questions as best he could and shared only what he felt was necessary. He kept out the truth of how often and long he would sit outside his ex-wife's house hoping to see her. He certainly didn't mention the truth about his time with Alexis. He believed everything the doctor wrote down in her notes would go directly to his captain, regardless of what she said about confidentiality. He counted the minutes until he would be excused and could get back to work.

Finally freed from the confines of the emotional self discovery session he was forced to endure every week with Dr Morrison, John returned to his apartment. It was a small, one-bedroom place not far from the station. After such a long night, all John wanted to do was sleep. He quickly made a call into forensics to inquire how far they had come in processing the evidence from last night's crime scene. Their final report wouldn't be completed for a few days. John had to wait until the evening before he could question everyone at Night Moves, so he decided to get some well-deserved sleep.

After tidying his compulsively neat apartment, John closed his blinds and lay on his couch. He popped a few pills prescribed from Dr Morrison to help with his anxiety and

obsessive thoughts and downed a glass of his favourite rum
mixed with cola over ice. He turned on the television and
found the sports channel to catch the highlights of games he
had missed while working his case the night before until
exhaustion caught up with him and forced him into slumber.
His dreams returned him to last night's events. He revisited
the feeling of capturing a suspect and being a hero, a good
guy.

* * *

Hot water poured from the showerhead in a powerful stream.
Steam filled the bathroom and misted up the mirrors. Selena
sat on the floor of the tub clutching her knees with her head
buried in her arms. She was trying to wash away the shame of
sleeping with yet another unknown stranger. After a long
while she stood and scrubbed herself from head to toe with her
favourite, coconut-scented soap. She shampooed and
conditioned her long black hair, the suds being swept from her
skin and washed down the drain. If only the pain of life could
be carried away so easily.

　　　Selena exited her shower and wrapped her towel
around her chest letting it hang to her knees. She wiped away
the cloudy residue on the mirror and examined her reflection
to make sure last night's make up was all removed. As she ran
a comb through her thick hair, she could hear her doorbell

ringing followed by the thumping of a fist pounding on her front door. She removed her towel and replaced it with her long bathrobe to cover her still wet and naked body. She quickly tied it closed and made her way to the door hoping it wasn't the young stranger she had kicked out hours earlier.

A quick glance revealed that it was Captain McGee outside her front door. On second thought, Selena would have rather it been the young man than her captain coming for a visit. Reluctantly, she opened the door and let the captain in. She was suddenly aware that she was still relatively nude and looked around her house in such disarray. She felt the sting of disgraceful humiliation. The captain walked into the living room and scanned over the mess with disapproving eyes then looked back at Selena, who was motioning for him to sit in the kitchen.

"I would ask how you're doing, but I think I already have that answer from looking at this dump," Captain McGee said. He sat at the kitchen table, pushing a pile of old newspapers out of his way. There was a look of pure disgust on his face as he looked around the kitchen. Old food containers, liquor bottles, drug paraphernalia, and days worth of dirtied dishes scattered upon every counter surface and table.

"I-I'm sorry captain. You want some coffee of something?" Selena asked shyly, pulling her robe closed.

"Selena, it pains me to see you like this. You're one of my best detectives. I know you've suffered an unspeakable tragedy, but you need to pull yourself together. I need you back kid," the captain said with his sincerest tone.

"Look at what's on the floor in front of my couch," Selena said as tears formed in her eyes. She directed the captain's attention to her living room where her empty pistol lay on the floor from her botched suicide attempt earlier that morning.

"After drunkenly bringing home a stray from the bar and screwing his brains out without even asking a name. I woke up and stuck my service pistol in my mouth and pulled the trigger. If it wasn't empty, you would've rolled up on a dead body. How's that for your prize detective huh?"

The captain didn't react. He looked away from the pistol and back at Selena who was sobbing harder now. He thought for a moment. He silently studied this young woman whom he thought of as a daughter and said, "Selena, look at me." She wiped her eyes and looked up, the captain cleared his throat and continued, "you are a prize detective. You're in a bad way right now. You might not realize, but you would have known on some level that that pistol was empty. You're an expert marksman."

"So, what are you saying?" Selena asked, grabbing a tissue to wipe her face.

"You're in pain but you're no fool. If you really wanted to kill yourself, you would've long before now. I think you need the job as much as it needs you. Your mind needs the challenge. So, get up off your ass, get your shit together and get back to work." The captain said sternly, switching tactics from caring and concerned to tough love.

"The department's shrink will never sign off, and I don't think I'm ready captain," Selena explained.

The captain knelt in front of Selena looking her straight in the eyes to strongly make his point. "You'll never be ready if you keep stewing in your own grief. Drowning your sorrows in booze, pot, and random sex. You keep telling yourself you're not ready, you never will be. You're a fighter. You're stronger than any man in my unit. You tell yourself you're ready and you will be. I'll always have your back and will help you the whole way. Climb out of this pit you're in girl. Come back to the world."

"What if I screw things up?" Selena replied.

"Then it'll be both our asses on the line," Captain McGee said through a slight chuckle. "I'll talk to the shrink and have her sign a conditional return. Okay?"

"Yes sir." Selena said, managing a smile.

"Good. Now clean this shithole up it stinks in here. I'll see you on Monday," the captain said as he stood to leave.

The Captain neared the front door and turned to find Selena directly behind him to walk him out. She wrapped her arms around him, hugged him tightly, and thanked him for believing in her. He gave her a kiss on the cheek before leaving the house.

Selena locked the door then turned and looked down at something touching her feet. It was her phone from where she had tossed it the night before. She turned it on to the picture of her daughter on her birthday. The image of her perfect smile and incredible beauty looked up at her. The happiness of her then proud husband as he had his arms around his wife and daughter frozen in the image. What a wonderful day that was.

As she stared down at the illuminated screen, Selena made a secret vow. A promise to her daughter. No longer would she wallow in her self-pity. No longer would she waste her life. If she was going back to the force, she would find her daughter's killer at all cost and make him pay.

* * *

The Lugar De Paz community park was a happy and peaceful place filled with people enjoying the hot, southern Californian sunshine. Couples walking together, hand-in-hand, stealing kisses and taking selfies to capture their memories. Joggers were working on keeping up with their fitness routines while games of sport were being played in the distance. Groups of children were at play running around and cheerfully screaming as other fellow park visitors quietly sat enjoying a novel or working on their laptops. All appeared as sheep to the wolf that sat observing them.

Among the peaceful quiet and beautiful serenity of the park, a killer sat on one of the many park benches in perfect disguise, completely invisible to those who passed by. People laughed and played around this entity who was void of the basest of human feeling. As the killer sat in observance of these people living their lives the urge to inflict pain upon them taunted this predator's troubled mind.

The parkgoers were completely unaware of the evil that was watching them, judging them, imagining hurting them in terrible ways. The eyes were scanning over each potential victim. Imagined visions of abduction and torture flowed through this troubled brain. There was no peace for a mind so disturbed.

A small puppy ran beneath the bench drawing the killer's attention. There was a pink leash attached to a sparkling collar. A precocious little girl broke free from her mother's side to recapture her furry playmate. The cheerful child skipped after her dog. The killer extinguished a freshly lit cigarette and wafted away the smoke as the girl approached. She was so innocent and trusting, speaking candidly when the killer inquired about the dog's name as well as her own.

The sweet child continued talking and the killer's predatory nature imagined unspeakable acts of hurting her. The mother was standing at the park's entrance, immersed in whatever appeared on her smartphone's screen, completely oblivious as to where her child had run off to. The killer scanned the area. It would be all too easy to take the child and remain entirely unnoticed. There was a van nearby with its door left open and its owner far from sight. Everyone's attentions were focused on their own lives. No one would notice if one little girl went missing from it.

The killer brushed a long, loose strand of the girl's silky blonde hair away from her face and tucked it behind her ear. This horrible predator thought of how easy it would be to overpower her and take her away. Cover her small mouth and place her in the vacant van. Her small form would be easy to carry away quickly. The little girl was so trusting of the killer's cover that she would gladly follow without protest. To kill her might be the lesson her incompetent, unobservant mother needed to put down her smart device and pay attention to what really mattered.

Alas, the killer patted the little girl's head and instructed her to take her dog back to her mother and never talk to strangers. This evil hunter watched her little legs carry her tiny form with her small dog in tow. She ran back to her mother who was too entranced with her phone she hadn't noticed the girl had run off. The mother had no idea how close she had come to losing what mattered most. The killer took one last look at the little girl. Luckily, she was far too young for the checklist this killer used as a template when choosing a victim. "Maybe in a few years," the killer thought.

Beyond where the unobservant mother stood with her curious little girl, sat the killer's true intended target. This hunter had been watching a second, beautiful young woman. A woman who met every criterion on the checklist. She would stop at this park every afternoon in her form-fitting yoga outfit and run several laps around the large area. This had been her routine each day before she started her evening of pleasuring her clients at the sleazy motel where she conducted her business.

As the young woman jogged past where the killer sat, the stalking continued as the hunter slowly followed its prey from a distance. The killer watched closely and intensely. It was discovered in the reconnaissance that this young woman knew Detective John Davis and would provide another glimpse into the hero cop's activities.

The brilliant light of the neon sign shone brightly in the night sky lighting up the heavy raindrops as they fell. The sign blinking the words: "MOTEL", "VACANCY", and "HOURLY RATES". A haven for seedy individuals seeking the comfort of those willing to sell their sexuality and bodies. The many customers, or "Johns", coming and going in the veil of darkness. Police officers ignoring the goings on at this establishment with half of its customers wearing badges.

Hiding in the shadows, intently watching the happenings at the hotel, a dark figure peered through the blackness. With eyes affixed upon the many people and the activities that transpired there. The dark figure glided unseen from room to room, peering through the windows to bear witness to various devious acts that were unfolding. Husbands were cheating on their wives. Lonely businessmen were seeking a little entertainment for the evening. The cops receiving payment to look the other way. It was a turn on for this figure to watch such debauchery.

The shadowy specter was focused on one room, listening intently as moans of orgasm turned to a heated argument. Through a crack in the window shade, a man was clearly visible with a look of pure embarrassment on his face for acting out his lesser desires and had taken things too far.

The figure smirked at the sight of the marks on the woman's neck and the blood on her wrists from the handcuffs used in the couple's sex play. Watching the man's face express a look of disgust and horror in what he had done. The figure quickly returned to the shadows and watched the man exit the room. He stopped himself several times and hesitated on returning to the young woman before he gave up and walked out into the rain.

The man hadn't noticed the dark figure watching from the shadows as he got into his car. The figure studied him. Watched as the man stared up at the motel room trying to decide whether to go back and apologize or leave. The unseen figure stood in the rain outside the man's car hoping he would get out. He dared him to go back to that room, wrap his large hands around the whore's slender neck and end her life. But the man drove away. The shadowy figure smiled slyly, and thought, "not tonight Detective Davis, but soon".

CHAPTER THREE

The coolness of the shower's strong stream was soothing on John's skin as he stood with his face directly under the flowing water to wake himself up. The exhaustion from last night's events had made John forget to switch on his air-conditioner before falling asleep. The late afternoon sun had turned the small apartment into a convection oven making sleep impossible. John had planned to wake up early regardless.

After the usual routine of getting ready and enjoying a quick bite to eat, John drove back to the station. He was scheduled to meet with the Internal Affairs division and review board to discuss the shooting he had been involved in. It was a frustrating practice. It was bothersome to John to have to justify his every action on duty to these pencil-pushers in their fancy suits, whose only goal is to bring down good cops for simply doing their jobs.

The meeting was thankfully short, and John had been cleared. The shooting the night before was deemed clean by the board. As he had many times before, John did his best to hide his contempt for the men and women that made up the judgemental review board and was quick to leave the building.

There was a sense of falling behind and John was eager to get started on his new case.

After exiting the police headquarters building, John had to walk through the community park to the only empty space where he could safely park his car. He walked up the narrow pathways, dodging groups of joggers. His mind was full of questions. He replayed the interview with Internal Affairs. Had he answered all the questions correctly? Did they believe his recollection of events? He stomped through the park with his head in the clouds, not paying attention to those around him.

John neared his sedan parked next to an open delivery van. He walked past an ice cream truck and stumbled over a dog's leash. He spun around to see if the dog was alright and the sight of a darling little girl in a sundress. She was holding the small animal's brightly colored leash which caught his eye. He apologized for tripping over her dog and asked her the playful pup's name. It was amazing to John how well children trusted police officers. As he playfully joked with the child, she acted as if she already knew him and chatted with him about how her puppy really liked him.

He struggled to hide his obvious frustration. John got the mother's attention and nonchalantly mentioned that she should keep a better eye on her daughter and be less focused on her cell phone. He couldn't help but think of what could be so important on that screen to take a parent's focus off their child. Mother and daughter walked away with the dog skipping happily behind them.

John couldn't help but fantasize about a life where he and his wife had never divorced and had a child of their own like this delightful little girl. He smiled as he imagined himself as a father, caring for a sweet child and spoiling her. As the pair walked put of sight, John returned his mind to the crime scene he had to visit. In that moment, he saw his job's true meaning. To protect sweet, innocent, vulnerable children, like that wonderful little girl with her dog, from the vile scum who might harm them.

The yellow crime scene tape marked off last night's gruesome display. Blood stains soaked the ground where the corpse had been laid out and fully exposed for all to see. John opened the case file and carefully tried to recreate the scene in his mind. He looked over the many photographs that had been taken by the crime scene team and set his detective brain to work to get a sense of who the killer might have been.

John carefully walked over the crime scene and let his imagination run wild. Like a twisted horror movie, John's mind played out the events as if he were committing the act himself. Some might consider him a heretic or some form of psychic with his ability to picture the scene through the killer's eyes. He imagined himself as the killer. He pictured himself positioning the nude body of the young woman in the specific way she had been discovered. John replayed this hypothetical movie over and over in his mind as he paced back and forth within the yellow tape's barricade.

The evening sun had dropped and turned to dusk. The lingering heat faded with the gentle, cooling, evening breeze. John remained patrolling the crime scene unaware that he had already spent hours pacing over the same area repeatedly. He had an incredible knack for imagining what had happened. His creative mind allowed him to step into a killer's shoes and picture the crime as it took place. This had proven a useful skill and helped him close a lot of cases. This dark skill made him appear a freak to those around him except for his partner, Detective Selena Lopez who had a similar ability.

Dusk was swiftly turning to night when John felt he had a firm grasp of what might have happened. Being a seasoned homicide detective, it was obvious at first glance that this was merely a drop site. The victim had been killed somewhere else and her body strategically placed behind the popular club "Night Moves". Why this club? The profession of prostitution was dangerous and everyday young women become victims. This young woman had been murdered for a reason and John intended to discover it.

The club's neon lighting had been switched on and the semi-pornographic sign was buzzing its bright lights into the night, enticing lonely and erotically charged customers to venture inside. The club's animated sign, the silhouette of a nude woman spinning up and down on a stripper's pole, stood high on the roof of the building and could be seen for miles around. The neon invited all manner of men and women to engage in their sexual desires and pass the time of a lonely evening with the beautiful dancers inside.

There were two massive men who looked more like boxers than bouncers guarding the front door of the club. Certainly, a formidable sight for most, but John wasn't intimidated. These men, along with most other employees knew John from his past dealings with the club's owner when John worked in narcotics. The men stepped aside to allow him entry without having to flash his badge.

The club was yet to open for the evening. Employees were buzzing around the interior preparing for another busy night. The bartenders were stocking the bar and the coolers with fresh bottles to serve. The servers were cleaning glasses and tidying up the tables. The DJ was busy setting up his sound system and preparing his track-lists. The dancers were arriving and heading to the dressing room to prepare for their performances. John followed his memory and headed to the back stairs which led to the manager's office that overlooked the entire club.

"Johnny," a familiar voice boomed as the door opened to let John in after knocking several times. The manager waved his hand to greet John into the office and give him a slight welcoming hug, "it has been too long man, how the hell are you?"

"Good," John replied, glancing around the large office casually looking for clues. "Is Business going well Sal?"

Salvatore Di Sano managed Night Moves for his father and had helped build the business from the ground up. To the public eye, he was a simple and successful club owner. In truth, he was involved in much more clandestine activities. His father and grandfather headed one of the more powerful crime families that had moved to California from back east in the early eighties.

The Di Sano Family was involved in many businesses and were greatly feared and respected in the criminal underworld. Back when he worked as a narcotics officer, John was considered on their payroll. He was often given a lot of cash to look the other way and had committed other crimes that helped keep the family out of law enforcement's crosshairs.

"Same shit, different day. You know how it is. What can I do for you Johnny-Boy?" Salvatore asked as he mixed a rum and cola over ice at the wet bar behind the large desk.

"As you're aware," John said as he accepted the drink offered to him by Salvatore and took a long sip, "I'm with homicide now. There was a young woman's body dumped in the vacant lot near the club and I've been assigned the case. I'm here as a courtesy to you and looking into what happened."

"I noticed the yellow tape as I drove in this afternoon. Any idea who the girl was?" Salvatore inquired as he sat behind his large desk, clutching a cigar between his teeth and igniting its tip.

John stifled his intense dislike for the smell of smoke and focused on studying his old friend's reaction for any sign that he might have been involved in the victim's demise. After a short pause he removed a picture taken of the corpse. It was a close-up image of her face. He handed the gruesome image to Salvatore. "Recognize her?" John asked, still watching Salvatore's reaction intently.

"Yeah," Salvatore said, a look of disgust swept over his face. "She's one of my girls. She hasn't been here in over a week as far as I know. Last Friday, I think, was her last show here."

"What's her name?" John inquired returning the picture to the file folder taking out his notepad and pen and wrote down his thoughts.

"Stephania Milovich, she went by the stage name, Eden. She's part of the circuit that we move between clubs up in L.A. and San Francisco, Vegas, Reno, Florida. You know. She's been here a few months." Salvatore slid his chair across the floor to the safe against the wall. He opened the heavy door and removed a small box with flash drives. He chose one from the collection and inserted it into his computer and opened the files on the monitor.

Salvatore printed out the paperwork confirming the identity of the slain exotic dancer. John took the opportunity to look around the office. It had been a long time since he had last been there. He thought of all the small jobs he used to do for Salvatore and the money he had made, both for himself and the Di Sano family. John knew Salvatore was a criminal, but the man followed a strict code and would never harm an innocent. He would never have killed one of his girls. John finished his drink and waited for Salvatore to finish what he was doing.

"This is all I have on the girl," Salvatore said as he removed several pages from the printer tray and handed them to John.

John graciously accepted the information and continued his conversation with his old friend which did not help much with the investigation. The girl was an illegal immigrant who had stayed in the country far beyond the date on her travel visa. She was hired originally by Salvatore's organization at one of their clubs in Florida but wanted to move to California with dreams of making it to Hollywood. There wasn't much information to work on.

The two old friends recalled their past dealings and chatted about various other things not pertaining to the case. John always kept an off-the-record policy with any information given to him by Sal as to keep his connection to a known criminal a secret. After a second drink John said he had to get back to work and mentioned he would have to question the staff before they opened for the night and required any security footage of the night before.

It was close to opening when John finished speaking to the staff inside the club. The bartenders and servers didn't know much of anything or were simply reluctant to cooperate. The bouncers knew Ms. Milovich well but hadn't seen anything out of the ordinary that would explain how the young woman had died. No one seemed to know this girl outside the club. John hoped the victim's fellow dancers would provide more assistance.

The backroom of the club, down the hall from where the storage locker and cooler were located, John found the entrance to the dressing room for the dancers. Salvatore had already told the girls it was allowed for them to speak to his detective friend. John spoke to each dancer individually about their fallen co-worker and did his best to be professional and keep his mind on the task at hand instead of admiring the bevy of barely dressed or nude beauties parading around in various costumes or lingerie.

With each interview it became clear John wasn't going to get any helpful information. Each of the dancers said that the victim was a nice girl who had a lot of admirers. There were always clients that might take things too far in the V.I.P. room or men that try to bother the girls outside the club but no one specific. John compiled a list of names of regulars who frequented the club that might have spent a lot of time with Stephania or asked for her time for private shows recently.

John thought he had gone through all the dancers and was gathering his files and notes and prepared to leave when a final dancer entered the makeshift interview room where he had been questioning everyone. The young woman caught him off guard with her immense beauty. She was olive skinned with raven black hair that glistened an almost blue hue. Her eyes were a dark brown and appeared black in the dim lighting of the small room. She shook John's hand and sat in the chair in front of him.

In what seemed like slow motion, the young woman settled into the chair and crossed her legs. John's eyes were affixed on the thigh-high, fishnet stockings that were connected to the garters that were held up by the lace belt around her abdomen. She wore a black sheer robe as a top and a sequinned bra that sparkled in the soft light. She flung her hair back as if auditioning for a shampoo commercial and moistened her twinkling red lips with her tongue. John realized he had been staring and settled back into his chair trying to compose himself.

The young woman smiled at the effect she had on John then finally spoke in a soft and sweet voice, "I'm Valentina, how can I help detective?"

John cleared his throat and struggled to return to his questioning form. "Hello Valentina. As I'm sure the other ladies have mentioned, I'm here to investigate the death of one the dancers here. Stephania Milovich. Did you know her?"

"Not very well," Valentina answered. She spoke with a strong Spanish accent but was easily understood. "I haven't been here too long. I'm new and only met her a few times."

"Have there been any customers that might have taken things too far since you've been here? Anyone who might have been threatening or might want to hurt you girls?" John asked. He kept his eyes down on his paper waiting for her response. He didn't want to reveal how much she attracted him.

"Yes," Valentina said finally, "an older man threatened me a few weeks ago. He wanted more than a dance and I don't do that. But he didn't want to take no for an answer."

"I see, did you mention this to your boss? Or the bouncers?" John asked as he jotted down notes.

"Yes. He was thrown out that night and I haven't seen him since. But this sort of thing happens a lot. Customers get carried away." Valentina said as she slowly shifted in her chair, crossing her long legs and casually fiddling with the garter straps watching John's reaction.

John swallowed hard and met her gaze to continue the interview, "if this happens all the time, why mention this one particular man? What made him different than every other jerk you come across?"

"He had something very dangerous in his eyes. They were pure black, no color. He scared me. There was just something dark about him altogether," Valentina replied. She went on to describe the man's appearance and that he called himself Duke.

John kept losing focus as Valentina spoke. He was fascinated by her lips as they formed her words. His eyes scanned over her body as she moved. He was imagining her naked and dancing on stage with the spotlight capturing her figure. He imagined kissing her, groping her, caressing her. He managed to write down her information amidst his racing imagination and was able to stifle his sexual response as the front of his slacks bulged. He hoped he wasn't being too obvious.

It was a relief when the interview was concluded. John took down Valentina's contact information and wrote down his personal cell phone number on his card in case she thought of anything else that might be helpful. Or if she happened to hear from this Duke person again. She flirtatiously and playfully wrote her name and number on John's notepad and signed it by kissing her lip marks onto the page. John admired her form as Valentina rose from the chair and slowly walked back into the dressing room. He had to catch his breath before leaving.

John searched Stephania's locker and found a ring with several keys on it which he hoped might unlock her apartment. Aside from make up and some clothing there was nothing else inside. He left the club with his notes from the staff and dancers. The information and camera footage from Salvatore, Stephania's keys, and a potential lead on a suspect named Duke. As he drove away, he couldn't shake the image of Valentina from his mind. He entered the destination listed as Stephania's home address into his car's GPS and sped away hoping working the case would clear his mind.

* * *

The bright rays of the morning's sun shone through the window to find Selena lying wide awake staring at her alarm clock. This morning would be her return to work, and she hadn't been able to sleep. She stopped drinking days before and was fighting the urge to down a mouthful of whiskey that had become her daily routine. She showered and dressed and braced herself for the day to come. Before leaving the house, she stared down at her daughter's picture and forced herself to remember the vow she had made to avenge her death. She was ready.

The station hadn't changed since she had been away Selena noticed as she walked down the crowded hallway. She did her best to avoid the concerned gazes and well wishes of her fellow officers. She didn't want to talk about anything and certainly did not want anyone's pity or advice on how best to move on. She entered the large collection of desks that made up the homicide division and found her way to her old workstation.

Selena met with Captain McGee who officially welcomed her back and caught her up on the latest cases. Armed with an armful of casework, Selena returned to her desk to start work. It hadn't been ten minutes and Selena already wanted to storm out of the station after meeting with the captain. For her to return to work she was required to speak with a therapist once a week to prove she was fit to proceed. It was the last thing Selena wanted to do was talk about what had happened. But she made the promise to her daughter and was determined to keep it.

File after file. Page after page. Selena read all the medical examiner's notes, witness statements, responding officer's reports of all the cold cases she was assigned to gradually return to full and active duty. She looked over the glossy pictures of dead bodies and the state of which they had been found. In every victim she saw her daughter. The gunshots, stabbings, drive-bys, beatings, and all the other acts of violence displayed across her desk like some demented museum of the horrors of humanity. It was almost too much to take.

Selena left her desk and went into the alley and lit a cigarette. She calmed herself down from having a full-blown panic attack. After several minutes of practicing breathing exercises and reassuring herself, she went back to her desk. She summoned her inner strength and forced herself to go through the cases. Forced herself to look at every photo and read every word. If these victims resembled her daughter than the promise, she made would extend to them all and she would find those responsible for their deaths.

Several days after her return to work, Selena had her first therapy session and managed to convince the doctor that she was over the tragedy of her daughter. With her keen detective's eye, she was able to solve several cases by simply reading over their respective files. The familiar rush she used to get when she solved cases with her partner was returning and she remembered how much she enjoyed being a detective. It was a calling she felt to help clean up the streets from the dangerous people committing such heinous acts.

During the morning briefing, after being back to work for over a week, Selena was finally put back to work with her old partner John Davis. They shared some awkward small-talk and discussed the current case John had been working on.

Things between them had changed. Selena used to look at her partner with admiration and wanted to become as good a detective as he was. Now, she looked at him with spite and disappointment. John was, after all, assigned to her daughter's case and failed to come up with so much as a suspect.

Selena waited for them to be alone in the field before asking the questions she had longed to ask. She demanded John tell her of any developments in the case, but John refused. Selena pleaded to at least have a look at the case file and to help with the investigation off-the-books. Again, John refused. He told her he thought she wasn't ready to come back to work and that she was obsessed. John tried his best to sway her from pursuing her desire for revenge, but his advice and concern went unheeded. Selena saw John as a mere distraction instead of the partner she used to feel so close to.

As days progressed with Selena and John working their cases the tensions between them continued to grow. Her distain for his inability to solve her daughter's murder and his unwillingness to show her the case file was all she could think of. John was considered the city's best detective with the highest solve rate over everyone, yet, in two years he couldn't solve the case of someone he claimed to love. Selena held him responsible for the continued pain she felt.

The collective voices of the large crowd inside the club sounded like mumbling. The loud music being blasted through the speakers made it impossible to carry on a conversation. Selena did not come here to talk. After her disappointing attempt to get her so called partner to help her find her daughter's killer, she needed something to forget her frustration and pain. It was well over a week since she had anything to drink, she decided to start with shots. She was three down before ordering a martini. Her destructive routine returned in full force and the last thing she remembered was struggling to walk to the ladies' room.

The next morning Selena awoke not knowing where she was or how she had gotten there. She was lying totally nude in the back of an SUV with a young, equally unclothed, woman in her arms. Selena sat up and found her clothes on the backseat. The young woman woke up and explained what Selena couldn't remember. In that moment, she hated herself. She listened to the missing details of another drunken night of making a fool of herself and having sex with another complete stranger. She couldn't believe how weak she allowed herself to become.

Selena and the young woman got dressed and they drove back to the bar where Selena had left her car. As they drove, the young woman continued to fill in the blank spots of last night's memory. She explained that it was Selena who initiated the brief relationship between them. Selena was in tears that she had lost control yet again. Her emotions had gotten the best of her and she was left with another shameful night to remember. The two women parted ways and Selena drove home utterly disappointed in herself.

After showering off the latest of a long string of regretful fornications and preparing for the day's work ahead, Selena made her morning coffee and headed out the door. She unlocked her car and got in. Her hand motioned to turn the key in the ignition when she noticed an envelope tucked under her windshield wipers. She got out and frustratedly grabbed the envelope thinking it was a parking ticket. She tore it open and prepared to crumple it up. She peered inside and what she saw forced her to violently vomit on her driveway.

Inside the small envelope was a neatly folded letter and several polaroid stills. The pictures were of Anna-Maria, Selena's late daughter. One of her clothed, tied-up on a mattress. One of her naked and chained to a chair. The final picture of her being assaulted by some sort of device. Her hands shook as she opened the letter to read what was written. The letter said simply, "Welcome back to the game mom. Yours truly, Shadow".

* * *

It had been years of waiting on the sidelines and hiding in plain sight. After weeks of stalking prey and preparing clues. The killer had finally scratched the itch that was always nagging. Always tormenting the mind with the insatiable need to inflict terror and pain upon others. To toy with those who aim to capture and imprison this hunter. The killer stood in the usual attire used to commit these crimes staring down at the latest victim.

The young blonde stripper who was chosen weeks earlier lay on a plastic covered mattress. She had suffered through days of this killer's sadistic ritual. Days of being raped repeatedly by the killer and experimented on with strange devices and toys as the killer took pictures to save as horrific souvenirs of the event. The young woman's death was a kindness after such suffering.

The broken corpse, stabbed, beaten, and strangled, was collected and placed carefully into a former delivery van with its interior covered in more plastic sheeting. It was early in the morning with the night sky slowly giving way to morning. The streets were empty and free of any onlookers or potential witnesses. The large van drove up to a vacant lot near the club where the young woman used to dance and came to a stop. The killer was careful to scan the area several more times before exiting the safety of the van's dark interior.

Using the shroud of darkness, this executioner removed the body from the back of the van and carefully and quickly placed it among the weeds. After collecting some more memorabilia from the body, the killer fled the area and returned to the dark base of operations to rid it of evidence and prepare the next stage of the game. Its not a game without an opponent and it was time for the kick-off.

This devious hunter had been watching Detective John Davis. The meticulous research had been done and the killer was confident that by staging the body at that club, John would be the detective working the case. The thrill of the city's best detective, the hero, as the opponent thrilled this killer. The clues intended to torment the pursuers were strategically crafted and placed with specific purpose. The killer wanted to target John Davis and wanted him to know that he, too, the hero, was being hunted.

An envelope with no postmark or address on it was dropped off at police headquarters. The envelope simply had, "for Detective John Davis", written on the front. There would be no hairs or fibres to collect within. No prints or DNA to incriminate anyone. Just a sample to connect the letter with the victim, a twisted way of taking ownership of the deed. This was a message. It was a taunt. A nudge to the detective that meant, the game is on.

CHAPTER FOUR

John always had a strange feeling when going through someone else's things. An entire life stuffed into a small apartment. The pictures held their memories and remained hanging on the walls or propped up on furniture. Their clothing left hanging neatly in the closet or folded into the dresser. A wide array of cosmetic bottles and tubes left on the surface of the bathroom sink, counter, and bedroom vanity. It always intrigued John how people left their living space one day not knowing it would be their last.

The small apartment was dusted and swept for physical evidence before John could do his walkthrough. He slowly moved from room to room to get a sense of what this young woman's life was like. Looking at the frozen smiles captured in the various pictures he felt he had seen this girl before. She was a beautiful blonde in California, John ignored the sense of familiarity since California was the land of beautiful blondes.

Long hours were spent combing through the remnants of the victim's apartment and had turned up nothing. There was no sign that a struggle had occurred there, nor evidence that anything was amiss. Cameras flashed taking pictures to capture an image of the state of each room. All the fingerprints were collected along with any fibres. John knew there was nothing here that would point to the killer. He had a hunch that she must have been taken from the club.

John returned to the station, went over his notes, and continued to read through the findings at the young dancer's apartment. His creative imagination was hard at work, trying to pick up a trail of the killer. Like a writer staring at a blank page, his mind seemed to be blocked. Among his notes was the lip-marked note given to him by the beautiful dancer at the club and as hard as he tried, he couldn't remove the thoughts of Valentina from his mind. Since his interview with her the day before it was difficult to concentrate on much else. He ran his finger around the lip marks left on his notebook and imagined he was touching her angelic face.

A nearby mail cart's wheels squealed and the distasteful smell of old cigarettes, cheap cologne, and coffee breath jolted John from his imagination. The shy, awkward, little intern had his hands full of envelopes and boxes. He hurriedly delivered them to their intended receivers. John shut his notebook and waited to see if there was any mail for him. There were several reports he was waiting for and hoped they were on the awkward man's cart. He had little patience for incompetence and was quickly annoyed when having to wait on others.

The small stack of neatly folded envelopes was placed in the plastic organizer that sat on the corner atop John's obsessively neat desk. The intern offered a slight smile as he removed the outgoing mail from the adjoining slot and quickly returned to the noisy cart and pushed it out of the room. John was quick to retrieve his delivery and start scanning who they were from.

There was nothing of significance as John slowly read the contents of each envelope. He shook his head in frustration, annoyed that he would still have to wait for his reports. The last envelope looked like a personal letter. It was a thick envelope with what felt like a card inside. John slid the slender blade of his letter opener under the top fold and sliced it open. He gently squeezed the envelope's edges to prop it open and look inside.

The contents of the mysterious envelope made John quickly drop it on the desk and shoot up from his chair. He stood for a long moment utterly confused. There were latex gloves in his bag next to the desk. John slid his hand into one of the gloves and picked up the envelope and placed it into a plastic evidence bag. He rushed to the elevator to head to the department's crime lab. What did this envelope mean? Was it a threat or a taunt? John's mind was racing.

The police headquarters crime lab was in the basement, several floors beneath the offices of its many divisions. John knew the technicians well and would often come down to get them to prioritize his cases. He handed the evidence bag to one of the young ladies who worked in the lab. She appeared busy and was working on something on her computer. With a little flirtation she was all too happy to stop her mundane task and help John. It helped that the girl was somewhat infatuated with the handsome detective and her full attention was easy to attain with a simple glance with his brilliant blue eyes.

The envelope was carefully removed from the plastic bag and its contents sprawled out on the surface of a UV lit tabletop. There was a computer typed letter, three polaroid stills, and a small plastic bag with strands of blood-stained, blonde hair. The technician used extreme magnification to look for any potential hairs or fibres on each of the items found in the envelope. There were no fingerprints on the items inside the envelope, just on the envelope itself which would belong to the mail handlers and John.

The pictures inside the envelope were images of Stephania Milovich, the victim of the latest case John had been assigned. The images showed her being whipped, raped, and stabbed. The young woman's body on plastic sheeting covered in blood. The blonde hair in the bag appeared to match the victim and it was a good bet that the blood that soaked into its fibres was hers. It was a gruesome and disturbing sight that made an already difficult case much harder.

The technician used forceps to unfold the letter. The paper was common printer paper and the font was neatly typed. The message mentioned John directly and appeared to be a challenge. John read the words on the page. Whoever had written this knew him and wanted his attention. Why John? Why kill a random stripper to target him? It made no sense.

The message said, "Detective J. Davis. Can the hero of Lugar De Paz City capture the devil before its too late? I look forward to finding out. Let's see if you deserve your title. Let the battle between good and evil commence. The game has begun. Yours truly, Shadow".

John left the disturbing mail delivery with the lab technicians after snapping several pictures with his cellphone. He returned to the fourth floor and to his desk. He knew he had to bring the captain up to speed and found him hard at work in his office. John entered and closed the door behind him.

"Captain, things just got a little more complicated," John said as he removed his cellphone and brought up the pictures of what had just been sent to him.

"What's this?" Captain McGee said taking the phone and adjusting his glasses to see the pictures more clearly.

"That was sent to me this afternoon. I just ran it downstairs to the lab. The killer dumped the body yesterday morning at the club. He knew I would get the case," John said as he sat down.

"Well this wouldn't be the first time a killer pursued his pursuers," Captain McGee replied, continuing to stare down at the pictures.

"This is going to wind up a serial," John said.

"Break up your routine. If you have somewhere else to stay, go there. Don't stay at your place. If this guy is targeting you, I can have some uniforms cover you if that will help?" Captain McGee replied, handing back the phone.

"This isn't targeting me to harm me. He's taunting me to catch him. He's attacking my reputation, not me," John added.

"Not yet." Captain McGee said sternly, "I also wanted to tell you that you're getting your partner back. Selena has been cleared to return Monday. With this, you could use her brilliance to catch this asshole."

The captain continued telling John about Selena's return to duty and trying to reassure him that she was ready. John thanked the Captain for the update on his partner and refused the need to have officers watch over him. If this killer was following John, he would make the perfect bait. If this killer made the mistake of coming after a cop, they would be able to catch him before he killed again.

He returned to his desk and John worked on his backed-up paperwork. He had mixed feelings about the news of his troubled partner returning. He didn't know how he would face her after all this time. She had refused to speak to him since her last attempt at returning to work. John wasn't sure bringing her back was the right thing for her. The last thing he needed while being targeted by a serial killer was to have to babysit someone so unstable.

* * *

"Hey, wake up," the loud voice demanded, "you okay lady?"

A firm hand grasped Selena's shoulder and gently shook her awake. She struggled to open her eyes and was completely disoriented. The cold morning air caused her to start shivering. Her clothes were damp and wrinkled from lying on the ground all night. A quick look around refreshed her memory. Selena had polished off another bottle of tequila and fell asleep at her daughter's grave clutching her headstone. She had fallen asleep and slept there all night.

"I'm fine, thanks, just please leave me alone," Selena said to the groundskeeper as she attempted to stand. The pleasant old man gave her a small towel and wished her a good day before leaving to go about his work.

Walking out of the shadows and into the sunlight stopped the shivering as Selena made her way to the parking lot to search for her car. It was another disappointing failure in her fight for sobriety. After seeing the photographs of her daughter's bloodied, bruised, and torn skin, she resorted back to drinking. The reminder of how her daughter suffered at her end and the fact the killer remained free and possibly targeting her as well was too much to handle. She required the aid of her good friend, Patron Silver to help her forget.

The parking lot of the funeral home was empty except for Selena's car and the groundskeeper's maintenance truck. She couldn't remember driving to the grave. The last thing she could recall was sitting in her car, parked outside a liquor store. She debated with herself of bringing in the envelope with the pictures of her daughter's body and the taunting letter to the station. She remembered purchasing her booze and choosing the drink over informing her captain and partner of the threat. She knew she had to pull herself together. In the state she was in, she was an easy target for a stalking killer.

Later that day, in midafternoon, after Selena had returned home to clean herself up once again, she showed up late to the station. It had been barely a week since her return to work and she was already struggling. She sat through another lecture from her partner of how she was late again and how they were falling behind on their case work because of her tardiness. She apologized but it was obvious he was already losing his patience with her. Or perhaps he simply didn't want to work with her anymore. John quickly switched off his computer and took a few thick file folders with him as he left.

Selena sat for a long time at her desk. She fought away tears thinking of how she was letting everyone down. Her partner, John, was her hero for so long and now he looked at her like she was a common junkie. She knew she had to find some way to snap out of this disastrous routine she kept repeating. There was a dust-covered, framed picture of her former family on her desk. Selena took it in her hands and wiped away the dirt to see the image clearly. Her ex-husband with his arms around both Selena and their daughter. She couldn't help but smile as she remembered the day the picture was taken.

As Selena returned the picture to its place on the edge of her desk, something on John's side of their shared cubicle caught her eye. John had a filing cabinet that he always kept locked. It contained his personal notes and case files he was working on. John always kept the key with him at all times. On this day, however, John had become so angry at Selena for making him late to an appointment that he stormed out and left the keys dangling in the lock. The case file for her daughter could've been in that cabinet.

With this realization, she sprung up from her desk and looking around the room to make sure John hadn't returned. Selena walked over to the cabinet and opened it up. There were several thick file folders, note pads and an old bottle of scotch. There was a small locked box as well that required a combination that looked like a pistol case. Selena removed all he files and searched through them. Her daughter's case file was near the top. She emptied the contents and replaced them with blank printer paper to make up for the missing bulk.

Selena returned to her desk and braced herself for what she was about to see. This would be the first time she would read the file on her daughter's murder. She would have to detach her emotion and read the file as a cop, not a mother. After several deep breaths, she finally turned the pages and read the coroner's report. She read John's reports and his personal notes that he had jotted down on various notepads. Fighting tears, she forced herself to look down at the crime scene photos. Forced herself to feel the pain she had spent so much time trying to run away from.

Among the pages of the file, Selena read the name Lucas Durante repeatedly. It occurred to Selena that John believed Durante to have returned to the city and targeted Anna-Maria to make the case personal and remove Selena from the investigation. The notes explained that John never believed that Lucas Durante had fled the city. It was apparent that John thought Durante was responsible for many cases over the years and his notes on the subject were borderline obsessive.

It was late into the evening when Selena finished going through the file. She had done her research on Lucas Durante and the latest cases her partner had been working on. There was no real history on Durante. He was born and raised in a small town in Oregon. From what she could see, Lucas Durante fled Oregon on a sexual assault charge that was still pending after all these years.

Various database searches came back with no results. Lucas Durante had never owned or registered a vehicle or property. There was no listing of next of kin. He wasn't on any social media outlets. The man had spent nearly a decade on the run after John had named him the prime suspect in the murders of several transient women and prostitutes. The latest activity she read on Durante was his capture by John, two weeks earlier.

A picture was left up on the computer monitor. Selena stared at the face of the man her partner suspected of killing her daughter. Her imagination tortured her with the image of this evil bastard touching her daughter. Hurting her. Raping her. She seared the man's face into her mind until she could no longer take it. She switched off her monitor and slid her daughter's file into her top desk drawer and locked it.

Slumped in her chair Selena looked back at her daughter's picture. The compulsion to drink was so powerful, she instinctively, without realizing, took out the squared bottle of tequila from her bottom desk drawer and removed its cap. She brought the opened bottle to her lips and nearly took a drink when she heard a voice that made her stop. It was a soft voice, softer than a whisper. It said one word. The voice said, "Mom".

Looking down at the bottle in her hand, then back at the picture of her daughter, Selena believed the voice she had heard was her beloved Anna-Maria's. Normally she considered herself a nonbeliever in anything spiritual despite being raised in a strict catholic household. The death of her daughter destroyed her belief system and she shut herself off to the idea of faith and religion. But this disembodied voice couldn't be explained. She was all alone in the office. There was no one around, no sound. She took this as a sign and threw the full bottle of tequila in the trash as she left the building.

Selena felt a powerful urge. It wasn't to drink or do drugs. It wasn't to pick up a stranger for another dirty one-night stand. The urge was to confront her daughter's killer. She knew that he was currently being guarded in the hospital as he recovered from being shot during his arrest. Selena needed a plan. She needed to look upon the man's face. She needed to see him suffer. She needed him to look at her beautiful daughter's picture, so he knew what he had done. She needed to kill this man by her own hand.

The next few days passed slowly, and Selena hadn't craved a drink. She felt a reinvigorated sense of purpose. The fire inside her had been stoked and she felt the energy course through her veins as she planned her vengeance. Killing Lucas Durante would be difficult. The man was being guarded by police day and night until he was fit to leave the hospital. She had been patient for two years; she knew she could wait a little while longer until she could plan a way to dispose of Lucas Durante and get away with it.

* * *

Another day faded into sunset and transitioned from blue to gold, orange to pink, then purple and dark blue, then black. A predator's watchful eyes adjusted perfectly in the darkness silently watching. The thirst for blood was stronger now. When an addict samples a fix, no matter how long it has been since the last one, the craving comes back with full vigor and there is no stopping it.

The blonde stripper was just a taste that tantalized the killer's senses. It provided an opportunity to return to the game and set the stage to challenge a formidable opponent. The clues had been delivered as intended and much to the killer's surprise, there would be two mice for this cat to prey upon. With Selena Lopez returning to work, along with her star veteran partner Detective John Davis, the game would be twice the fun.

The beautiful young detective would need to be reminded of her loss. There had to be a test to see how worthy she was to play this game. The killer removed some devious mementos from an old collection that had been accrued over a long time and prepared a special message to Ms. Lopez. The pictures taken as the detective's daughter met her end would either break the woman's spirit or set her rage ablaze. The killer prepared the package in the same fashion as John's envelope, which contained images and evidence of the blonde stripper's death. The killer wanted to prove the sender of each package was the one who committed these acts.

It was humorous watching John open his special delivery. The expression on the hero's face. The killer was able to enter the building and move freely through its halls and offices without anyone paying close attention. It was all too easy for this hunter to remain unseen. Carrying on conversations with random people with nobody suspecting a thing. All the while watching John's reactions, studying his methods, being in the same room without the hero even realizing it. For this killer, it was almost too much excitement to be contained.

It had been a long time, months, since the killer paid attention to the hero's sidekick, Selena. This prowler watched her descend into alcoholism and drug abuse. Watched her take home random strangers, men and women alike, to try and screw away the pain of her loss. She was too weak to take this hunter down. The killer thought her to be damaged goods, too broken to return to her role as a police officer.

The reaction to the envelope left under Detective Lopez's windshield wiper was unexpected. The days that followed she returned to her former self. Maybe she was worthy to chase this killer after all. Watching her prepare to face their prime suspect. The angered and determined expression on her face revealed her intention to kill. The killer watched intently trying to determine what she might do next. This might have been the most fun the killer ever had playing this game.

The killer's surveillance of his pawns was continuous, and Detectives Davis and Lopez were closely observed as they continued their crusades. John found a new friend to enjoy in the bedroom. Selena was preparing for her first kill. The killer thought it was time for them to be reunified as partners. There needed to be another piece of work for them to bond together as a team. There needed to be something to hit home. The next display would make them feel vulnerable, especially John.

The killer had already chosen the next victim. The research had already been done. The woman's routine was already memorized, and the apprehension was planned and scheduled. The room where the next victim's blood would be spilled had been prepared to perfection. The tools were set at the ready for when the time would come to use them. The mode of transportation was set-up in its usual fashion. It was time for the next play of the game.

The damp air was cool that night. It was clear with a full moon casting its pale light. The hour was late, and the streets were relatively empty. Traffic was light, and there were very few pedestrians on the sidewalks. The blacked-out van drove through the streets avoiding the intersections with traffic cameras. The van's destination was located in a rough part of the city where little money was spent in the neighbourhood's upkeep.

The van was brought to a stop in an alleyway not far from where the woman lived. The killer got out of the van and moved through the shadows, creeping up to the building. A sleazy motel that was used for prostitutes to conduct their business. The killer had discovered where the security cameras were situated from the reconnaissance of this next intended victim. The security system was easily deactivated along with the bright sign that illuminated the property in a demonic red glow. The dark hunter could proceed without danger of being seen.

Of the twenty-four rooms that made up this haven for the sexually depraved, there were only a few lights on. The building was mostly shrouded in darkness. The shadows draped heavily allowing the dark specter to move effortlessly without making a sound. The cunning predator slithered up to the correct door. The door's lock was all too easy to pick and did not take much time. The door had a hook that acted as a secondary lock that, when applied, would only allow the door to open a crack. The killer came prepared with a makeshift tool equipped with a magnet to disarm the latch.

Inside the room, lying on the bed, the young woman was in deep slumber. There was no sound to warn her or wake her. The killer removed a rag and a small bottle of chloroform and poured the liquid onto the rough material, soaking it completely. The intense smell woke up the woman just as it was forced down hard to cover her mouth and nose. She tried to fight and struggle but was overpowered. There was nothing she could do to fight off the force that held her down. The strength was near supernatural.

A short time later, the frightened woman awoke from the sting of smelling salts being forced into her nostrils. A bright light shone down on her making it hard to see with her eyes fighting to adjust. She tried to sit up but soon realized her wrists were tied down to the edge of the bed. Panic shot through her entire body and she thrashed around in a wild attempt to free herself. Her ankles had been tied down as well. The gag that covered her mouth was so tight it was cutting the sides of her mouth and made screaming impossible.

A shadow blocked the light as it loomed over her. She squinted her eyes to try see a face, but it was too dark. The shadowed figure produced a pair of large scissors and dragged the cold metal along the woman's skin. She tried to plead and beg for this to stop but could not form the words. The left-handed scissors chomped into the fabric of her clothing cutting off her shirt first, then her pajama pants. Then the straps of her bra, then her panties. Surprisingly, then the scissors cut off the gag.

"Please don't do this, Please," the terrified woman begged. The figure remained silent, "I don't know who you are. I haven't seen your face. Let me go. You won't get in trouble. Please."

The figure moved behind the light. There were camera flashes and the sound of pictures being printed. The woman continued pleading but it was no use. She could hear metal clanging together, the plastic ruffling. There was a buzzing that sounded like an electric razor. The terror was rising within her and she screamed for help. Her voice echoed far into the distance. There were no other sounds to be heard. Tears poured out of her eyes not knowing what was about to happen.

The sound of footsteps drew her attention to the bright halogen light. The shadowy dark figure stepped into its beam and suddenly she could see who it was. It was a man who was a customer of hers from the motel. Without saying a word, he stood before her completely still, staring down at her with an expression of pure evil on his face. After allowing her to see his identity, he paused briefly then dropped the robe exposing himself to her.

"Don't do this. Please. You know me. It's me. Alexis. Please let me go," she cried out through tears.

The man didn't respond. He leapt on top of her and grabbed her face in his massive hand pulling her close to him. He leaned closer and said in a menacing, growling voice, "I want you to scream for me, whore."

CHAPTER FIVE

It was late in the day when John arrived at Dr Morrison's office. Later than her usual office hours, but she would make such accommodations for her patients when needed. John was preoccupied with his latest case earlier and wouldn't be able to make his appointment for that week. He felt, for reasons unknown, overwhelmed. He would never admit this, but he really needed to vent his frustrations and Dr Morrison's sessions were the safest place to do so.

The usual secretary had been sent home for the day and it was just Dr Morrison in her office. She usually kept her dark hair pinned-up, but today had it down and let it flow freely along her neck then down her shoulders. Her usual sports coat or blazer was hung over the back of her chair and she wore a loose, silk blouse that flattered her cleavage and a knee-length, tight skirt that accentuated her voluptuous curves. The doctor's beauty always captivated John, making it difficult to concentrate on their sessions.

"Good evening John. You sounded stressed on the phone earlier today when changing your appointment. Is everything okay?" Dr Morrison asked, gesturing for John to take his usual seat, closing the door behind him.

"Yeah," John replied, sneaking a glimpse of the doctor's behind as she swayed over to her chair and sat down across from him. "Just caught up in this case. Its not going to be an easy one to solve."

"Well I'm sure you'll find a way. How is everything else going? In our last session you mentioned that you had recently broken up with your girlfriend, is that still over?" She asked.

"Yes, it is, I haven't spoken to her since. She has been on my mind at times. The last few nights I've been having these daydreams of her," John explained. He went on to describe how he had seen images of Alexis in his daydream tied to a bed. John also added that during his relationship with Alexis they would often engage in playfully rough sex.

"Well maybe you're thinking of her in that way because you're sexually frustrated. Have you had sex with anyone else since the breakup?" Dr Morrison inquired, jotting down notes as she listened.

"No." John answered. "You're probably right doc. I haven't been sleeping well either. Probably why I keep daydreaming at work."

"Why aren't you sleeping?" Dr Morrison asked.

"I keep getting these awful headaches. I usually get them when I'm stumped on a case, my ex-wife used to say it was part of my process," John said, adjusting in his chair to get more comfortable.

"So, you've had these headaches before?" Dr Morrison asked.

"Yeah, every so often when I can't quite figure out a case, or when I'm stressed out," John explained.

"And these headaches are the cause of your sleep problem?" Dr Morrison inquired.

"I'm not sure. I know I sleep. I go to bed. Lay down shut my eyes. But when I wake up hours later, I still feel exhausted, like I've been out working or something. Then I start my day, working on my cases then the headaches begin," John said.

"Maybe try taking some melatonin or drinking some chamomile tea before bed. Or there are always meditation techniques that can relax you. I think the break-up, combined with this new and difficult case are causing you to stress yourself out. I can also run some tests to see if there is another reason you feel lethargic. Perhaps your iron levels are low or maybe your vitamin b-twelve?" Dr Morrison said, tugging at the material of her skirt pulling over her exposed knees. She had noticed John glimpsing at them and didn't want to give the wrong impression.

The appointment continued for the scheduled hour. John spoke vaguely about his latest case and the threatening letter he had received at work. He told the doctor of his concerns of his partner, Selena, who had returned to work after losing her daughter. John shared his concerns that he believed his partner to be too unbalanced to come back and she wasn't ready. By the end of the session, John felt more at ease with everything. Dr Morrison had a calming effect on him.

It was beginning to get dark as the session ended and John offered to walk Dr Morrison to her car. They continued talking about their session as they walked the short distance from the building to the parking lot. John opened her car door and watched her drive away. He considered all of Dr Morrison's advice from the session and wondered if any of it would help him get a restful sleep.

John returned to his car and had more images of Alexis suddenly run through his mind. He remembered their last time together and how perfectly she played along in his desires. His attractions to Dr Morrison always left him slightly aroused after his appointments. Perhaps that's why Alexis came to his mind now. John thought maybe he should call her. Maybe he should go apologize. Her anger towards him might have cooled down by now and they could continue with their usual appointments.

John fumbled through his pockets and removed his cell phone. He swiped through his apps until he found the contact icon. He struck the small square with his large, right thumb and scrolled down to Alexis's number. He was about to hit the call button when an incoming call blacked out the screen. It was a number he didn't recognize. He hoped it wasn't his snitch, Tricks, with more information. He felt far too tired for another late-night goose chase.

"Hello, this is Detective John Davis," John said reluctantly, not sure who this would be calling him.

"Detective, this is Valentina, from Night Moves," the sultry voice replied.

"Of course, hello Valentina how can I help you?" John asked. His mind replayed the brief interview he had with her, remembering how gorgeous and sexy he thought she was.

"I think someone has been following me. I've seen him in the club a few times, if you remember I told you about him when we spoke at the club? He calls himself, 'Duke'. I'm afraid he knows where I live," Valentina said with obvious fear in her voice.

"Okay, can you give me a description? When was the last time you saw him?" John asked, trying to focus on the job and not his sexual frustrations. He removed his notebook and prepared to jot down the scared woman's description.

"I think he is outside my apartment building right now," Valentina whispered.

John ordered Valentina to get somewhere safe in her apartment and took down her address and said he would be right over. He started his car and sped through the dark streets. Valentina's apartment was across town, but at that time of night, it wouldn't take John long to get there. His mind was laser-focused, as it always was when chasing down a perpetrator. His excitement caused his heart to race. This could be the killer preparing for his next victim and John could stop him.

The tires screamed as the large sedan slid to a stop nearest the curb close to the apartment building. The street looked empty. John armed himself with his pistol and flashlight and locked his car as he left for his patrol. He cautiously walked around the building, but there was no one. He went up and down the alley and still no one to be seen. He entered the building and searched each of the narrow hallways all the way up to the twelfth floor where Valentina said her apartment was located.

It wasn't his snitch that caused it this time, but John felt annoyed that this was another evening wasted. He could be home in bed catching up on sleep. John found Valentina's apartment in the corner of the building, at the end of the hall. As he knocked on the door, he tried to calm himself and to not seem too annoyed with his potential witness. He announced his name and took several deep breaths to calm down as he waited for her to open the door.

When she finally opened the door, Valentina stood wearing a long bathrobe. Her hair was still wet and from the opening in the robe's front, it appeared she wasn't wearing anything underneath. John entered the apartment trying to keep his mind on the job. He was quick to reassure Valentina that whoever she thought was following her wasn't outside anymore. He told her he had checked all around the building as well as every floor all the way up and had seen no one.

Valentina was gracious for John coming out this time of night. She apologized that it was all for nothing and offered him a cup of coffee or something harder to drink to make up for wasting his time. John accepted the offer and asked for his drink of choice, rum and coke over ice. John casually looked over the apartment as he waited for his drink. A detective's mind was never fully relaxed.

The apartment was very neat and tidy, much like his own, and filled with vintage items. There was an old-fashioned record player and a collection of albums. The pictures that hung on the walls were mostly old-time pin-up girl posters from the world war two era. John peered through the open door to Valentina's bedroom and noticed lit candles on the night tables and could smell the scent of strong perfume that smelled familiar to him, but he couldn't place it.

Valentina returned with his drink and offered him a seat. She had turned off the light in her kitchen and it was obvious she was trying to set a mood. She said she had felt embarrassed about being caught in her bathrobe and was going to change. John reminded himself of the code of ethics. He couldn't possibly allow this to progress any further. He couldn't allow this to become something sexual. Sleeping with Valentina would put his case, and possibly his career in jeopardy. He decided he had better leave.

John quickly finished his drink before the ice cubes had a chance to melt and placed his glass on the kitchen counter. He turned to make his way to the door, racking his brain to come up with an excuse to leave. As he neared the door Valentina's voice tickled his ears like soft music and asked him for help with something in the bedroom. John paused for a moment. He knew he should just leave. He knew he should just go home, but instead succumbed to his desire.

The bedroom was small and only lit with candles. John walked through the open French doors and found Valentina lying on the bed wearing nothing but the rose pedals she had draped over the surface of her bedspread. The room was filled with the powerful scent of roses. John struggled to say doing this would be inappropriate, but Valentina had risen from the bed and walked towards him. She ran her fingers along the zipper of his jacket, pulled it open, then slid it off his shoulders. He was powerless to resist.

Valentina moved her lips to John's and gently pressed them together. The tip of her tongue ran along his lips until he opened his mouth and slid his tongue against hers. His hands were freed from his jacket as it fell to the floor and were quick to find the warm flesh of her hips. Her hands tore at his clothing until she pulled his shirt over his head. She admired his manly physique, running her fingers down the lines of his muscles towards the belt which held up his jeans.

The heat between John and Valentina intensified. She had removed his pants and lowered her mouth to perform oral sex. She brought him in and out of her mouth. Using her gentle suction and the movements of her tongue to tantalize and entice him. John could no longer take it. He motioned to stand her up then tossed her onto the bed and moved between her legs. He brought his fully erect phallus to her moist opening, then slid himself inside her. He found her mouth with his to continue wrestling their tongues, then with his right hand, he gently tugged at her hair.

The pair explored several different positions as their sex lasted for well over an hour. John had brought her to climax several times and she returned the favor. Their fornications had begun in the bedroom and somehow ended up on the living room couch. After their final climax, with their bodies teeming with sweat, they fell asleep from the effort. John held Valentina as close as he once did with his wife so long ago.

In the morning, John and Valentina shared a hot shower before John left for work. As he drove away from the apartment building, he compared the previous night's sexual experience with what he used to have with Alexis. He didn't feel dirty or disgusted with himself. He could fully remember what had happened instead of blocking it out and the sex itself was passionate without delving into simulating rape. Perhaps the reason he had always felt that way afterward was that Alexis was a prostitute

John arrived at the station ready for the day. He wasn't necessarily well rested after what had transpired the night before, but he felt he was reenergized and ready to take on his case. He felt elated and relaxed as he sipped his first coffee and settled in to start his day. A smile curved his lips as he replayed the events with Valentina. He couldn't wait to see her again, feeling like a teenager having just gone on his first date. His smile quickly faded when he went through his mail inbox.

Under folders of files and reports was another envelope addressed to John in the same writing as before. Did this contain pictures of the latest victim? More hair? More blood? John put his mug down and slid on latex gloves. He carefully opened the envelope and emptied its contents onto the surface of the desk. There was no letter this time. There was only a key with a plastic keychain with a bloody thumbprint on its surface covering the number twelve. There was also a polaroid picture of a shady motel, Alexis's motel. Another picture of the door to a room. Room number twelve. Alexis's room.

* * *

Working with her old partner had become intolerable for Selena. She could no longer focus on her daily tasks. Her mind was set on killing Lucas Durante, the man listed in her partner's secret file as being the one responsible for killing her daughter. She kept puzzling with questions. If Lucas Durante was responsible, he must have been working with someone since he was in the hospital when someone tried taunting her with that ghastly envelope left under her windshield. There must be some other person, or persons involved, who would also face her justice.

The daily routine was tedious. The bodies would be discovered. The police were called in to collect evidence and take pictures. It was amazing how something so gruesome over time can become so common place. Seasoned detectives become desensitized to the sight of death, blood, and body parts. The cruelty of human beings and what they are capable of no longer surprised or shocked the men and women working homicide.

In every corpse carried away, Selena would see her daughter. This newly reinvigorated sense of passion for the job made her a tougher cop. In the weeks since her return, her solve rate had increased. Detectives Davis and Lopez had returned to their former glory as they solved most cases within the first forty-eight hours of discovery. Selena respected John's imagination and intuition, combined with her intellect, there seemed to be no case too difficult for them to solve.

There was a difference between the way things used to be and the present dynamic between the two partners. Selena felt John had forgotten about her daughter and no longer cared to find her murderer. In the past she had great respect for John. For a brief time, though they both had spouses, she had been attracted to John and they had almost acted on their urges nearly committing adultery on their former marriages. She would defend John against the allegations of corruption and being on the take with the Di Sano crime family. But times had changed.

The more Selena investigated her daughter's case, the more distain she felt for her partner. She felt there must be some external reason why it had taken so long to find Lucas Durante. According to the arrest report filed when John apprehended Durante, there was a confidential informant whose name was not listed. This informant had mentioned to John that Durante had been in town for a long time despite there being a manhunt for him for nearly a decade. Why wasn't this informant named in the report? There had to be more to the story.

Selena took it upon herself to start looking into her partner. She had to find this informant for herself and question him. Lucas Durante was still listed as critical and was protected and sleeping comfortably in the hospital's intensive care unit. Confronting him could wait. Selena applied her skills, learned from her misspent youth as a troubled teen, and broke into the personnel department of police headquarters. To find out more about her partner's informants, she must first delve into his past. Finding this informant might reveal who else might be involved in her daughter's murder.

There were long rows upon rows of large file cabinets filled with thick files with wads of paper clipped together. It was surprising that there were still paper files in this digital age. It took Selena the better part of an hour of searching before finally finding Detective John Davis' personnel files. The file explained his years on patrol. It listed his many commendations and awards and his transition to the narcotics division. There were several internal affairs injunctions that claimed corruption that appeared to be halted by the chief of police.

Selena couldn't possibly finish reading the entire file without being caught. She escaped the dark storeroom where all the files had been kept and returned to her home. She had replaced her evening bottle of tequila, that was recently her method of coping, with pots of coffee and cans of energy drinks. She had to stay awake and focused as she read report after report of her former partner. She read up on his past, his application to the academy and his background check which seemed overly vague. A whirlpool of questions tormented her mind and she was left more confused and perplexed. There was something not right about her partner, but what?

The next morning's briefing came and went as any other. New cases were assigned to detectives and progress reports were shared then the meeting was adjourned. Selena couldn't help staring at her partner. His past was a mystery according to the files she had stolen from the human resources' personnel files. She went through every conversation they ever had of their pasts in hopes of remembering something that could clear up this feeling she now felt. Was he still the valiant detective she respected? Or was he a disgraced cop on the take protecting his own interests.

The day was underway, and Selena put her off-duty investigation of her daughter's murder and her partner's past aside to keep up her day job. John arrived in what appeared to be the same clothes as the day before. He smelled of cheap perfume and sweat. He changed his shirt at his desk, applying his deodorant, and drank several cups of coffee. When asked where he had been the previous night, he mentioned he had met someone who kept him out all night. Selena faked a chuckle to maintain their comradery and not reveal her doubt in his credibility.

The pair discussed their latest cases. Selena shared her reports with John, and they were prepared to file them. Together they looked at their open cases. John hadn't gotten anywhere with the Night Moves case and was planning on following up with the club's owner to see if there had been more incidents with unruly customers troubling the dancers.

Selena read over the case file and was looking at the photographs trying to get acquainted with the case that had become cold.

Selena continued reading the reports of the medical examiner on scene, the coroner's autopsy, and John's personal notes. She read over the interview transcripts and a mental picture was forming. The brutal beating and rape that the victim had suffered was eerily similar to the file she had read on her daughter. The polaroid stills sent to John in the same type of envelope as what had been left under her windshield made it clear they were connected. Selena was glad she had kept the pictures of her daughter's body a secret from John and Captain McGee. If she had brought them in, she wouldn't be able to work the case.

Selena read over the file of the murdered stripper to get caught up on their cold case. John went through his mail inbox and fell silent. The disturbed expression that came over his face drew Selena's attention. She watched as he put on evidence gloves and took hold of another envelope. It was the same as the ones both her and John had received containing evidence. The writing on its face looked the same as before. John carefully opened it and emptied its contents.

Both John and Selena put their planned visit to the club Night Moves on hold. They brought the envelope and what was inside to the lab then left the station driving immediately over to the motel featured in the pictures contained in the envelope that was delivered to John. John hardly spoke to Selena during the entire drive. He remained silent as he sped through the wet streets of the city as it poured rain from above. He narrowly escaped several collisions as he raced towards their next clue. Selena was about to call for back-up on their radio, but John told her not to, not yet.

They pulled up to the motel and entered the manager's office. The manager looked like an unkempt ex-convict, sipping from a beer can at nine o'clock in the morning. He was quick to comply to John's threatening order to hand over the master key to room twelve. Selena had never saw John this emotional. There was something personal driving him to react this way. John seemed scared in a way Selena had never witnessed. They had been on many raids together and he was always calm and collected, never one to let his emotions take control. But now he seemed panicked, reluctant to enter the room.

With their pistols drawn and following their tactical police training, Selena and John moved towards the room. Selena covered John's back as they moved forward up to the door. There were streaks of blood on the floor in front of the door and on the door jam. John slid the key into the lock and turned it slowly. The lock released, and John forcibly opened the door and burst into the dark, small room. Selena was second in the room ready to protect her partner, not knowing what was lying in wait beyond the doorway.

Red streaks of blood smeared the walls. There was blood on the beige carpeting. The broken body, bruised, naked, and sliced up, lay spread out across the bed. Police handcuffs holding her wrists to the headboard. John was frozen in place as he stared down at the body. Selena took over and checked the closet, then the bathroom to make sure there wasn't anyone else in the room. The letter S was streaked in blood on the bathroom mirror.

Outside the room, Selena tried to snap John out of his stoic state. He seemed devastated. They had worked more cases than she could remember, and John never reacted like this before. It was as if he wasn't present. Selena managed to get John out of the room and called back to the station. She ordered the crime scene investigative team and medical examiner out to the motel's location and called out the respective codes pertaining to the situation.

Selena returned to John. He was standing outside the room staring inside through the open door. He looked saddened and distraught. Selena tried to get his attention, but he wouldn't budge. She studied him closely not sure what had happened. Who was this girl in the room? From the location where the body was discovered, it was a fair assumption that she was a prostitute, but who was she to John? Selena continued to probe to get John to answer.

"John," Selena said loudly, "who is that girl in there? Do you know her?"

"Yes," John said finally, his voice was tight, and he was fighting the urge to cry.

"What's going on here John? What the hell happened here?" Selena asked placing a concerned hand on her partner's arm.

"It's me," John replied pulling away from Selena's concerned touch.

"What do you mean?" Selena asked confused.

"I did this," John said as he walked away.

* * *

Hot water washed away the blood of the latest kill. Standing under the powerful stream, the water forced the sticky, red liquid to flow like a crimson river off the killer's body and onto the floor of the shower. After applying soap, the collection of blood and water travelled into the drain. The memory of the latest victim arousing him as he replayed his twisted events and heinous acts.

The hideout had been rigorously steam cleaned of all evidence. If the police somehow managed to piece together who the killer was, they wouldn't find any physical evidence to link him to the victim. After carrying out the routine of rape and torture, once the whore's light had been extinguished, this disturbed fiend cleansed his bodily fluids out of the orifices where he had forced himself inside his victim. He had washed the corpse thoroughly with bleach once he was finished having his fun and wore a rubber jumpsuit when moving the body.

After decades of playing this game and honing his skills, this killer knew everything the police would look for. He knew how to leave no trace of his identity. Not even star detectives like Selena Lopez and John Davis stood a chance against this evil expert. He had been doing this longer than either of them had been on the police force and they would never piece it together.

It was another clear night, completely dark with no one around to witness this shadow at his work. This dark specter returned the prostitute's torn body to her room at the motel where she conducted her filthy business. The killer despised hookers. He found them disgusting. They sell themselves night after night like dirty magazines, spreading their legs and letting anyone inside them for the price of a few hundred dollars. He hated them. Disposing of them was a kindness to society.

The body had been returned, and the scene set. The killer set up the scene, painting the walls in his victim's blood which he had collected while enjoying his unspeakable torture of her. Leaving no trace was like a second nature to him with all his experience. He moved so quickly, so quietly, that no one would ever see him in his work. Especially at this motel-turned-brothel, where no one wants to see or be seen conducting business there.

The killer prepared another special delivery to be sent to the desk of John Davis. Another envelope filled with goodies. Another taunt in the game. This time it would be personal. This time John would know he was being watched and that no one around him would be safe. This always made the chase more thrilling for the killer. The torment of his pursuers. It was almost as thrilling as committing the acts themselves, but not quite.

After the delivery of yet another envelope to Detective Davis, the killer enjoyed another cigarette as he waited in the rain. He watched as John and Selena sped away from the police station. He also watched anxiously as they risked hitting innocent travellers on the freeway and roads, barely avoiding several accidents along the way. He watched the pair ascend the stairs, guns at the ready. He was almost laughing as they stormed into the whore's room. The look on John's face was satisfying. Detective Lopez looking confused trying to piece together the connection.

As the team arrived at the small motel the killer followed his self-developed code and returned to the safety of the shadows. He had gotten the thrill of tormenting and toying with his pursuers. He had displayed his work like some horrendous art showing. He faded from the crime scene like a ghostly fog to plan the next stage of the game. It was time to fuel Selena's confusion, to pit her against her partner. It was time to test her loyalty and see how John responds. It was time to choose the next victim.

CHAPTER SIX

Rain pelted the roof of the police cruiser. Its soothing rhythm was mesmerizing and relaxing. John was sitting behind the steering wheel staring blankly through the windshield as the swaying wipers shot back and forth pushing the water out of view. John stared at his partner as she was barking orders at the crime scene team members. They all wore their rain gear, carefully preserving the evidence collected from the small room.

John kept thinking of the last time he had seen Alexis alive. They had just finished having sex where they simulated rape in a session of rather rough roleplay. He recalled the look of fear and disgust on her face when he had taken the act too far. That would have been her last thought of him. He never wanted to hurt her. She provided comfort and distraction from the troubles of his destructed life. She didn't deserve the end she had met.

After sitting alone for a long time, John emerged from the comfort of the car's warm interior and joined Selena as she helped the uniformed officers question the patrons of the motel. Selena had the same fearful look on her face as Alexis had that long-ago night. John couldn't hide his emotions. On any other occasion, he felt detached from feeling when it came to a crime scene. This time, however, was different. He cared for this young woman and it devastated him thinking of how she had met her end.

"We need to talk," Selena said finally as John approached.

John followed Selena as she told the remaining officers to continue their interviews. They entered the motel's office which had been closed due to what had transpired. John took a seat behind the desk and ran his fingers through his rain-soaked, long hair, and waited for Selena to conduct her interview. He anticipated her questions and wasn't sure if he should tell her the truth.

"What did you mean out there?" Selena asked finally, once she made sure there was no one in the cramped office. "What did you mean, 'I did this'?"

"It's my fault that girl is dead," John answered, surprised that he could find the words.

"How's that?" Selena shot back.

"I was sleeping with her," John explained, "I used to meet her here. I was one of her clients."

Selena stood stunned not sure how she should respond. She sat across from John and softened her tone feeling pity for her tormented partner. "How does that make this your fault?" she asked finally.

"This killer has addressed me personally with his demented letters. He's targeting me for some reason. He's going after anyone connected to me. If she hadn't been with me, she would still be alive. She didn't, no one, deserves what happened to her in there," John replied holding back tears.

"For now," Selena responded, taking John's hand in hers, "this stays between us. If anyone gets wind of this scandal it will be bad for you. The captain already has units watching over your ex and mine as a precaution since you were addressed with the first letter personally. We'll catch this asshole, okay?"

John felt comforted by his partner's words. He wanted to mention Valentina and that he had recently been sleeping with her but resisted. Already having revealed that he had had sex with their latest victim, a known prostitute, was enough information for one night. He wanted to preserve some self-respect by keeping the fact he was now bedding a stripper and potential witness to the case. They left the office and went back to the room where Alexis's body had been displayed and waited for the team to be finished with their work.

As difficult as it was, John removed his feelings for Alexis and returned to his usual calm and collected posture. He walked the room and let his imagination take control. Once again placing himself into the killer's shoes. He imagined the scene from the murderer's perspective. He tried to see everything through the killer's eyes. Trying to go over every detail and uncover any clue as to the identity of who might have wanted to kill Alexis and the stripper before her.

The methods and inspiration hit every detective in different ways. For John, it always came from his vivid imagination, playing out the events in his mind like the scene of a horror movie. Often details would return to him hours, or even days later when he would least expect it. He exited Alexis's room and ordered that the reports of all evidence and all witness interviews be completed and handed over to him as soon as possible.

The drive back to the station was silent. Selena knew better than to push him to talk. She was good at reading his body language and knew to keep quiet. John replayed the days' events carefully as he drove, and one thought troubled him. The reaction of the manager of the motel. He seemed to recognize Selena. John of course had seen and met the manager many times as he frequented the motel on his visits with Alexis, but how did he know Selena? And why did he seem scared of her? She had always done everything by the book, why now was she so eager to keep Alexis and John's sexual relationship a secret?

John dropped Selena off at her car and drove away. As he always did when faced with a dilemma or a victory, he found himself parked down the street overlooking his ex-wife's house once more. He just wanted to see her, even from a distance. The very sight of her calmed him and set things at ease. Whenever he had been stumped with questions, he would always talk to her about it. She would lay his head in her lap and stroke his hair till he fell asleep and when he would wake up, he would usually find the one missing piece of the puzzle. She was his muse.

Unfortunately, the house was dark. No one was home. John left and was about to head home when suddenly he found himself parked outside Valentina's building. It was almost as if he drove there on automatic pilot. He ventured inside and climbed the stairs. He hesitated before knocking on the door not knowing how she would react to him showing up unannounced. He walked away without knocking and was just about to leave when he heard the door open.

Valentina had heard his heavy footsteps and saw him through the peephole of her door. She could see that he was troubled and welcomed him inside for a drink. She was wearing a long, baggy shirt that hung just below her waist. Her long, tantalizing legs protruding from its base. John didn't want a drink. He wanted to forget the day. He wanted the distraction of physical connection.

Without warning, hint, or preview. John spun Valentina around and lifted her off the ground and sat her atop her kitchen table. Their mouths found each other again. Their tongues playfully sliding and slapping against one another. John tore away her shirt, then her panties. He removed his pants and boxers and dropped them to the floor. He slid himself inside her. Their collective moans echoing off the walls could be heard in the hallway. His powerful thrusts slid the table across the floor until it contacted the wall and came to a stop.

Valentina took control of the situation and forced John onto the floor and straddled him. Riding him to completion. Her juices flowing over his skin with his pumping inside her. She fell onto him. Her bare breasts pressed against his shirt. Their chests were both heaving as they fought to catch their breath from the effort of their passions. They managed to settle, and she laughed playfully at his urgency to have her. He apologized for being so forceful. There was an unspoken connection between them that John couldn't understand. And he didn't care.

Standing from the floor, Valentina led John into the bathroom and ran him a bath. They sat there together with the candlelight illuminating the small room. She sat behind him and he leaned against her with bubbles surrounding them and covering their exposed skin. She massaged his tense muscles as they sipped from the same wine glass. They remained in the water for a long time as he opened-up about what was troubling him. He had never felt so comfortable opening up to anyone. Not even Dr Morrison. Even more so than his ex-wife.

After the bath, John fell asleep laying in bed with Valentina stroking his hair. He must have had too much wine, he felt dizzy and drowsy and finally fell into a deep sleep. He awoke hours later in a panic, struggling to breath. His heart was racing as he remembered the dream that he had woken up from. It was a recurring dream that he had suffered from over the years.

In the dream, John walked down a narrow hallway. The ceiling seemed to be dropping slowly. The blood red walls would be closing in on him. There were black doors with gold lettering on their front, but the words were blurred from sight. At the end of the hall was an exit door. He would run towards it to escape but could never seem to get there. He could hear muffled voices as he fought to get out of the shrinking hallway.

John would always wake up in a panic when having the dream, never knowing if he was able to escape or not. He sat on the bed, covered in sweat and breathing heavily. He scanned the dark room for Valentina, hoping he hadn't frightened her. In her place on the bed was a note left on the pillow that read, "I'm sorry I had to go baby, but I had to get to work. Lock up when you leave and call me later," she signed it with her lipstick marks.

Finally, at home, John showered and climbed into his own bed. He felt as if he hadn't been there in days. He was nervous to sleep, not wanting to face the hallway again. His thoughts went back to Valentina and their time together. It wasn't long before he was asleep again, sleeping comfortably. He tried not to dwell on the thought that he would have to start investigating his partner Selena the next day for the murders of the unknown blonde stripper from Night Moves, and Alexis.

* * *

Beads of condensation slowly dripped down the glass and formed a ring around its base, then soaked into the coaster. The clear liquid was floating the ice cubes like boats in a still harbor. Selena sat across the bar staring at another customer's drink. She had ordered a club soda and was battling that little voice inside her that wanted her to breakdown and order a shot of tequila. Or maybe a little vodka, or some rum. She was hoping the noise of the bar would drown out the confusion of the days' events. All she was left with was having to fight her addiction.

Selena paid for her drink and left the bar hoping to avoid succumbing to her need for alcohol. As she neared the door, she recognized one of the young men at the door as the man she had taken home and had sex with recently. He looked like he wanted to come over and try for another night of fun with her. She slid her holstered pistol and badge to the front of her belt and walked past the young man without saying a word. It was difficult, but she had found her inner strength to continue battling her temptations and remain focused on her goals.

As she left the bar, Selena returned to the station instead of home. She was worried that being at home, alone, she might find one of her hidden bottles and drink herself into oblivion again. Then she might be compelled to invite another stranger into her pants leaving her to regret it the next morning. Though the hour was late, she decided to focus on work. She wanted to review Alexis's murder and the murder of the stripper dumped outside Night Moves. Whoever did this was targeting John for some reason. These murders were also connected to her daughter, since the pictures of her body had been delivered to her in the same manner the killer had sent the taunts to John.

Alone at her desk, Selena was scouring both files. Reading every note and staring at each photograph. As she looked through the crime scene photos of the Night Moves body dump, she noticed something. In the mud, next to the body, there was the shape of the letter S deliberately carved into the earth. Something clicked in Selena's mind. She had seen another symbol like that. She forced herself to venture into her purse and remove the envelope that contained the photos of her daughter's body.

The elastic of the latex gloves snapped against Selena's skin as she slid her hand in. She removed the plastic evidence bag from her purse and laid it on her desk. She slowly removed the envelope from the bag and took a deep breath to brace herself to look at the photos of her daughter again. As she stared down at the photos of her daughter, she saw something that was further confirmation that these murders were definitely connected. There was a red-letter S on the jersey her daughter was wearing. It appeared in each of the three photographs clearly and purposefully.

Selena shot up from her chair. She felt that familiar rush, finding a clue that ties a crime together. This case was far from solved but at least she knew she was getting somewhere. She knew that she was getting close to catching Anna-Maria's killer. She was getting closer to fulfilling her promise of vengeance. Though she could prove, if only to herself, that these cases were all connected, she had even more questions. There was one man she needed to ask them to. Lucas Durante.

It was the middle of the night, but Selena tried calling John anyway. The call went directly to his voicemail. She thought about going over to wake him. He was honest with her about having a sexual relationship with their latest victim, she thought she should share the discovery of her daughter's killer. The engine of her car rumbled as it idled as if waiting for her to decide where to go. She changed her mind and chose to go to the hospital instead without John.

All the evidence showed that Lucas Durante was involved with this latest killer somehow. John captured Durante in a secret room with the same polaroid pictures scattered everywhere. There was a soundproof torture room that looked the same as the one pictured in her daughter's pictures. There was a box of trophies in the very room where John was attacked by Durante. It was all in John's report of the arrest. Lucas Durante had to know who this killer was, that was copycatting his methods and continuing this sick game.

The hospital was quiet. The emergency room was slow with very few patients filling the beds. Selena followed the directions guiding her to where she knew she could find Lucas Durante. She had to flash her badge to get past the security guard protecting the patients and doctors of the hospital. Her previous desire to kill Lucas Durante entered her mind and she quickly realized how difficult that would be. The cameras captured her image as she made her way to question him. The security guard would surely remember her. She tried to remove all thoughts of revenge as she neared the room.

The young officer stationed outside the room was clearly a rookie. He was standing at full attention, ready for action as if he were a secret service agent guarding the president. Selena applied her charms. She was an extremely beautiful woman and knew how to use this when needed, especially when dealing with men. She unpinned her hair and let it hang low and changed her posture to accentuate the view of her breasts. The young officer tried to remain focused, but no man can resist the charm of a woman so gorgeous, especially one so inexperienced with members of the opposite sex.

A playful smile, a flash of the badge and a flirtatious glance were enough to get Selena around the guard. To his credit, the young officer thoroughly checked her credentials and mentioned he had recognized her from around the station. Once in the room, she felt that burning urge. That hot anger that had been building up inside her until her entire body was quivering with fury. Her hand instinctively palmed her pistol as she neared the foot of the bed.

Selena stared down at the man responsible for the deaths of countless young women. The man she knew in her heart, was connected to the murder of her baby girl. Her hands trembled. Her teeth clenched. She almost didn't care what happened to her anymore. She could put a bullet in this son-of-a-bitch's forehead and be done with it. Her thumb unclasped the holster. Her fingers wrapped around the grip and tightened. She pulled her hand up and felt the pistol sliding out of its leather prison.

Just as the pistol was near fully unsheathed, Lucas Durante woke up and stared up at Selena. His eyes opened wide and he motioned towards the bandages and tubes that protruded from the wound on his throat. She dropped the pistol back into place within its holster and instead removed her cell phone. She brought up Anna-Maria's portrait and showed it to Lucas Durante.

"Do you remember her?" Selena growled.

Lucas looked confused and shook his head. He kept motioning towards his throat. His eyes were filled with tears.

His confusion turned to terror as he could sense Selena's rage. It took everything for Selena not to carry out her desire to end his life. She wouldn't have to shoot him. All she would have to do is pull out these hoses and wires keeping him alive. She brought her phone closer to Durante's face and grabbed onto the tubes preparing to pull.

"Look at her. You raped her. You tortured and killed her, you, sick bastard. Look at her. Look at what you took from me," Selena shouted as she tugged on the hose that protruded from inside Durante's throat and was helping him breathe.

Lucas Durante had a panicked look on his face trying to mouth the words, "It wasn't me", and, "I didn't do it". He motioned with his hands for something to write with. Selena returned to a sense of calm and self-control. She had noticed the young officer had entered the room and saw what she was about to do.

"Detective, what are you doing?" the young officer demanded. He motioned towards her to stop what she was doing.

"Look Skippy," Selena said. then took a step back and removed her weapon, "just get the hell out of here."

"I can't do that ma'am. Back away from the bed, now," he ordered as he aimed his service pistol at Selena. "Lower your weapon and leave the room. It'll end here."

As the young officer walked closer to disarm her, Selena put her training to use. She was the more experienced officer and knew how to defend against a larger attacker. In one swift motion, she removed the pistol from the young officer's extended arms and knocked him to the ground, breaking his nose in the process. She aimed his own pistol at the officer and demanded he get out of the room. He didn't argue and stumbled his way out the door struggling to find his footing.

Selena knew she didn't have much time. She removed her note pad and pen and gave it to Durante. She placed the muzzle of the gun hard against his testicles and demanded he write down everything he knew, and that he had better write quickly before she pulled the trigger. Terrified, Lucas's hands furiously scribbled down what he could. It wasn't long before there was the commotion of the officer and security guard in the hall.

"Hurry up Lucas, I'll pull this trigger. I swear to Christ," Selena screamed as she heard the footsteps getting closer and closer.

The overweight security guard chased close behind the bloodied officer down the hall. He had removed his pistol and charged forward towards the room at the end of the hall where the beautiful but dangerous detective had just struck an officer and was threatening to kill a patient. The security officer and young cop could hear screaming from the room as they neared. The young cop kicked the door as they security officer burst in with his pistol aimed.

Selena heard the footsteps draw closer and quickly took the notepad back from Lucas Durante's hands and returned it to her purse before the door was kicked open. Selena dropped the young officer's pistol to the ground and complied with their orders to turn around and place her hands behind her back. The young officer clasped the handcuffs onto her wrists and shoved her out of the room.

The doctor and several nurses entered the room to check the patient. Other than evacuating his bladder, and being utterly petrified, Lucas Durante was in no worse shape than before Selena had entered his hospital room. The young officer led Selena down to his squad car and stepped away to make a private phone call. Selena was curious why the young man didn't follow procedure and call the incident into the station. She sat silently waiting for what punishment surely awaited her for this stunt.

It was nearly an hour of waiting in the back of the squad car, handcuffed like a common criminal before the young man returned. Walking alongside him was Captain McGee. Selena bowed her head in shame. The captain was the last man she wanted to see. The officer removed her from the car, then unlocked the handcuffs. The doctors had bandaged his damaged nose and he seemed to be quite embarrassed by the whole event. The captain thanked the young man and took Selena by the arm and led her to his car.

"You want to tell me what in God's name you were thinking tonight? Have you just completely lost your goddamn mind? Is that it?" the captain shouted once inside his car.

"I had to look him in the eyes. I had to see if he is the one who killed Anna," Selena shouted back.

"So instead of doing things the right way, you destroy any chance of prosecuting him? You give his lawyer grounds for dismissal, a lawsuit. You'll be lucky if all you lose is your job after this," the captain yelled, like a father scolding a petulant teenager.

"I don't care about my job. I had to know," Selena said then lost her battle to hold back her tears and cried into her hands.

"What did your idiotic little stunt prove then? What information did he give you?" the captain asked frustratedly.

"He didn't kill Anna," Selena said once she had calmed herself.

"You know that how? How did a man who can't speak tell you that?" the captain shot back sardonically.

"His eyes," Selena replied. "I could see it in his eyes. He had no idea what I was talking about, and he was telling the truth."

The captain and Selena sat in the car for a long time. Captain McGee didn't know what to do. He wasn't sure he could save Selena from herself anymore. If Lucas Durante presses charges, she will lose the one thing that could've brought her back to her former self, her career. They sat in silence until he finally ordered that at the very least, after the night's events she would be required to see the department psychiatrist on an even more frequent basis. He demanded that she be in his office first thing in the morning to try and fix what she had done.

Selena returned to her car and watched the captain drive away wiping the tears from her eyes. In her mind she replayed what went on in that hospital room and she knew now that Lucas Durante was no killer. She could see it in his eyes. How could John have gotten it so wrong? John's instincts were never wrong, how could he have missed this?

Why was Lucas Durante his only suspect? Nothing about this case made sense.

After being taken into custody and scolded by Captain McGee, Selena had almost forgotten her notebook. She removed the leather-bound book from her bag and opened it up and flipped through the pages until she found what Lucas Durante had written. As she read the roughly written note. Her eyes widened. Her mind raced with even more confusion. This case had gone from difficult to impossible. If what Lucas Durante had written was true, it could destroy the entire homicide division.

* * *

The latest kill had satiated the killer's thirst. He returned to the cover life he had created. Smiling and posturing, pretending to be a normal person. He walked among the citizens of Lugar De Paz City and revelled in the thought that they had no idea of the danger that walked next to them. He considered himself the Grim Reaper and these fools were none the wiser.

The pictures taken of Alexis kept his need for sexual release in check. He would stare at the photos and videos of her abuse, the captured images of her torture and rape. In his deeply disturbed mind, he thought he had given her what she deserved. All these filthy women who can sell themselves so carelessly deserved his punishment. Where normal people look to the words of poets and writers, great leaders and men and women of history for inspiration, this killer was inspired by the likes of Jack the Ripper and Ted Bundy.

The killer continued following Detective Lopez. He watched her struggle with her decision to kill. He had hoped she had the courage to dispatch that pathetic excuse of a man laying in the hospital bed. He watched her drive to the hospital that night and followed her inside. He was there, watching from the shadows as she failed to dispose of Lucas Durante. She allowed herself to be arrested by a rent-a-cop and a rookie policeman barely out of diapers. His hopes of her being worthy were fading.

This experienced hunter prided himself on years of perfecting his methods. He had killed more people than he could remember and was never even suspected for it. Yet this time, in his most favourite of games, he had left a major loose end. He left this one detail to throw John off the scent for awhile. He had hoped John had the spine to remove this stone from his shoe, but alas he couldn't either. John and Selena were exceptional detectives, but they were not killers.

The doctors finished their check up on Lucas Durante after Selena's botched attempt on his life. They left the room after cleaning up their patient's sheets and administering a sedative to help him sleep. Moving in darkness, the killer entered the room. There was a small light left on above the bed where Lucas Durante slept. The killer slowly moved towards the bed. He stared down at the sleeping scapegoat he had arranged. He underestimated his pursuers' abilities and now the deaths of these women contradicted the frame of Mr. Durante. For how could he be the killer if he was already in custody while the bodies continued to drop?

The killer moved in closer. He moved the alarm button just out of reach and applied the restraints to Durante's wrists to prevent him from moving. He removed the smelling salts from his pocket and brought it to Durante's nostrils, jolting him awake from his medicated slumber. He struggled to focus. The room was dark, and he could barely see until the killer leaned out of the shadows and let the light hit the curves of his face, revealing his identity to Durante.

Lucas panicked at the sight and struggled to free himself from the restraints. He could see the alarm button to call the nurse. It was right next to his hand. He stretched as far as he could but couldn't grasp it. He struggled to take hold of it while the killer stood watching with disturbed amusement. Like a cat watching a mouse try to scurry away from its claws.

"You remember me, don't you Lucas?" the gravely, growling voice hissed.

Lucas tried to avoid looking back into the man's face. He remained focused on retrieving the button to call the nurse. The killer moved to the other side of the bed and handed the button to Lucas, placing the remote in his hand. Lucas pressed the red button repeatedly. Again, and again it clicked.

"I suppose I had better leave now," the killer's haunting voice said. Then he reached down and raised the cord. It had been cut, completely disabling its signal to the nursing staff. The killer removed a syringe from his dark jacket and waved it in front Lucas' face.

"You know what this is don't you Lucas? You know what it does?" the killer asked rhetorically. "Its time to kill you for good this time old friend."

The killer walked over to the life support system and entered a code that deactivated its alarms. He brought the needle of the syringe to the intravenous line and slid it into the injection port and slowly depressed the plunger. Lucas sat in horror as he watched the fluid leave the syringe and enter his line that fed into his veins. He tried to remove the line from his arm, but the restraints held him firmly in place. The drug made its way through the array of tubes then into Lucas's bloodstream.

As the drug hit Lucas's system, its effect caused a seizure. Lucas's body jolted back and forth. His muscles seized and spasmed. He was wracked in complete agony until his heart took its last beat. Lucas Durante looked directly into the killer's face and that horrible, evil grin would be the last thing he would ever see as his pupils dilated completely. His muscles relaxed as the air left his lungs for the last time.

Lucas Durante was dead. The killer had tied off the one loose end that could sink him and vanished from the room as swiftly as he had entered it. Unbeknownst to the killer. When Lucas was struggling to reach the call button for the nurse, he was using Selena Lopez's pen that she had dropped earlier to write the identity of the killer on the plastic side rail of the gurney.

CHAPTER SEVEN

The smell of fresh-made coffee filled the air of the small diner, combined with the delicious food being prepared in the kitchen. John sat at his usual booth and stirred the cream and sugar into his mug of steaming hot coffee. As he slowly sipped the hot beverage, he pretended to engage in the small talk the waitress was trying to intrigue him with. He counted the seconds until she left his table then went over his notes. The strange fact was that John related better with victims and killers than with regular people.

It had been several days since Alexis's body was found at the motel and, just as it was with the blonde stripper's murder, there was little to go on. John had secretly been looking into his partner's recent behaviour. There was something in the look of the motel manager that night. John knew fear when he saw it and when Selena spoke to that manager it swept over him. What could Selena have done to make this man so terrified of her? Had she threatened him? Did he see her doing something? John forced his loyalty to Selena as his partner and fellow officer aside. He had to delve more into his partner's life to know what she was capable of.

In the two years since her daughter's death, Selena had ventured down a dark path of destruction. John had uncovered several arrests for being drunk and disorderly where the reports were filed without any formal charges laid. There were many citations of driving while intoxicated where her car was impounded, and her driver's license suspended for three months. In every instance, Captain McGee was there to keep the troubled detective's record clean.

John had interviewed several bartenders, as well as bouncers, and some of the regulars at some of the bars Detective Lopez was known to be frequenting. There was a clear pattern emerging. Selena had been drowning her sorrows on almost a nightly basis. She was sleeping with anyone who would have her and that ultimately sacrificed her marriage. John tried to contact Selena's ex-husband to ask his side of things but was denied. John knew his partner was grieving the loss of her daughter but had no idea she had fallen so far from her former self.

The motel manager had gone into hiding and couldn't be tracked down anywhere. John had spoken with his usual snitches and the word on the street was that the manager had fled town. There was nothing more to go on. John decided he would have to keep a closer watch on his partner. Everything he had uncovered pointed to her being unstable. She clearly returned to work with the sole purpose to solve her daughter's murder at all cost. John had to protect her. From herself.

The investigation into Selena made things between the two detectives extra tense. John was trying to maintain the usual friendliness that had always existed between them. All the while he thought she was hiding something. Before, they spent nearly every day together. They never got tired of each other's company and, at times, acted like a brother and sister act. They used to be attached at the hip, solving cases left and right. Now, the bodies were piling up. The pair could hardly stand each other for more than a few minutes at a time and their daily cases weren't getting solved.

With breakfast over, John drove over to Dr Morrison's office. It was time for his usual appointment and John wanted to get something to help him sleep. His recurring dream of the shrinking hallway was happening more often. He would always have these dreams during periods of heightened stress or increased pressure. Since Alexis's death and investigating Selena, the dream came every night. He would wake up gasping for air and feeling the same crushing feeling on his chest.

The session was its typical back and forth. Dr Morrison attributed the dream to stress and told John to try some meditation techniques to take his mind off all the recent stresses to avoid having the dream. At least she had prescribed a light sedative that should help. John left the office in the usual fashion, more confused than he was before the appointment started. Dr Morrison always dressed so provocatively, and John suspected she wanted to sleep with him. He certainly wanted to oblige but knew it wouldn't bode well with the captain if word ever got out.

John was turned on as he left the medical building where Dr Morrison's office was. He took a small detour and drove over to Valentina's. Being with her made him forget all his stress. He wouldn't have to think about Selena and her instability. He didn't have to think about his ex-wife or Alexis's last judgemental impression of him. It was the one place where he could be totally in the moment and free. Being with her was the highlight of his days.

Traffic was heavy for that time of day and it took John longer to get to Valentina's side of town. He had stopped to pick up some flowers and her favourite bottle of wine. He finally reached her apartment and made his way up to her door. He could hear some commotion inside, but she wouldn't answer. John pounded on the door urging Valentina to respond, but still there was no answer at the door. Concern took over, as there were sounds from behind the door, yet she still wouldn't answer.

A scream and several loud thuds, that sounded like something heavy being dropped onto the floor, alerted John.

He quickly drew his pistol and dropped the wine and flowers before taking a step back. John raised his foot and hurled his weight into a heavy kick shooting the door open with a thunderous crack as it slammed against the wall. He entered the apartment with his pistol aimed, announcing his presence and calling out for Valentina. There was no answer or sign of her.

As John neared the French doors which led into the bedroom, he took a deep breath and hesitated, not knowing what he might find. He turned the handle and pulled the door towards him. As the door opened, John moved to look inside when a shadowy figure bolted towards him with a baseball bat. John quickly ducked as the bat narrowly missed his head and struck the glass of the door behind him. John fell to the floor and the figure ran out of the apartment. John got off the floor and gave chase.

Pounding footsteps echoed in the empty hallways as the shadowy figure ran away. John stayed a safe distance behind to make sure the figure wouldn't get too far from sight and to avoid being attacked or shot. As the chase went through the halls, down the stairs and finally out of the building, for some reason John was reminded of his shrinking hallway dream. John ignored his déjà vu and demanded that the fleeing figure stop.

John followed the figure around the corner of the building and was getting closer. He pushed himself to run faster but the figure was too quick. John couldn't discern whether the figure was male of female. He couldn't see any skin to determine race. John reached to grab hold of the black flowing fabric but stretched too far and briefly lost his footing and stumbled allowing the figure to break free. John didn't give up. He regained his footing and sprinted down the alleyway where Valentina had said a strange man had followed her before.

Nearing the end of the alley, John had lost sight of the quick figure. He felt winded and wanted to give up but knew he had to catch whoever this was. This might be Alexis's killer. John ignored his burning lungs and the spots in his line of vision as he turned the corner into the street. A sharp pain struck his head. His vision went all white as he was taken clear off his feet and hit the pavement. John was knocked unconscious.

* * *

The hands of the clock ticked away slowly. It felt like an eternity had passed and yet the intended hour of the appointment was still counting down with time remaining. After what she had done at the hospital, threatening a suspect and striking an officer, Selena was meeting with the division's psychiatrist to prove herself fit to remain on active duty. This was the first of what would be many more meetings in the near-future and Selena thoroughly hated every second.

This elderly woman had no idea what it was to be a detective. To be through the things Selena had. Selena had found out the woman had never had children. She had been married several times and remained close with her ex-husbands. How could she pass judgement on Selena with no experience in the very matters that cause Selena her pain? Selena found herself judging the woman throughout the entire appointment. She would have to play nice if she wanted to continue working. If she wanted to catch her daughter's killer.

Since the evening at the hospital, Selena had been setting out to prove Lucas Durante's claim in the note that he had scribbled down before she was forced to leave. She had to tread lightly due to what might be involved. If she was wrong, she would lose her career. She had pulled up old files to research the claim made by a suspected murderer. She knew this could have been a clever smokescreen by Durante, but she had a strong hunch. A detective's greatest weapon is their intellect and the best detectives follow their gut reactions and intuitions to solve cases. Selena spent most of her appointment praying for it to be over so she could return to more important things.

The appointment came to its end and Selena managed to hide her contempt for this old fool who held her career as a detective within her grasp. Selena carefully chose her responses to make sure she would be cleared to remain active. She couldn't get out of the office fast enough. A thought occurred to Selena as she left the building. What if this woman could help with her grief? She had too much to contend with. This case had become much more difficult and she had to be extra careful how she would proceed.

The troubled and confusing thoughts that scurried about in Selena's mind were instantly silenced by the ringing tone of her cell phone. It was Captain McGee. Selena didn't want to answer. He probably wanted a full status report on her appointment with the department shrink. Selena hated herself for letting the captain down. He was a good man who had risked a great deal to help her through her grief. He had always treated her like a daughter, and she thought of him like the father she had lost as a young girl. She hoped the day would come where she could make him proud of her again.

Selena avoided the phone call since she was headed back to the homicide department and would be seeing the captain shortly. Her mind was dissecting the doctor's analysis as she returned to her desk. The doctor had struck a sensitive chord with Selena and though she had put up her strongest armor, the doctor's comments and observations made her look at herself. She was left contemplating her recent actions and felt rather shameful.

The deep self reflection was interrupted by the captain knocking his massive fist against his office window to get Selena's attention. She put away her thoughts of the doctor and prepared what she would say to the captain. She couldn't mention what Lucas had written in that note. Not yet. There was still some information she needed to put together. She needed to make sure she had a case before involving the captain.

"Shut the door and sit down," Captain McGee said. Not quite angry but certainly not himself. "You weren't answering your cell."

"I'm sorry captain, was just finishing up with the shrink," Selena answered.

"Good. I told her you needed to be there twice a week. No one knows about what happened at the hospital the other night. As long as you keep up with the doctor, no one will," the captain said.

"Yes sir," Selena complied, trying to find an easy way to bring up Lucas Durante.

"Speaking of the hospital, did you hear what happened after you left the other night?" Captain McGee asked, studying Selena's reaction.

"No sir. What?" Selena returned, confused.

"Lucas Durante had some sort of seizure. It dislodged the tube in his throat somehow and his heart gave out. He's dead," Captain McGee answered.

"Now what?" Selena asked staring down at her collection of file folders.

"Well, forensics has linked the victims to his collection of trophies. His pictures and videos. Obviously, what we have going on here is a copycat, with that stripper outside the club and that hooker at the motel," Captain McGee said.

"We'll get the bastard sir," Selena said.

"Did Lucas Say anything to you that night? What did you say to him?" He asked like a cop would ask a suspect.

"I showed him Anna-Maria's picture. Made him look at it and asked if he remembered her. He didn't. He couldn't talk, kept pointing at his throat. It was just his eyes. I've stared into the eyes of many killers captain and just didn't see one in him." Selena answered.

"I see," Captain McGee said, thinking carefully about what Selena had said and watching her intently. It was quite clear he had lost faith in his favourite detective. "Where is John today? He isn't answering his phone either."

"I'm not sure sir, I haven't seen much of him outside of work since coming back," Selena replied.

"Well get in touch with him. I want movement on these cases. Your guys' day-to-day cases are beginning to pile up," the captain ordered. Selena stood to leave but as she neared the door he added, "Selena, Internal Affairs is going to want to speak with you about Lucas Durante. You were the last to see him alive. I've done my best to keep you clear of the dirt, but you seem hellbent on running through it. Just be prepared."

Selena left the captain's office and returned to her desk. It was never easy being scorned by a superior, but to have the captain look at her with such disappointment broke her heart. She would have to work extra hard to win back his trust. She knew now wasn't the time to bring up what Lucas Durante had written to her. Whoever's name was written in that notebook did not want Lucas talking to the police. Whoever was killing these women and copycatting Lucas Durante wanted him silenced. This killer must be watching closely and covering their tracks.

The rest of the evening was spent behind her desk going over the files of recent cases. Selena had called John several times and there was no answer. She had grown tired of trying to keep track of her partner. He was hardly ever at the station anymore. He was always out, claiming to be working on cases without her and he seemed to trust her less than the captain. Everything between them had changed and John was different now. There was something in his royal blue eyes that disturbed Selena. He used to look at her with pride, now his gaze reminded her of how he looked when interrogating a suspect.

It was long into the evening hours when Selena set out for home. She had caught herself up on her recent cases and had some more leads to look-into to further investigate Lucas Durante's claims. She was feeling drowsy and was nearly falling asleep as she drove home. As her car drove by the bars she used to drink at, she realized she no longer felt that urgency to go in. Perhaps she was over her habit. Or maybe she was just too tired to have a drink, either way, she continued to her home and wanted to shut her eyes.

The neighbourhood where Selena lived was quiet. It was lined up with small bungalows with their red-clay shingles. The streetlamps were few and far between keeping the streets relatively dark this time of night. Selena slowed down as she turned the tight corners leading up to her house.

As she neared her house, she could see the beam of a flashlight from inside her front window.

Selena switched off her headlights and parked her car up the street. She watched the flashlight move from her front window into her kitchen. She quickly called in back-up and gave her location. She removed her pistol and crept her way up to her house. As Selena neared the door, she could hear hushed voices. It sounded like a man's voice and a woman's voice arguing about finding something.

The door opened slowly without making a sound as Selena pushed her way through. She followed the whispering voices into the kitchen. She turned the corner and accidentally bumped a framed picture that hung low on the wall. The frame fell and exploded glass onto the hardwood floor alerting the prowler in the kitchen. Selena shone her flashlight into the kitchen to see who it was and how many burglars there were.

There were two loud shots fired from inside the kitchen. Selena quickly took cover behind the wall. The bullets hit the drywall and caused two small craters in its smoothed surface. Selena got low and peaked around the corner to see a massive figure break open her back door and flee into her backyard. Selena rose to her feet and made her way to the door.

Three more shots were fired at Selena before she could exit the house. Each bullet hit the sliding glass doors which led to the backyard. Selena returned fire. She pulled the trigger, firing three rounds into the black of night hitting the wood of her fence as she saw the prowler scale its tall height. She ran up to the fence and hopped over then ran through her neighbour's backyard chasing the armed burglar who had just broken into her house. Once she reached the street, there was no sign of anyone.

Selena returned to her house as patrol cars pulled up with their flashing blue and red lights. She gave her report to the officers and searched through the house. There was nothing stolen or missing. The office where she kept all her files and her computer was ransacked. Papers were strewn about. Her desk had been rifled through. Whoever broke in was looking for what she knew. They weren't looking for money or jewelry. They wanted what she had been looking into and any information she might have found.

It was late into the night by the time Selena had settled her report. The officers left, and Selena locked up her house and packed a few bags. She was careful that no one followed her as she went and found a small, cheap, motel to stay at until she could have the locks at her house changed. There was no doubt that the killer was the one who had just broken into her home. Suddenly, any doubt Selena might have felt towards Lucas Durante's innocence faded. The name he had written in her notebook went to the forefront of her mind as her prime suspect.

* * *

The killer had once more returned to the hunt. He had spent his relaxing hours watching his two mice struggle through the maze he had been creating. The craving was coming back, much sooner than ever before. That urge and thirst had gotten stronger. That tireless need to kill was more potent. He had watched the videos and scoured the photographs taken of his victims, but the mere images weren't enough to hold the need at bay. He needed the feel of flesh, that look of terror. The screams of horror in his ears like a terrible symphony.

It had been mere weeks since his scene at the motel, killing that hooker whom Detective Davis had been sleeping with. John had since moved on to another beautiful plaything. Like the first victim in this round of kills, she, too, was a stripper from the club Night Moves. She was young and gorgeous, and the killer could tell she meant a great deal to John. He had spent a lot of time watching the star detective. Studying him closely, watching the way he worked, and what made him tick. He would be broken if another of his lady friends were taken from him.

The tenement Valentina called home was in a rather forgotten part of the city. Very little foot traffic on the sidewalks and even fewer cars on the street. Everyone who lived there kept their business to themselves and didn't want to know what other people were in to. The people that made up this neighbourhood were well accustomed to the way the city works. They had their own laws and existed on their own terms. They took care of themselves and rarely called upon outsiders for help.

This neighbourhood was perfect hunting grounds for a killer in need of a new victim. He had been watching Valentina since she first caught Detective Davis's eye. The killer had been to the club and watched her dance. He admired her control of the crowd with a simple gesture or move of her body. Her beauty outshone all the other dancers. The killer could see why Detective Davis was so taken with her and respected his eye for beauty.

There had been a few nights when the killer had purchased time in the Champagne Room for a private dance with Valentina. His urges had gotten the better of him and he was asked to leave several times for being too physical. He waited in the dark for the dancer's shift to end and followed her home. She caught him the first night he had tried following her and called in the hero detective to her rescue.

She rewarded Detective Davis that night by spreading her legs and letting him inside. The killer managed to spy on the whole event.

Watching Detective Davis enjoy her flesh made the killer want her more and more. Like a jealous child wanting every toy as his own, he needed to make her his. He kept watching from a distance as John and Valentina kept up their relationship in secret. Detective Davis would arrive at all hours and spend the night. The killer decided it was time for another round in the game. This would be a blow John would struggle greatly with. The killer set his sites on Valentina.

Detective Davis had spent another night and left early in the morning. He went home and showered, then went off to his usual diner for breakfast. The killer knew Detective Davis had his usual meeting at the psychiatrist's office across town. He had a brief window of opportunity. He left Detective Davis to enjoy his breakfast at his favourite diner and set out to take away another of his beautiful companions. It was time to turn up the heat in the game.

The killer returned to Valentina's apartment building. He picked the lock and crept inside to find Valentina had left the apartment. He snooped through her things. Looked through her music collection, her magazines, and books. He looked through her underwear drawer, inventoried her lingerie and costumes she wore when she danced. He found her toys and devices she used in her sex-play. He carefully set the stage for his next victim. He arranged his tools and prepared to carry out his next murder.

Valentina had been out shopping and was gone for a few hours. She returned home and was in the middle of stocking her shelves in the kitchen and refrigerator, when strong and powerful arms suddenly wrapped around her neck. The killer put her in a choke hold, cutting off the blood flow and oxygen to her brain. After several minutes of her trying to struggle, she fell asleep and went limp. The killer dragged her unconscious body to the bedroom.

The sting of smelling salts returned Valentina to awareness. She awoke to find herself tied to her own bed. She was wearing one of her costumes and there was a ball gag strapped tightly between her teeth. She couldn't move or make a sound. She fought and tried to free herself until the silhouette of a massive figure walked in front one of the bright lights set up to shine directly upon her. She couldn't see his face.

The killer had picked red lingerie and dressed Valentina up while she was knocked-out. He ran his hands slowly up and down her body. He took his knife with his left hand and sliced away the fabric one strap at a time. He enjoyed every shutter and squirm Valentina made as he kept cutting away until she lay fully nude atop her bed. He felt himself harden beneath his pants. The urge was taking over, and he imagined the light leaving her eyes. Making her heart stop as his pounded within his ribcage. It was his turn to taste Valentina's flesh.

The killer placed himself between Valentina's muscular legs. He was about to remove his pants when there was loud banging from the other room. Detective Davis had returned unexpectedly. The killer shut the French doors to the bedroom and armed himself with a baseball bat. It wasn't John's time to die just yet. The killer listened to John enter the apartment and make his way to the bedroom. The French door opened slowly, and the killer gave a powerful warning swing just above John's head to scare him off.

Sprinting down the narrow halls and stairways, then out the door, the killer developed more respect for John being able to keep up so closely. He quickly tried to lose John down an alley, but the detective persisted, coming close to catching him several times. It wasn't time for John to know who his nemesis was just yet. The killer managed to get ahead of John and darted around the corner, arming the bat, waiting for him to exit the alley.

One powerful swing sent the baseball bat's polished, hard surface into John's skull. The sudden strike coupled with John's momentum of running, took his body off his feet. His back slammed down against the hard pavement. The killer checked his pulse and breathing before disappearing, unseen, into the safety of the shadows. He had never been interrupted while conducting his work before. He smirked as he had finally found a worthy adversary that brought a whole new level of danger to his game.

Detective John and Valentina had gone into hiding after the attempt on the stripper's life. The killer returned to watching the second mouse in this maze he had created. He followed Detective Lopez on her daily routine. He knew about that night back in the hospital, Lucas Durante gave her something to work with. He had stood in the shadows watching her and saw that look in her eye when she sat alone staring at her notebook. What did Lucas Durante give her?

Lucas Durante was supposed to be his scapegoat. All those years ago he had arranged the evidence against Durante and made him the police's number one suspect. Before the killer could subdue Durante and set him up to be captured, he fled the city. Lucas Durante had been on the run ever since until he returned to town. The killer spotted him in a well-known drug den while searching for a new victim. The plan had formed. He went to work. His plan was to add to Durante's body count.

The killer underestimated Detective John's connections. His snitch had recognized Lucas Durante and told John where to find him. Now, the killer would have to find a new scapegoat. He knew he would have to eventually kill the snitch who ruined his plans, he had already disposed of Lucas Durante, but he must have given Detective Lopez something, but what? If she knew the killer's identity, she would've already arrested him by now. Unless she wasn't sure. He had to make sure she couldn't ruin the game.

With Detective Davis hiding his girlfriend, Detective Lopez was working her cases alone. Due to her overzealousness at the hospital, she was now required to see a psychiatrist. The killer would love to be a bug in the wall during those conversations. He had listened in on a few of John's sessions with his therapist. It was a good way to learn more about the man chasing him. The killer remained at a distance, to be careful of whatever information Lucas Durante had given to Selena.

After the therapist's appointment Detective Lopez returned to the station and went to work. If she stuck to her new routine, she would remain at the office long into the night. The killer knew he would have enough time to search her house. He had been watching her ever since the hospital but hadn't seen her with her black notebook since that night. She must have hidden it somewhere and he already combed through everything on her desk and computer at the police station.

With Detective Lopez hard at work, the killer turned her house upside down searching for her notebook. He searched her desk, every file she kept there, and all through her computer. There was nothing. He was nearly about to give up when he heard Detective Lopez open the door. He had to scramble to flee the small home, firing several warning shots to keep her from chasing him. The darkness of night made it easy for him to escape.

These two detectives were both accomplished and in a span of a few days, they both had nearly caught this once impeccable killer. He had never made a mistake. He had never come so close to being caught. He loved the thrill. The hunter being hunted. Narrowly avoiding capture. It was all too much fun. He had successfully pitted the two partners against one another. They were now suspecting each other instead of looking for who the killer really was. It was all too much fun. And he was just getting started.

CHAPTER EIGHT

The fluorescent tubes flickered and fluttered, blinking their dim light up and down the narrow hallway. The walls were painted with a glossy, deep, dark, red which appeared wet. The walls looked as if they had been sprayed and covered with fresh blood. The floor was black marble that reflected the strobing fluorescent lighting. Each step on the floor echoed loudly in the narrow space like the inside of some blood-soaked cave. The sight alone was unnerving.

There were tall, slender doors, painted deathly black which lined-up and down the hallway on either side. At the hall's end, there was a door with a small window beneath a glowing red neon exit sign. John felt familiar with this place. Walking towards the exit he had the feeling that he had been here before. He was suddenly stricken with fear as he stared down the hall.

Muffled voices could be heard all around, John couldn't source exactly where the voices were coming from and wasn't able to discern what was being said. There was a feeling of intense paranoia that fueled the fear surging through John's entire body. He didn't recognize the voices but was certain whatever was being said was about him. He struggled to hear what was being said but it was no use. It was as if he wasn't meant to hear.

Panic activated John's fight/flight response in his brain, and he tried running as fast as he could towards the exit sign. There was a darkness behind him swallowing all the light and getting closer and closer. John knew he had to escape. As hard as he tried, he couldn't make his legs run faster. The darkness was getting closer. John could feel it directly behind him. He forced himself to run as his legs became heavier and heavier. The air left his lungs from the struggle making it extremely difficult to breath.

John stretched-out his hand reaching for the door at the end of the hall. He was nearly there when the walls closed in on him and narrowed the hall. The light in the hall was quickly disappearing. The impending darkness was closing in. John couldn't breathe. His legs struggled to move as the walls shrunk inward more and more. His heart thumped in his chest from his desperate effort. He truly felt this might be the end.

The darkness was upon John's back. The only light was the hellish glow of the red exit sign above the door and the light from the small window. The walls continued shrinking making it almost impossible to reach the door. John used the last of his strength and forced his legs to jump as he hurled himself towards the door, slamming the palms of his hands against the handlebar pushing the heavy door open.

John's body shot off the bed as he awoke from his nightmare. He was covered in sweat as wet as if he had just been swimming. His hair was drenched. His chest was heaving as he fought to catch his breath. His lungs were on fire and his legs tingled as if he had just finished running on the treadmill. John's intensely blue eyes scanned the room and returned him to a sense of calm revealing that he was in the bedroom of his neatly compartmentalized apartment.

The cool floor felt good against the heat of John's sweat-soaked skin. He laid there for a long time, angry and frustrated that this dream continued to torment him. John finally raised from the floor and left the bedroom to go to the kitchen for a drink of water. Valentina was still asleep in his bed and John was amazed at her ability to remain in slumber after he awoke in such a panic. He closed the door behind him knowing he wouldn't be able to go back to sleep after this.

There was something easier about working in the late-night hours. There was something about working so late that made the brain work easier. John always found the answers would come to him easier in the night. He made himself a pot of coffee and sat at the small table of his kitchen. If he couldn't make himself sleep, he might as well try and find this killer. If he could just close this case, he might be able to stop this nightmare and have a decent night's sleep.

John was reading over the paperwork and going over each crime scene. He read over his notes and employed his creative imagination to form a picture of this killer who had taken Alexis's life and had nearly killed Valentina. John flipped through the pages of notes he had scribbled down. He imagined each of the women being attacked. He imagined their deaths and tried to see himself as their attacker. This disturbing process had always worked in the past for him. His enlightened sense helped him imagine everything from the killer's perspective.

There was page after page written of John's thoughts on each crime. He reread his writing until he reached his latest entry. He had interviewed Valentina after rescuing her from her attack days before. John asked her everything she could remember from the event which wasn't much. He read the vague description of what she could recall, and his imagination returned him to her apartment.

Valentina remembered walking into her apartment then everything went black. She woke up on her bed with her wrists and ankles tied to the four corners of the bed not allowing her to move at all. There was a ball gag in her mouth keeping her from making any sound. Bright work lights had been set-up and shone down on her, blinding her sight. She could smell menthol cigarettes in the air and hear the whispered conversation of two people before a dark figure stepped into the light.

The lights prevented Valentina from identifying the figure, the size and shape of its shadow, together with the immense strength, made it obvious this was a man. There was a second person in the background directing what was to happen next. This second person stood out of Valentina's line of sight and tried to disguise their voice, but it was female. Whoever stood in the background taking pictures and directed this horrifying scene was in charge.

The next thing Valentina recalled was hearing John's voice from outside the apartment. The two figures panicked and hid after arming themselves. Valentina lay helpless unable to warn John as the male figure had risen a baseball bat above his head and prepared to strike John as he entered. The male figure tried to hit John then fled, making John give chase out of the apartment, leaving Valentina exposed and vulnerable, still tied to the bed.

After John chased the would be killer out of the apartment, the second assailant emerged from Valentina's closet. There was a moment when the figure stood still, briefly, staring down at her then left the apartment. As this second shadowy figure motioned towards the bedroom door to leave, they knocked over the bright light's stand, making the bright beam shine upward towards the ceiling. The figure stepped over the fallen light and through the beam, glancing over their shoulder for a split-second, then left the apartment.

John's imagination played out this description as if he were Valentina lying on that bed as he read the description of events. The second figure, the smaller figure who was directing what was happening in the room, turned their face into the fallen light's beam just enough for Valentina to catch a quick glimpse. This figure was a woman. It was a woman who was telling this killer what to do and watching as the deed was carried out.

This case had gone from the glorious capture of a killer John had been chasing for nearly a decade, to an apparent copycat, now to a pair of killers that were targeting John and now Valentina. John read over Valentina's description of the features of this second suspect, this female in charge of the killer. He put himself in Valentina's place and pictured it. He imagined being on that bed. He could see the figure step into the light.

Along with a powerfully creative imagination, John also possessed some drawing ability. When he had trouble imagining a certain crime or killer, he would try sketching the

"Hey," Valentina said softly after kissing John, "what is it?"

"I read your description and sketched out the woman who attacked you," John answered. He handed the sketchbook to Valentina, "is this her?"

Valentina took a moment and looked over the picture, "oh my god, how did you do this?"

"Is this her?" John asked insistently, eager to know.

"Yes. That looks exactly like her," Valentina answered and handed the picture back to John and watched his expression as he studied the sketch. He had a look of concern on his face, "why? Who is it?"

John didn't answer. He left the room to get a picture and returned seconds later. "Okay, look at this picture. Is this who you saw in your apartment? Is this the woman?"

"That's her," Valentina answered. She sat up and touched John's face to comfort him. Whoever this was in the picture was someone close to John and she could see he was in pain. "John. Who is it?"

"The woman in the picture," John said, but had trouble forming the words from his utter disbelief. "Is my partner, Detective Selena Lopez."

* * *

The small motel room was cramped, and the paper-thin walls made it difficult to sleep. Selena had too much on her mind, too many questions to allow her mind to rest. On the faded wallpaper that covered the walls of her room, Selena had pinned the crime scene photos along with all the reports and notes. She sat on the edge of the small bed and gazed at the killer's work and tried see the one clue that would connect these crimes with Lucas Durante's information, and her daughter's murder.

Selena knew she was getting close to something, or someone, who must have been watching her. She knew it was the killer who broke into her house. She knew there had to be a connection with what Lucas Durante had told her and thanks to him, she had a name and a lead to work with.

The note Lucas Durante had written that night at the hospital wasn't altogether clear. It had implicated someone along with another name, Nathanial Whittaker. Along with the names, Lucas wrote down the name of a boy's home and an address from a small town in Washington state near the border of Oregon and a date, May the twelfth, nineteen-ninety-seven. Selena had searched for what information she could track down via the internet but there wasn't much to turn up. The only way to decipher Durante's message was to go to Washington.

At the station, Captain McGee continued his harsh demeanor towards Selena making her aware of his disappointment in her. She knew she couldn't bring her information to him, not yet. The captain would see it as wild ramblings of an unstable mind. She had to come up with a reason to leave California for a few days without raising suspicion and without anyone knowing where exactly she was going and why.

The morning briefing concluded and despite his obvious discontent with her, Captain McGee congratulated Selena and John for returning the overall murder solve rate for the month back up. With everything that had been going on and despite the tensions between them. Even with the discontent they felt for one another, it was surprising Selena and John managed to solve nearly a dozen murders while a far more dangerous killer surrounded them and taunted them with messages.

Selena sat next to John in the meeting and asked him what had happened to his head. There was bruising at the top of his forehead just near his hairline and he did his best to cover it up. He mentioned it was nothing and changed the subject as they returned to their desks. He inquired about the findings of the break-in at her house. He asked if she was alright and if anything had been stolen. It had become difficult to maintain small talk with her friend and partner.

There seemed to be something John was hiding when talking with Selena. She could tell there was something more going on with him, but he wasn't letting on. He used to be the most anal person when it came to be at work on time. Lately, he was always late. He never seemed to be present when working a crime scene. She could tell he was seeing someone new and was keeping the relationship hidden. John had become unreliable and someone she couldn't trust. Especially with the new information she had uncovered.

The most recent cases had been closed and Selena looked at the board and saw that the only outstanding cases attached to herself and John was the motel murder and the body dump outside Night Moves that were listed as being connected. What no one else knew, what Selena couldn't share, was the killer that committed these crimes had also killed her daughter and Lucas Durante to cover his tracks.

This killer was also the one taunting Selena and broke into her house to find out what she knew. To solve this crime, she knew she had to follow her instincts and go up to Washington. These murders were connected and to find the killer she had to follow the source. She had to find out what Lucas Durante's note meant. Why he had written down that address, that boy's home, and those names? Selena knew she could solve not only these murders but her daughter's.

Selena waited for the time to be right. She watched Captain McGee finish his meeting and handout assignments to the other detectives in the unit. He had some random conversations before returning to his office. She knew she had to approach this subject softly. She had to fool the captain into allowing her to leave for a few days without letting him know where she was going. She went into his office and closed the door hoping she could pull this off. She had to pull it off.

"Good morning captain. Thanks for the commendation out there," Selena said to break the ice.

"Well thank you and John for solving those cases. You haven't gone upstairs and had your meeting with Internal Affairs about Lucas Durante yet. They keep pestering me about it, saying you haven't returned their calls," Captain McGee said in his authoritative tone.

"Sorry, I just haven't had time with the break-in, my caseload, meeting with the shrink, it's been a busy month," Selena responded trying to dodge Captain McGee's inquisitive gaze.

"Well find a way to make it work. I'm through covering your ass and cleaning up for you Selena. If you don't keep up with them, they could suspend you. There won't be anything I can do to help," he said curtly, showing his pure disappointment.

"I will, sir," Selena returned somewhat sarcastically. "With our numbers down this month, I have some personal matters to tend to out of town. I was wondering if I could take a few days. There have been some things that have come up in therapy that I need to take care of. You know, to stay *'on the wagon'*," Selena said, hoping that if she mentioned keeping up with her sobriety, the captain would agree without asking too many questions.

"How long? I mean you haven't been back all that long Selena, now you want time off? In order to keep the solve rate up and our caseload down I need the detectives of my department here doing their jobs," he fired back angrily.

"Not long. Just a few days," she replied, shocked at the captain's outburst. Something she had rarely experienced directed towards her.

The captain told her she could have her few days off as long as Selena checked in with Internal Affairs about the meeting regarding the events surrounding Lucas Durante's death. She left his office and returned to her desk. She called the I.A. officer that wanted to arrange her meeting and set a meeting for when she got back, stating that she had personal matters to tend to out of town.

Before leaving the station, Selena gave John her notes on their most recent cases and told him she would be gone for a few days. He didn't seem impressed or surprised. He barely reacted to her at all, giving the same cold shoulder treatment Captain McGee had given her. Selena knew she had only one chance to get to Washington to get the information she needed to solve these cases. When she returned with what she believed she was going to find, the department would never be the same.

Another requirement for Selena's sudden departure out of town, as directed by Captain McGee, Selena had to keep up her appointment with her therapist. Selena made sure she made her last appointment. It was another hour of saying what she thought the doctor wanted to hear. She mentioned her need to get away from town and mentioned she was going to Nevada for a few days. She also mentioned her false destination to Internal Affairs as well as John to mask her true destination.

With everything tended to, her motel room paid up for the month, the shrink, John, Internal Affairs, and Captain McGee were led to believe she was heading to Nevada, Selena was ready to leave. She purchased a burner cell phone, a secondary cell phone with a prepaid card for minutes and no sim-card to track her location. Selena intentionally turned off her usual phone and put it in her motel room's safe. She left her car in the motel's parking lot and rented another for her trip.

Selena had covered her intended destination well and prepared for her trip. She entered her destination into the rental car's global positioning system and set out for Washington. She had the files she needed to keep her mind on the case and her notebook with Lucas Durante's cryptic note. There wasn't much to help her with the case, but she was hopeful she could find what she was looking for.

For the first time since before her daughter's murder, Selena felt that strong drive, that passion for the job when chasing down leads. She had lost that side of her for so long and never thought it would ever return. She knew these cases were connected to the killer who had taken her daughter and the answers that would help catch him were in Washington. Her instincts had returned her focus and determination. She had the feeling of being the hunter again instead of the prey.

The trip would take a full day's drive to get there if all Selena stopped for was gas. The only other times she had left California was for her honeymoon when she went to Maui, Hawaii with her newlywed husband and when she had taken her daughter and husband to New York City for a family trip. Selena reminisced as she drove. Memories of her daughter and the family she had filled her mind and she felt a great sense of purpose. She would avenge all she had lost.

The scenic drive took her through the redwood forests of Oregon, Selena couldn't help but admire the beauty of the land. She had spent so much of her adult life facing the ugliest things of society that she never really took the time to enjoy the simple pleasures the world had to offer. The beautiful green growth of the plant life and trees. There was so much for the eye to take in. She could imagine leaving her life chasing the filth of the big city and escaping to a simple life on the lake surrounded by this beautiful nature. She knew Anna-Maria, her late daughter, would have loved to have visited this place.

Coffee and energy drinks helped fight Selena's fatigue as she persisted onward. The long hours in the car had stiffened her body and she considered stopping but her spirit and determination wouldn't let her stop. No matter how tired or sore she was, she had to continue onward. Finally, the robotic voice of the G.P.S. announced the arrival at the intended destination. Selena pulled over at the roadside turnoff where the sign announced the arrival at the small town.

Down the road, at the bottom of a long hill, nestled in trees, were the lights of the town Lucas Durante had written down for Selena to find. Pine Valley. She got out of the car and stared down at the twinkling lights of the town. In this small town she would find the answers she needed. In this town she would find the source to catch this killer that had been chasing her. She could finally catch her daughter's murderer.

* * *

The loud music vibrated out of massive speakers. The lights went off in the room except for the spotlight on the stage. The blue accent lighting illuminated the edges of the platform. The announcer had mentioned the name of the next performer to come on stage. The music changed, and the lights flashed as a woman emerged from the dark and stepped into the light. The crowd of mostly men roared with excitement as the stunning woman walked around the stage beginning her performance.

The music continued and the woman on stage moved her body to match its rhythm. She was wearing a pantsuit and dancing to the song, Hot for Teacher performed by, Van Halen. The lights on stage came on to reveal a mock teacher's desk. There was a blackboard behind it with the word, "Detention" written boldly in chalk. The scene depicting the fantasy of a sexy teacher in a classroom that was shared by most teenage boys who have endured puberty.

The show went on. As the beat of the song got faster, the steamier the show became. The pantsuit was torn off to reveal a black and red, lace corset, garter belt, thigh-high black stockings, and high heels. The fake-teacher's dance skills and physical agility were displayed as she danced around the stage. Working the shiny stripper's pole with various spins and tricks guided by the music.

The crowd got louder as the corset was slowly removed to reveal the dancer's breasts glistening with body glitter and sweat. She teased and taunted her devoted fans covering her nipples with her hands then turning her back to the crowd. She removed her garter belt, then slowly slid off her G-string panties, dancing now only in her stockings and high heels. The men roared and begged her to get closer to the stage's edge. She worked their excitement perfectly. Her tantalizingly gyrating form charmed these men into throwing dollar bills of all denominations onto the stage.

There was one observer who sat in the corner of the room unknown to anyone. All eyes were on the stage watching the blonde play her role as the naughty teacher. He had been coming to the show for the past several nights searching for a woman with the right look. This was this dancer's first appearance at this club, and she fit the mold of what he was looking for. She had the look of both innocence and deviance. She would make a suitable replacement for his failed attempt on Valentina's life.

In all the times he had killed, with all the lives he had taken, all the women he had tortured, this killer had never missed his target. There was an infallible process he followed when choosing his victims that had never been interrupted before. He had always begun with exotic dancers, then prostitutes, women that were easily forgotten. That is how he managed to survive and keep up his twisted hobby. Now, his pride was shattered.

In every cycle of this game, the killer always required a worth-while pursuer. In one case the killer managed to get the man chasing him convicted of the very crimes he was investigating. Though the killer enjoyed the challenge, as much as he needed to be chased for the thrill to keep him focused, he had never chosen a detective as good as John Davis. No cop had ever prevented one of his kills before and taken a victim away from his grasp. He intended to right this wrong he had felt deep inside.

After the attack on Valentina, John had hidden her away and even the killer couldn't find where she was. John had become very adept at losing potential followers tailing him, so locating the safe house was near impossible. The couple had returned to his small apartment for a few nights and were now off the killer's radar. The killer would pick up John's trail when he would arrive at work, and would watch him during the day, watch him work his cases, but afterwards he would vanish.

When following John proved fruitless, the killer returned his focus to Selena. But Detective Lopez too, had vanished. After he had broken into her house to search for what she knew, she had moved into a drab motel. Her belongings remained in the room. Her car remained in the parking lot. But Selena had left town and now the killer felt completely lost. He felt like he was hunting blind.

The killer needed to set things right in his mind. He felt that he had lost his advantage and didn't like the feeling of vulnerability. He needed another kill to return that feeling of strength and control. Providing another victim for John and Selena to chase would throw them off and give him back his edge. And this blonde on stage, gyrating and exposing herself to these drooling fools would provide ample distraction from his recent failure.

It was closing time at Night Moves and its patrons stumbled out the door with slobber and spilled alcohol on their lips and the semen of blown erections soaking in their boxer-shorts and briefs. The killer had fled the club hours before, after the teacher's performance and returned to his perch. If the police had any brains they would be staking-out these hunting grounds, but they stopped visiting after the first stripper's body was dumped. The killer remained at the ready, waiting for the blonde.

The bouncers escorted her to a waiting car service. The killer hadn't studied her routine like his usual victims. He hadn't completely vetted this woman and had no idea where she would be going. This was an impromptu kill, a spontaneous act, and the level of risk aroused him. The car had two more girls in it from another club. The blonde dancer got in and they sped away from the curb, the killer wasn't far behind.

The car was a black SUV, and it was large and bulky. The heavy vehicle had to slow down for sharp corners and made it easy for the killer to stay close. Like a swift lion pouncing on a lone wildebeest. The large vehicle drove through the city until finally coming to a stop at an expensive apartment building. There were doormen and security who came out and brought the three women inside, checking their identification and walking them through the lobby.

Under normal circumstances, the killer would never dare risk his safety and follow this urge. There were cameras, guards, and witnesses. He would be too exposed, but he desperately needed the kill. The urge wouldn't let him walk away. It taunted him. The failure of not killing Valentina fueled this deviant need. This attack would be daring, unexpected, and would certainly make his detectives respect the danger he could impose.

The killer found a place to park, not too far away, but well hidden. He put his talent to remain among the shadows and move invisibly to good use, he breezed into the building's rear exit like a phantom. He found the security room and after disabling the two guards, he located the floor where the girls had gone. The cameras were deactivated, and the killer made his way to the penthouse. There were two guards posted in the hallway outside the penthouse entrance that he would have to handle.

The guards were no match for the killer's skill and strength. They were easily subdued and secured. He took the guard's keys and entered the apartment. There was music playing and the lights were off. A search of the array of rooms revealed there was no one else in the apartment. The owner was in the main den area enjoying a private show from the three girls performing various sex acts on him and on each other. The lights were dimmed and the music blaring. There was alcohol and drugs on the table. It was quite the private party.

The killer stood in the back of the room enjoying this pornographic scene as it played out. He gathered what he needed to commit his work. He waited for the opportune moment then subdued his latest victims. As he tied the wrists and ankles of those he was about to torture and kill. He looked around and imagined the scene he was about to create for Detectives Davis and Lopez to find. His pride returned with an evil grin upon his lips. His eyes were ablaze with evil desire as he started his latest work. There would be no one to interrupt him this time.

CHAPTER NINE

The car's engine was idling, the exhaust rumbling, as it sat parked alongside the curb. Rain showered from overhead and was dripping off the paint. John sat in his car, once again parked outside his former wife's house. He was confident that he had hidden Valentina well, and she was safe. He was lost in thought thinking about his partner. Questions and theories rattled in his head as he sat in silence hoping to catch a glimpse of the woman he let go.

The sketch he had drawn, that matched Valentina's description of the woman who was directing her attacker, was held tight in his hands. He had spent a long time staring down at the drawing and at the picture of his partner Selena Lopez. Could she have really lost her mind and be capable of this? Was she now involved with the killer he was chasing? Did she have anything to do with Alexis's death?

John's confusion was profound. Everything seemed to point to Selena but why would she do these things? What would she gain from these deaths? Nothing made sense. Valentina could be mistaken but she identified the drawing and then the picture of Selena with absolute certainty. John knew he had to look-into his partner's recent activity more closely. He wanted to bring this to Captain McGee but knew how biased the man was when it came to Detective Lopez. John knew he had to keep this quiet for now.

At the station, John started his day working his cases. He had no more leads on the Night Moves body dump or Alexis's murder. Most of his recent cases had been closed with the help of Selena and the captain had rewarded her with a few days off. John found it difficult to play the concerned friend while talking to Selena now, when she could possibly be involved with this killer who attacked his new girlfriend.

Selena told John about her need to get out of town to go to Nevada on personal business. He recalled their previous conversations long before her daughter's murder. He couldn't remember ever hearing her mention family or anything of significance in Nevada. It seemed suspicious to John she was suddenly so urgently in need of leaving town in the middle of this investigation immediately after the failed attempt on Valentina's life.

Though it was difficult, John played his role. He appeared annoyed with her leaving him with all the work on these cases but still concerned with her continued sobriety. He watched her leave the building, then went through her desk. There was nothing there that was out of the ordinary. She had disposed of the expensive bottle of tequila she kept in her desk and had even gotten rid of the cigarettes she used to smoke. John certainly wouldn't miss those filthy things.

There was nothing out of the ordinary on her computer. John was able to access her most recent searches into old cases, but it connected with their recent list of victims. There was nothing incriminating at her desk. He left the floor and went to the elevator and headed down two floors where the burglary/robbery/auto-theft department was located. There was a young woman working the switchboard and was assistant to the department's captain. John flirted his way into having a look at the file on the break-in at Detective Lopez's house.

The reports all showed nothing special or strange. There was nothing stolen but the house was ransacked and trashed. Whoever did this to her house, the act appeared to be personal. Maybe if she was involved with this killer, this could have been a message to her, or it could have been a threat of some kind. The official conclusion surmised that it was a random act of vandalism since there had been similar break-ins in the area. There were no suspects.

John collected his things and drove to Selena's neighborhood to have a look at her house. Her car wasn't in the driveway and the police tape hadn't been disturbed. The board on the door was still secure. John went around to the backyard and entered the house from the rear entrance. He pried away the board that had been nailed over the shattered, sliding, glass doors. He entered the house and quietly snooped around.

Inside the house, John had to be careful where he stepped. There were items everywhere. Furniture had been overturned, the contents of all the drawers of various cabinets had been emptied and tossed across the floor. The shelves had been cleared of any objects, which were also knocked to the floor. The pictures had been knocked off the walls. There were broken pieces of glass scattered everywhere.

Each room seemed worse than the next as John ventured further. The office was where the burglars seemed to concentrate the bulk of their efforts. It appeared whoever did this was searching for something, then smashed-up the rest of the house to make it look like vandals had targeted Selena's house. Nothing too suspicious about young thugs tearing up a police officer's home. John had gone to the house for answers and instead left with more questions.

Selena had mentioned she was going to stay at a motel in the meantime but didn't mention which one. John had friends back at the station who owed him a favor that could help him locate his partner and would keep what he was doing a secret in the event John was caught investigating a fellow officer. He called into the station to his tech-savvy friend and after reminding him of the favors he owed, John convinced him to help.

"Look, its probably nothing. I just want you to locate Detective Lopez's cell phone and check her most recent credit card activity," John asked intently.

"Why? Has she done something wrong or what? She into some bad shit?" the nervous voice replied.

"I don't know. Probably not, I'm just checking out a claim and keeping her reputation clear. She's my partner and I'm just looking out for her," John returned, trying his best to be convincing.

"Yeah, but you wouldn't be doing this all cloak-and-dagger type shit if she wasn't into something bad, what did she do man? You can tell me," The voice said.

"I told you I'm just looking out for my partner," John responded, his voice tightened. "Now are you going to get me the info I need, or am I going to have to uncover some of your hidden truths?"

"Alright, calm down. I'll call you right back," The frightened voice shot back.

John hung up the phone and waited. He remembered helping this friend out of trouble back when he worked narcotics. This guy worked for the police in technical services and was a genius when it came to computers but had a weakness for prostitutes. Particularly, transgendered prostitutes. John had arrested a pimp on suspicion of heroin trafficking and in the process found his computer genius friend in the middle of some disturbing playtime with a rather large he/she hooker. John had used this information to get this computer nerd to do a lot of clandestine computer work ever since.

The cell phone rang, and the rattled computer geek provided a location of Selena's cell phone as well as the credit card records which he sent to John's email. John vaguely threatened his friend again to keep this request for Selena's information quiet. He hung up and checked his email for the credit card records. She prepaid for the motel, from the amount it looked like she rented it for the month. She had rented a car, two hours after she had left the office then took out several thousand dollars in cash.

It appeared Selena was keeping her activities off the radar. John knew she was up to something more than her sobriety. He headed to the last address of where her cell signal was tracked, it was the same motel she had prepaid for the month. John went into the office and considered himself lucky that there was a kid in his early twenties working the counter. John flashed his badge, then offered a fifty-dollar bill for the room number and its spare key for where Detective Lopez was staying.

The kid checked his records and was quick to give out the key and mentioned she was staying in room number eight. John took the key and headed for the room. Selena's car was parked directly in front of room eight. It was locked, and it looked like she had removed everything from its interior. John opened the door and went inside the small room.

The walls were covered, floor to ceiling with crime scene reports and pictures. There were the case files of the body dump at Night Moves and Alexis's murder. There was also Lucas Durante's file that John had believed to still be locked up in his cabinet at work. There was Anna-Maria's case file pinned up next to all of it. John stood back and read over all the reports and the yellow post-it notes taped up along side all the pictures of corpses. It looked like the work of a mind, very broken and unstable.

John took a step back from reading everything. It was clear his partner had snapped somehow and was now obsessed. There was a section of wall with holes from thumbtacks and the remanence of tape residue but whatever had been attached to the wall had been removed very recently. All that remained was a picture from Anna-Maria's, Selena's daughter's, case file. It was a picture of her naked corpse, horribly broken and beaten and left out for display. Next to the picture was a post-it that read, "John Davis?"

It was hard for John to see these pictures. It was even worse that now it was obvious Selena suspected John for her daughter's murder. John's head felt like it was going to explode as a sudden headache swept over him. He felt dizzy and nauseous and had to leave the room. He didn't know what to think of what he had just discovered in Selena's room. He removed his cell phone and briefly considered calling Captain McGee. Maybe he could help bring Selena in and question her.

There was a long moment of deep thought. John didn't know what to do. He brought up Captain McGee's number on his phone and was about to hit the call button when the phone rang. It was dispatch. There was a collection of bodies found downtown at the penthouse of some rich lawyer. Apparently, the crime scene had John's name written all over it, literally.

* * *

The alarm's annoying melody woke Selena from a deep sleep. She had arrived at the small town late into the evening and went straight to bed and fell fast asleep. The long day of driving up from California, coupled with the previous nights of not being able to sleep since the break-in at her house, completely exhausted her. She rose from her bed and hopped into a hot shower hoping it would help her wash away the drowsiness.

The small town of Pine Valley had a pleasant peacefulness to it. The people on the street were friendly, accommodating, and helpful. With her dusky, exotic, appearance, Selena stood out from everyone in the small town. The men were all twisting their necks to catch an extended look at her. The women stared some intense glaring looks towards her, especially those whose husbands or boyfriends were admiring Selena's beauty and form showing through her tight clothing.

There was a corner diner advertising that it served the best coffee and breakfast in the northwest. Selena went in and took a seat. The waitress was friendly and inquired where Selena was visiting from and seemed interested in hearing more about the city Lugar De Paz, California. After a brief conversation the cheerful woman headed off behind the counter to put in Selena's order and get a fresh pot of coffee. Being from a large city her entire life it was unfamiliar for Selena to experience such kind service from strangers.

As she waited patiently for her breakfast, Selena sipped her coffee and looked around the diner's interior. She was reminded of John's favourite diner near their station. It was where Anna-Maria worked before she was murdered.

There were pictures of the small town's past hung proudly on the walls along with various pop culture items. It was difficult not to think of Anna-Maria sitting in a restaurant so similar. She imagined her daughter in an apron serving coffee and smiling with the customers. Selena quickly returned her thoughts to what she needed to do. She had to remain steadfast and clear.

Selena finished her breakfast and went to the till at the counter to pay for her meal. As the friendly cashier punched in the amount owing and handed back the exact change, Selena noticed a framed newspaper clipping behind the till with the headline, "The Heroes of the Pine Valley Fire". The date was May nineteenth, nineteen-ninety-seven. The date was one week after the date written in the note given to her by Lucas Durante that night at the hospital. Selena removed her cell phone and casually snapped a clear picture of the article.

After a few hours touring the town and asking the locals about their home, Selena decided to pay a visit to the local sheriff. She had received directions from the people at the diner and she found the small building quite easily. Inside the local police station, it appeared time had stood still, much like the rest of the town. Compared to what Selena was used to in her precinct back in Lugar De Paz, this was like entering the stone age.

The building was small and quaint. There seemed to be a small number of police officers for the size of the town. The computers looked as though they hadn't been upgraded in well over a decade and the officers' equipment seemed very limited. Back in the precinct in California the officers had access to the latest self-defence equipment available. In this small town, the police most likely didn't face the same dangers and problems as the cops in the big city.

The receptionist was friendly and escorted Selena inside offering various drinks or even a homemade snack of muffins, which she was proud to admit she baked herself. Selena politely refused and smiled at the hospitality of this town. In a mere few hours in this sleepy little town she had seen more politeness than a decade of living in the city. The receptionist, dressed in her flower-print summer dress, walked Selena right into the Sheriff's office, where they found the sheriff practicing with his putter on a small strip of turf with a thick beer mug laying on its side as a makeshift golf hole.

The sheriff was a kindly, elderly man. He looked like he was near retirement in his mid-sixties with a cheerful kindness in his eyes. He had short-cropped hair and a white beard. He reminded Selena of a perfect depiction of Santa Claus, with his heavy stature, plump cheeks, and twinkle in his eye with a propensity to hold his face in a permanent smile.

The man's massive grip swallowed Selena's petite hand when he offered his greeting and motioned for her to take a seat.

"Good morning ma'am, I am Sheriff Gerald Rasmussen. How can I help you my dear?" the large sheriff said with a mostly diluted accent that sounded slightly German.

"Good morning, I am Detective Selena Lopez from Lugar De Paz, California. We spoke on the phone last week about my coming up," Selena answered.

"Oh, that's right," The large man said with a laugh. Selena smiled at the image of the man wearing a bright red suit and smoking a pipe as the man's round belly shook while laughing. "Something to do with a cold case you're working on that may have started here?" he said finally.

"Yes sir," Selena replied. "I was given a name, along with a date and mention of a boy's home, as well as the name of this town itself. I couldn't find much information via the internet, and since I had some days off, I thought it might be worthwhile to visit your beautiful town and possibly have a look at some of your old files?"

"And who, may I ask, gave you this information?" Sheriff Rasmussen asked.

"A suspect in multiple homicides by the name of Lucas Durante," Selena replied.

"Doesn't sound familiar, but you'll have to forgive me dear, my memory isn't what it used to be," the Sheriff said with another friendly chuckle. "What else did this, Mr. Durante, tell you?"

Selena paused, not sure if she should divulge everything. There would be little harm in telling this old man the information Lucas Durante had given her. Deciding to leave out the information that could potentially ruin her department and the real reason for her visit to this small town, Selena continued, "Durante mentioned the name, Nathaniel Whittaker. The Mother Mary's Home for Boys. He also mentioned the date, May twelfth, nineteen-ninety-seven."

"Interesting," the Sheriff replied after a moment of introspection. "I know Mother Mary's burnt down that year. It was involved in a terrible forest fire in May of ninety-seven. It was a converted mansion just outside of town that accepted troubled boys in need of a home from various communities. As for the names, I'm not sure who they are."

"Well if it is possible, I would like to have a look at your old files. Learning about this killer's past could better help me build a case against him," Selena asked, giving her slightly flirtatious and innocent look to aid in the old man's decision.

"I assume you don't have a warrant, or court order for this information?" Sheriff Rasmussen responded, trying to hide his blushing at noticing Selena's beauty.

"You assume correctly sir," Selena suddenly doubted whether this old-fashioned cop would go against protocol and allow her to view the files. He might be a by-the-book officer. She decided to share something personal to help her cause. "My daughter was murdered several years ago. Her case remains unsolved and I have reason to believe this case is connected with hers. I could never forgive myself if I didn't at least look into every potential led for information."

"I'm terribly sorry for your loss my dear," the Sheriff said with pure sincerity in his voice. He reached across his desk and patted Selena's hand gently with his. There was a slight tear forming in his eye as he took another long pause before responding. "I share the loss of a child. Not from murder, but the loss hurts just as much, and the pain is never fully gone. I can't imagine the pain and anger you must feel. If this will help you, then by-all-means, you can look through my files all you want, and we'll help in any way we can. Just remember, whatever you find can't be used directly without going through proper channels."

Selena thanked the old sheriff and they remained in the office for a time, sharing small talk before he finally walked her out of the room. The receptionist was asked to lead Selena to the basement file room where she could go through the files in search of whatever she could find. Two floors down, the receptionist walked Selena up to a small door and unlocked it. Once opened, Selena peered inside to find a vast collection of filing cabinets and long rows of shelving with boxes and what appeared to be ledger books. This was quite the haystack, and Selena was determined to find the needle she needed to find.

Dust particles coated the air in the massive room. With no windows to ventilate, it was hard to breath without coughing each time Selena opened a drawer or removed an item from the shelf. Thankfully, there was a simple but effective filing system in place that left this massive collection of paperwork in relative order. There were files dating back to the early sixties and probably further. If this were a larger center, all this information would be digitized.

Hours passed, and Selena was no closer to finding any information. She had managed to locate the files from the year nineteen-ninety-seven but hadn't found the month of May. The station was closing for the night and Selena thought it best to take a break. She had a good jumping off point for the next morning and took the advice of the receptionist and shut down her search for the evening.

As she left the station, the receptionist mentioned to Selena that she had phoned the local newspaper and they were going to pull their old issues for the month of May for ninety-seven as well as anything on Lucas Durante or Nathaniel Whittaker. Selena thanked the young woman for her help and suspected that she might be the granddaughter of Sheriff Rasmussen, bearing a slight resemblance. It was funny to Selena, the eagerness of the officers and the receptionist to help in a big city murder investigation. She appreciated the assistance. Tomorrow would hopefully yield better results.

Selena found a local pub that served food and bravely ordered a cheeseburger and cola. The officers of the station had recommended the place as being the best in town for a burger and a beer. Perhaps it was a nonchalant way of asking her out. Selena finished her dinner and was pleasantly surprised at how good it was. She enjoyed a game of eight ball with the officers and the sheriff's receptionist. It was a nice distraction to the true reason for her visit to this delightful little town.

* * *

The screams and muffled moans of gagged mouths had ceased. There was so much blood surrounding the room, the smell of metal was choking throughout the apartment. There were streaks of red across the silver colored walls. Blood had covered the lampshades and provided a hellish hue to the lighting. Rivers of the thick, near black, red blood saturated the area rug and pooled in various areas around the floor. Each room was decorated in the same horrifyingly gruesome manner.

The killer had satisfied his thirst for a kill after his failure to eliminate Valentina. He sat in a chair in the main living room enjoying the sight of his work and was replaying the events in his mind. He didn't have to worry about the security guards. He managed to subdue them quietly and disabled the cameras and security system. The guards outside the front door in the main lobby were instructed to wait until called by the apartment's owner when his night had reached its end. A call that would never come.

The lawyer who owned this newly made house of horrors had confided in the killer under threat of death. He told the killer he had purchased an entire night of pleasure from the young dancers. The security staff had been well paid to keep quiet and ignore all sounds and complaints of noise from the penthouse as it was supposed to be a wild night. The killer had hours to fulfill his desires with each victim without any interruption from pesky guards.

There were three bedrooms in the apartment and the killer put them all to use. He had secured each of the dancers to a bed and fastened the lawyer to a chair, taping his eyelids open and forcing him watch what was about to happen. This killer normally worked without an audience but found the thrill of someone watching all-the-more exciting. He took his time with each dancer and enjoyed each hit. Each cut. Every scream and terrified look on their face. He had broken from his usual routine but to him, it was well worth all the risk.

The three women had suffered for hours. The killer spent equal time with each of them. He started with the beatings. He slapped and choked them, struck them with a belt or paddle. He punched them to raise their level of fear. Once tied to the bed the killer penetrated them with various phallic-shaped objects both rectally and vaginally until he was ready to rape them himself. He forced himself inside them forcing them to make eye contact while he committed his unspeakable acts upon them.

Once he had ejaculated, the killer brought out his knives. He would begin cutting the limbs and torso in long, shallow slashes to simply draw blood. Once he had one dancer beaten, raped, and bleeding, the killer dragged the tied-up lawyer to the next room and continued the process with the next. He did the same a third time. He left the other girls terrified and bleeding. Beaten and raped tied to the bed, praying for someone to save them.

Throughout the arduous and disturbing process, the killer paused to take pictures. He had taken dozens of each victim in every stage of his process and then finally of his completed work when the light had gone from their eyes and they remained mere corpses. The lawyer had evacuated his bladder and bowels from the fear he felt. He had nearly choked on his own vomit. The killer removed his gag to allow him to expel the consumed alcohol and dinner he had earlier that evening, then reapplied the sullied rag into his mouth and returned to his torture of the women.

Once each of the women had drew their final breath, the killer stripped the lawyer and performed the same terrible deeds upon him. It was the first time the killer had killed a man using his process. He was unchained from the shackles of his routine and acting on pure desire to inflict pain and terror. The killer ended the lawyer's life by hanging him from the ceiling fan in the main living room area, putting him on display.

The killer had worn a plastic suit to keep from leaving trace elements of his DNA. If this were his usual kill, the killer would set up a controlled environment and be able to touch his victims freely and clean them with bleach afterward. This was out of his routine and element. He wore the suit and latex gloves. He wore a condom with each victim and collected them afterward. He retraced his steps and removed any trace he had been there.

After he was confident that he had removed all trace of his presence, the killer decorated the apartment in the blood of his victims and left his usual taunting messages along with his signature. This kill was payback for interrupting his process with Valentina. It was John having broken the routine that had infuriated the killer. This was a challenge to the star detective. John had taken one intended victim away, so the killer returned with four for him to solve.

The killer painted the walls like some deranged artist. He signed each victim as he had done previously and wrote John's name in blood on the walls. He carved a taunting message into the flesh of the deceased lawyer's chest and scattered some of the polaroid pictures he had taken so the police would know who exactly committed these crimes. This crime scene would confuse and torment them. The game had changed, and the killer wanted to turn up the pressure on John and Selena. He couldn't wait to see how the pair would react to this one.

CHAPTER TEN

The flashing red and blue lights lit up the façade of the buildings up and down the busy street. Squad cars had positioned themselves strategically to block traffic and to form a barrier for onlookers and reporters. Patrol officers had strung the yellow police tape and were standing watch to make sure no one got through who didn't need to be in the building. A large crowd of people had formed outside, curious to know what all the commotion was and why there were so many police.

The crime scene team's mobile laboratory, a large van that held all their equipment, was backed up to the main doors of the building. Members of the forensic team were dressed in their coveralls and gloves and went inside first to get a look at what they were dealing with. There were private security guards that had been posted outside the front door that had been detained for questioning along with several other security personnel who had been tied-up and rendered unconscious inside the building.

An anonymous call through the nine-one-one emergency call center had led the police to the building. The security staff had said they had been hired by their client, who resided in the penthouse on the top floor, and were to remain at the front of the building until requested. They mentioned the building's security team were stationed inside and two other members of their team had been posted outside the main doors of the penthouse and hadn't reported anything strange or out of place.

The police ordered the guards to call the remaining members of their team. When they didn't answer, the police told the security team to remain at the door as they ventured inside. They found the building's security staff tied-up and unconscious in the security office with nothing but snow showing up on the monitors for the building's security camera system. The police called for back-up and proceeded to the penthouse where they found more guards knocked-out and fastened together on the floor.

John arrived at the scene after being called in from dispatch. He parked outside the taped barricade and displayed his badge for the patrol officers who immediately let him through. The crowd of media reporters were shouting in the background asking for a comment. There were camera flashes and large news cameras filming the police as they secured the perimeter of the building's entrance. John avoided them as he quickly made his way inside, not wanting his face captured for the evening news or some internet blog.

The lobby had been converted into a makeshift interrogation room with officers taking statements from the private security team as well as the building rent-a-cops who were being administered first-aid for whatever had struck them to put them to sleep. John demanded an immediate copy of their statements once completed before he went further into the building where he found Captain McGee speaking to members of the forensics team.

"Good evening sir," John said as he approached. "What have we got here?"

"Hey John, I haven't gone up to the penthouse yet but apparently it's a bad one. I'm told as many as three, maybe four bodies. You better get up there," the captain said as he turned to answer another officer's question.

"Sure thing. Sir, can I talk to you afterwards? In private," John said. He was reluctant to tell the captain of his concern for his partner Selena and what he had discovered earlier in her motel room but felt a responsibility to do so.

"Regarding?" Captain McGee asked annoyed, thinking this was some personal request of some kind, like time-off or some other inappropriate request to ask at a crime scene.

"Regarding Detective Lopez," John replied.

"What about her? I know you're shorthanded and that she just got back but her therapist recommended she tend to some personal business," the captain said sharply, clearly not wanting to talk about Selena.

"I don't care about that sir. I have other concerns about her recent behaviour that I can't exactly bring up right now," John returned, motioning his head to gesture the many people around that he didn't want to hear the conversation.

"Find me when you're done here," Captain McGee ordered. He felt he knew what John was going to bring up. Perhaps he found out about Selena's drinking problem and other vices. He motioned for John to go to work and returned to where the officers were questioning the security staff, thinking of how he could protect Selena from John's potential inquiry.

John turned from Captain McGee and boarded the elevator. He was regretting mentioning Selena to the captain. He knew the captain and Selena had a father-daughter type of relationship. If his speculations were wrong, John knew he would further drive the captain's intense discontent with him. John never knew why there was such friction between them but bringing accusations against someone the captain cared about would make matters worse. He could only hope the captain would hear him out with an open mind.

The elevator doors opened, and John stepped out. There was a narrow hallway which led up to the penthouse with several doors on either side. In John's mind he had flashes, images of the hallway in his dream as he walked closer. He closed his eyes and tried to force himself to focus. Why would that image be in his mind now? Perhaps it was because the area looked like that of his dream. John tried to return his mind to the present but felt that same panic he had always felt in his dream.

The officer standing outside the penthouse entrance could see John shaking his head and closing his eyes as if strained by a headache or as if he might faint. John said he was okay and forced himself to focus as he entered the penthouse. He placed the latex gloves on and watched his footing as he sidestepped the marked, bloody footprints on the floor of the entranceway. He carefully walked around members of the forensic team as they continued their work. The display in the main living room snapped John into absolute clarity.

There was the nude body of a man hung from the fan and secured to the ceiling. His arms were outstretched, and his body appeared to be covered in bruises and large cuts. There were rope burns on the man's wrists and ankles and his genitalia had been removed. There were words carved into the man's chest but from the angle, and with all the blood that had poured from the wounds it couldn't be read.

John stepped back as members of the team were going to lower the man's body to the floor since they had taken all the required pictures and samples. He watched as the team carefully laid the body onto a stretcher and inside the large, black, plastic body bag. Before zipping it up, a member of the team attempted to get photographs of the message carved into the chest of the victim.

The living room walls had been painted in blood. Massive streaks and sprays of blood dripped down the walls with the words, "For Detective John Davis", and the ominous "S" were written in blood on the wall directly behind where the body was hanging. It looked like a scene from a disturbing horror film. John continued to walk through the apartment, heading out of the living room to where the team had mentioned the remaining victim's bodies had been found.

The first bedroom. There was the body of a redheaded female victim, face down on the bed with her hands tied behind her back and her ankles fastened together with barbwire which had punctured the skin. The woman was nude and propped up in a kneeling position on the bed. The body was heavily bruised and cut up like the first victim with on object protruding from between her legs that looked like part of a broom handle.

John looked around the room. The bed was covered in blood that had dripped onto the floor. There were pieces of rope and cut zip-ties scattered amidst the pools of blood where the killer must have changed her position and retied her multiple times. The woman's clothes had been neatly folded and placed in a plastic bag with her wallet opened to her driver's license to let the police know exactly who she was. Above the headboard, painted in blood, was the message, "Catch me Johnny", with the same "S" underneath.

The second bedroom. Another nude female, this time with black hair. Her body was bruised and cut in the same way. She was sitting up against the wall with her arms spread outward and her palms had been nailed to the wall behind her. The back of her skull had been smashed-in from a heavy object. Her legs had been spread and ankles secured to the edge of the bed with zip-ties. Her abdomen had been sliced wide open with her innards spilling out onto the bed between her legs.

Another blood bath with red covering the bed's surface and pouring onto the floor. More rope and zip-tie fragments surrounded the bed. There was another plastic bag with the victim's clothes and displayed wallet left open on the desk next to the door. In this room, there were devices left on the nightstand that had been used in the torture. There were several knives, a hammer, and various masturbatory aids. On the wall above the bed was another message streaked in blood, "Are you good enough to find me Johnny?", with yet another "S" signed beneath.

The third and final bedroom. This time a blonde victim who had been beaten and cut up in the same way as the others. This victim had the same marks on her wrists and ankles from having been secured but her restraints had been removed. She was displayed laying flat on her back as if she had simply fallen asleep. There was immense bruising around her neck and the whites of her eyes had blood spots from petechial hemorrhaging. This woman was killed by strangulation.

This room had less blood than the others. Though the victim's body had been stabbed in her chest and stomach and cut in various locations on her body. The blood on the bed was limited compared to the other rooms with more rope and zip-ties on the floor. Various sexual devices and tools on the table coated in what looked like Vaseline mixed with small streaks of blood. The same display of the victim's clothing bagged and left for easy identification. The woman's arm had been moved to rest on her chest as if to display the stamp from the club Night Moves on her hand. This room's bloody message read, "Your Time's Almost Up Johnny", and another "S".

John left the bedrooms and returned to the living room to speak with the leader of the crime scene team. This crime scene was set up for him and now the killer was escalating his thrill. This was a risky situation to put himself in. Why would he go to such lengths to target John? What did his messages mean? Why single-out John specifically? John had seen a great many terrible and disturbing things during his career, but he had never seen anything like this before.

"The other victims' clothes and identification were found in the bedrooms close to their bodies, where is this guy's?" John asked the crime scene technician, trying to put his concerns to the back of his mind and activate his imagination to work the case.

"Well we searched the entire place and couldn't find his clothes or identification. The penthouse is owned by a law firm, its listed as corporate property. The private security downstairs said the guy who paid them was a lawyer named Alfred Rothstein," the technician replied.

"Okay, well snap a shot of the victim's face and confirm it before you leave. Make sure its him. What about his missing appendage?" John asked.

"Missing. Probably a trophy of some kind. Who knows? Maybe the guy's wife caught wind of his extracurricular activities. She went nuts, then took his," the technician replied sarcastically. It was a poor attempt to lighten the mood with his poorly timed joke.

"What about the words on his chest?" John asked.

The technician directed John's attention to the body, which was still laying on the gurney. John asked for some light to be shone on the man's chest and struggled to read what had been carved. It was difficult to delineate with so much blood covering the skin and some of the cuts not being very deep. John's heart raced with panic. His eyes-widened and his jaw clenched in anger as he finally deciphered the message. It was a threat from the killer. The message said, "Can Valentina Come Out'n'Play? - S".

The message hit John like a boxer's right hook. He stepped out of the room and onto the apartment's balcony for privacy. He closed the glass door behind him so no one would hear. After taking out his secret cell phone, John hit the first number on the speed dial. He had purchased Valentina a matching cell phone that couldn't be traced and set up a system to keep her location hidden. He gave her a pistol and instructed her that if anyone was to come in the door who wasn't John, she was to pull the trigger.

It took several tries before Valentina answered the phone. She must have been asleep. John alerted her vaguely about the threat not mentioning the full details of how it had been delivered. He told her to make sure everything was securely locked and told her to keep the pistol close. She did as he asked, and everything was fine. With a crime scene like this, John knew he was going to be there for a long time, he told Valentina he would be there as soon as he could then hung up before anyone could ask who he was talking to.

Before he could return to the inside of the apartment, Captain McGee had made his way to the balcony and joined John outside. The man had on his usual unreadable expression that one couldn't tell if he was angry, tired, or concerned. The captain was acting strange and wanted to make sure no one could hear what he was about to say to John. He made his way close to John and offered him a cigarette.

"Thanks," John said, holding up his right hand with a stopping gesture to refuse the slender tube of tobacco. "You know I hate those things sir, I don't smoke."

"Right, sorry," Captain McGee said as he lit his cigarette and took a long drag. "What do you think of what happened here? Why is this guy calling you out?"

"I think it has something to do with the Lucas Durante case," John said after taking a moment to consider the captain's question. "Durante targeted strippers, hookers, and runaways. He signed his victims and taunted detectives with letters too remember?"

"Yes, but the Lucas Durante case had long since gone cold before you caught him. It certainly didn't have the notoriety that these killers go for. Why copycat him?" Captain McGee asked, taking long drags on his cigarette.

"I'm not sure it is a copycat. Maybe it's a former accomplice, or maybe Lucas Durante was innocent all those years ago. Maybe this killer was going to use him as a scapegoat, a patsy," John explained.

"What makes you think that?" the captain asked.

"Just a hunch," John replied, trying to think of how to approach the conversation he needed to have about Selena.

"That imagination of yours?" the captain asked.

"Yeah, something like that. I'll vet it carefully as I go forward," John answered.

"Alright, I trust your hunches. You're usually right when you get them," Captain McGee said patting John's shoulder. He stared directly into John's royal blue eyes and his face bore an expression of gentle concern. "So, what did you mean before? What are your concerns of Selena's behaviour?"

John took his time and carefully went through his suspicions. He showed the captain the pictures he had taken of the break-in at Selena's house and how it appeared staged. The pictures of the collage found on Selena's motel room wall and how unstable she appeared to be. John finally mentioned who

Valentina was and about the attack at her apartment. He explained that Valentina positively identified Selena as being in the room during the attack and was directing the male attacker's actions.

Together, Captain McGee and John discussed all they knew about Detective Lopez. They discussed her drinking and use of drugs. The dissolution of her marriage and her new-found promiscuity. The captain didn't want to see it before but hearing John's suspicions and considering all that he had found, Selena seemed more out of control than he wanted to admit. They agreed to keep this information among themselves and John promised to watch Selena closely when she returned to work from wherever she had taken off to, which certainly wasn't Nevada.

The night wore on and John was able to proceed with his investigation. The more he considered the facts, the more he suspected his partner. She must have had some sort of mental breakdown to be able to be involved in these heinous crimes. She must have snapped after her daughter, Anna-Maria's death. Whenever she returned from her trip, Selena would be number one on John's list of suspects.

* * *

The second day in the small town of Pine Valley, Washington, started very much the same as the first. Selena had returned to

enjoy breakfast at the small diner and chatted with her
waitress and the cook. She spoke with several people from
around the town and asked if they knew of the town's history.
It certainly was the perfect, peaceful, little town time had
forgotten. The locals had the friendliness that stereotypically
only existed up in Canada. Selena wondered if such a town
could spawn the evil that had committed the murders that had
ultimately sent her here.

It was still early when Selena made her way to the
sheriff's office. She returned to her table in the basement
searching through the seemingly endless collection of papers.
One of the officers who had accompanied her to the pub the
night before came in to see if she needed help. He was
bragging during the billiards game that the next day was his
day off and yet he showed up to go through files with Selena.
She feared she might have led him on. Though she could use
the help, she politely declined.

Hours passed quickly, and the determined detective
remained undeterred from her vastly daunting task. Fueled by
the drive to solve her daughter's murder, and several pots of
coffee, Selena remained in the file room until she had gone
through all she had uncovered for the year nineteen-ninety-
seven. She had found everything she could on Nathaniel
Whittaker and Lucas Durante, which wasn't much. She found

all associated files and read through them to find their connection.

Lucas Durante moved to Pine Valley when he was a young boy to live with his Grandmother, Agatha Hammond, the widow of a millwright at the local mill just outside of town. Richard Hammond, Lucas Durante's Grandfather, was killed in the winter of nineteen-ninety-one in an accident on the highway caused by a drunk driver and poor road conditions. Agatha was a nurse at the hospital before she retired and received a sizeable payout from the insurance company of the drunk driver who was deemed responsible for causing her husband's death.

Desmond Durante, Lucas' paternal father, was an automotive mechanic in Seattle and an abusive drug addict, as mentioned in the reports. He repeatedly beat his wife Sarah Hammond, Lucas' mother, until she divorced him when Lucas was just two years old. Sarah had remarried while her ex-husband languished for eighteen months in prison for the assault on his wife. According to the report, Sarah, Lucas, and her new husband Joel Cheney moved to the city of Tacoma.

Several years after his release from prison, Desmond tracked down his ex-wife and her newlywed husband and, in a drunken rage, beat them to death with an aluminum baseball bat. Lucas had seen the entire event at the age of six. After killing Sarah and Joel Cheney, Desmond Durante fell asleep from the alcohol he had consumed. When he came-to and saw what he had done, he panicked. He found Joel Cheney's shotgun and shot himself before the police could arrest him and send him back to prison.

The police took Lucas into custody that night and placed him into emergency childcare while they searched for any relatives. There was no one on Desmond Durante's side of the family that could be reached. The police found Agatha and Richard Hammond's phone number among their daughter's personal things and Lucas was placed in their care. It wasn't long before Lucas displayed his father's abusive nature and violent temper.

As his childhood continued in Pine Valley, Lucas' troubles escalated. There were reports of vandalism and random acts of public disturbances. He had been caught setting fires, shoplifting, and doing drugs all in his early teenage years. In February of nineteen-ninety-six, when Lucas was sixteen, he assaulted his grandmother while under the influence of cocaine and stole the money from her purse and her car. Being a loving grandmother, Agatha didn't want to press charges but surrendered her rights as guardian and signed his placement into Mother Mary's home for boys.

Nathaniel Whitaker, the name given to Selena by Lucas Durante on his death bed, shared a similar story, though more tragic. Nathaniel's mother, Cora Duvall was an exotic dancer based in Portland. She often came into Washington state to perform shows in various cities at clubs owned by an infamous motorcycle club known as, The Devil's Hand. She often moonlighted as a prostitute for extra money to support her drug habit.

Douglas "Duke" Whitaker, Nathaniel's father, was one of Cora's clients who supplied her with drugs. The troubled couple was never officially married. Douglas, or Duke as he preferred to be called, would often act as Cora's pimp, selling her body to the many fans she had at the club and making money from her efforts. Duke was highly intelligent, yet extremely dangerous, and was quick to violence. Cora was equally intelligent, conniving and manipulative. Together, they resembled a modern-day Bonnie and Clyde.

The police had eventually caught up with Duke's side empire outside his dealings with the motorcycle club. He fled Oregon with Cora and moved to Washington, where they lived in hiding in a small town. Duke had betrayed his club with his business and was a wanted man by both his club members and the police. As the couple waited for the heat to die down, Cora made herself get pregnant. When the police finally found her, the judge showed her leniency due to her being with child and let her go with a sentence of house arrest followed by a term of probation. Duke was arrested for drug-trafficking.

Before making it to trial, Duke was murdered by his former club members while being transported to a holding facility. Cora, who had since given birth, traveled around Washington supporting her child and her habits by prostituting herself. She hooked up with several different men, whoever she could latch onto for money and support. The men she often spent her time with were not well-intentioned individuals and it wasn't long before a bad situation for any child to be involved in, became much worse.

When Nathaniel was the young age of eight, the abuse started. His mother and her boyfriends would smack him around and neglect him. Leave him for days without food while they would fornicate and get drunk or high. She would give Nathaniel alcohol to force him to sleep to keep him quiet while conducting business. She would use his skin as an ashtray when he misbehaved, putting cigarettes out on his flesh in places no one in public could see.

As he got older and more developed, his mother forced Nathaniel to perform sexual acts on her and do the same to him. Some of her more disturbed clientele would pay to fulfill their disturbed sexual fantasies on the young boy. Cora abused and allowed others to do the same to her son for years. He appeared in homemade pornographic films and was the subject of many disgusting, deviant photoshoots where he was shown with both men and women.

The police had been tracking a case of child pornography, prostitution, and drug abuse. One of Cora's most dedicated clients was a schoolteacher whom the police had been trying to capture for a long time. Cora and her many clients, including the teacher, were eventually arrested and Nathaniel was removed and placed into a group home. He had no living relatives. No one came forward to take him in. He had turned to violent behaviour just as Lucas Durante had, and in October of nineteen-ninety-five, at the age of fifteen. Nathaniel was remanded to the care of Mother Mary's home for boys.

That was the connection. Selena had found that Lucas Durante was at the same boy's home as this Nathaniel Whitaker. Both Lucas and Nathaniel shared a terrible past. But what happened after their time at the boy's home? Selena couldn't find anything online about this Nathaniel Whitaker. Was he Lucas Durante's first victim? Was this Nathaniel the one who killed Lucas? It was all too confusing, and Selena knew there had to be more to the story.

It was the cooling evening hours when Selena finished repacking the files away. She found all she was going to find in these dusty, forgotten files in the basement of the sheriff's office. She knew that she had to start looking into Mother Mary's Home for Boys further if she was to find out why Lucas Durante made the effort to give Selena, Nathaniel Whitaker's name. As she drove away from the sheriff's office, she couldn't shake the reports she had read from her mind. The terrible abuse that Nathaniel had endured. Whoever he is, it is likely that he could have very well become a killer from all that he had suffered.

Selena returned to the pub for another late dinner and was met once again by the handsome officer. She was pleasantly surprised and after the day's difficult reading, she welcomed the distraction. They enjoyed their meal and talked for a long time. It was the first time since her husband, Selena felt comfortable sharing herself with another man, emotionally. Much to her surprise at the end of the evening, the officer remained a perfect gentleman. He walked her to her motel room and said good evening. Selena eventually went to sleep to prepare to continue her investigation the next morning.

* * *

The thrill of murdering the lawyer and his whores should have satisfied the killer. He would often go months, even years without feeling such urgency to quench his desires. He had just slaughtered four people days earlier and it didn't accomplish anything. He couldn't replace that hole he felt deep within him. That disgrace for not being able to follow through in killing Valentina. It was a wrong he had become obsessed with setting right, and the only way to return the balance in himself and his demented game.

The stress of the carefully constructed cover life's day job was getting to the killer as well. Under normal circumstances he could maintain his calm resolve while pretending to be this good person. Any stresses that came up could be managed or forgotten until he could put a victim under his knife. He could feel his mask slipping and his world spinning out of control and didn't know if he could return to usual perfect form.

After the penthouse murders, the killer stalked Detective Davis as he had been doing since the beginning. John had done an excellent job in hiding Valentina. The killer had trouble following John as he continued to be as slippery as a snake. The killer knew that if he was ever to return to his position of power, if he was ever to regain control of this game, he would have to kill Valentina.

When following John proved fruitless, the killer continued his search for the missing Detective Lopez. Where had she gone? The killer managed to track her to her motel room and slipped inside. It pleased him to see his intention of pitting John versus Selena in suspecting who the murderer was, had worked. From what that note said, that she had hung up on the wall, it was apparent she was considering John as the murderer. This small victory returned some sense of peace.

The killer used his day job resources and attempted to track Detective Lopez's whereabouts. A trace of her cell phone revealed it to have been deactivated for days and its last location was the motel where she was staying. Her bank account and credit cards remained inactive since she charged the motel and rental car and withdrew several thousand dollars in cash. Her personal vehicle remained in the motel parking lot. The killer went as far as questioning the clerk at the rental car agency who revealed Detective Lopez mentioned Nevada as a potential location for the assumed mileage she intended to put on the rental.

Detective Lopez was nowhere to be found. It was clear she wasn't going to Nevada and didn't want to be tracked. John was keeping Valentina well-hidden and out of the killer's reach. He remained in his perpetual state of torment. There was seemingly nothing to be done to change his plight. The thought of more victims constantly came to his mind, it was his way of centering himself, but the emptiness of failing to kill Valentina would remain. There was one thing that could be done, had to be done, to take credit for his latest kill.

The killer took extra care and attention preparing his latest package for Detectives Davis and Lopez. He picked out a special box. He placed the dry items in neatly and carefully. He then packaged the wet items on top and wrapped them together. He carefully combed over every inch, every item, every fibre, to make sure it was free of anything incriminating. When he was confident it was clear, he placed in the equally, carefully prepared letters to his pawns and packaged everything together.

If he couldn't kill Valentina. If he couldn't locate and taunt Detective Lopez directly. He could, at the very least, stir the pot. This was his game. Sending in pieces of his kill, something to prove he was the one who killed the victim, this was his signature. Detective Davis was about to receive the killer's latest piece of work.

CHAPTER ELEVEN

The crisp morning air welcomed the dawn. The night sky was giving way to morning as the sun rose. The black canvas turned to dark blue then brightened, scaring away the lingering shadows that clung to the buildings. It wouldn't be long before the city's citizens started their day. The peaceful silence of the morning would soon be filled with the sound of rumbling exhaust and annoying car horns.

It had been yet another night in the presence of death. John had wrapped up his work in the crime scene inside the penthouse and was directing everyone to finish their work. The bodies had been removed without being seen by the crowd, which had since dispersed in the early morning hours. The penthouse had been rendered off-limits and was taped off and the elevator access locked out.

The crime scene investigative team had taken all their pictures, collected all their samples, and had removed all their equipment and findings from the apartment and returned to their laboratory. The witnesses had given their statements and the security staff members, whom had been rendered unconscious, were all transported to the hospital. The patrol officers were removing their barricades as the scene was about to be released, returning the front of the building to its normal elegant appearance.

It was still early as John drove away from the building. He was confident that Valentina was safe. She had locked the apartment and had the pistol John had given to her and shown her how to shoot. John realized as he drove away that if this killer was hunting him and threatening him directly, anyone connected to him was at risk. He had officers patrolling his ex-wife's house just in case but as he drove away from the horror of this latest collection of victims, with his name scattered in blood throughout the apartment, John felt he had to warn his ex-wife.

It had been a long time since John had spoken to her. Though he often parked outside her house attempting to catch a glimpse of her, he never wanted to disrupt her new life. He found himself feeling as nervous as he had when he had asked her to marry him so long ago. He struggled to catch his breath as he approached the door and could feel his pulse pounding and his knees felt weak. Her lingering effect on him was always intoxicating.

It was still early as John was about to ring the doorbell. He could see there was a light on within the house and could hear the commotion of people inside. "At least I won't be waking anyone," he thought to himself. He decided to knock instead of ring the doorbell. It was less alerting and annoying to hear someone knocking as opposed to the chiming melody of the doorbell.

The door opened, and to John's disappointment, it was his ex-wife's new husband that answered. After a few awkward seconds of silence, John apologized for the early hour and briefly mentioned the reason for the visit and why it was so urgent to speak with his ex-wife. The new husband was in the process of preparing for his day with his shirt untucked and his necktie simply draped around his neck and hanging low on his chest. He invited John in and led him to the kitchen table where he offered a mug of coffee. John politely accepted.

The doctor left John in the kitchen to go and get John's ex-wife. John couldn't help but wonder what his ex-wife saw in this guy. He hated to admit that he was jealous of their house and its extravagance as he looked around the vast kitchen area. He could never have afforded such a place for them. When they were married, John's ex-wife always seemed content with the simpler things in life, it appeared her tastes had since changed.

John's admiration of the home was halted when his ex-wife entered the kitchen. Her hair was wet from her morning shower and she had on a long flowing bathrobe. John swallowed hard and tried to mask his attraction to her. He stood from his chair as she entered and greeted her. The doctor, John's ex-wife's new husband, entered the kitchen behind her and poured them each a cup of coffee and refilled John's mug. It was obvious that his ex-wife was less than thrilled to have John in her kitchen.

After several moments of awkward small-talk, John thought it wise to simply cut to the chase and dive into the real reason he was there. He went on to describe what had been going on over the past few weeks. The letters, the threats sent into the station, the clues left behind at the crime scene. John told them about the attack on his new girlfriend and how she narrowly escaped. His intent was to scare them out of town until he could catch this killer. He left out that he believed his partner might be involved.

It was a long conversation and John had certainly struck a chord with them. They agreed that they would find somewhere else to stay for a few days until they could arrange their schedules for some time off. They thanked John for the warning and mentioned they were going to be late for work and had to finish getting ready. John left them with the promise to keep them safe until he was able to find this killer. He did his best to hide the love he still carried for his ex.

Exhaustion was starting to kick-in. It had been nearly thirty-six hours since John had rested and all he wanted to do was crawl in bed next to Valentina and shut off his mind for a few hours. He carefully drove to the safe house he had arranged. He lost several vehicles that might be following him, then parked several blocks away and walked down the back alleyways and backyards until finally reaching the apartment building.

Inside the apartment John was expecting to find Valentina asleep in bed. Instead, he found her seated at the small kitchen table puffing a cigarette and sipping a glass of scotch. She glared at John as he entered the apartment. Her anger could be felt without anything being said. John approached her cautiously and attempted a kiss which she immediately refused, pushing him away from her.

"Where the hell have you been?" Valentina shouted, jolting out of her chair and stepping away from John.

"Keep your voice down," John said softly, looking out the window to see if anyone had heard the shout.

"Fuck you," Valentina shot back, "where the hell were you? I've been up all goddamn night, terrified."

"Baby, I'm sorry. I called you from the crime scene. I was working that all night." John replied trying to touch her to calm her.

"All night? It's mid-morning and you called me almost ten hours ago. Why are you just getting back now?" Valentina growled angrily. She shoved John aside to leave the room.

"After what I saw last night, it wasn't just a threat against me and you. It's a threat against anyone connected to me," John explained. "I had to go warn my ex-wife."

"So, you leave me here, exposed, with a killer hunting me to go console your ex-wife?" Valentina replied, throwing a heavy picture frame at John narrowly missing his head.

"Hey, calm down," John shouted back as metal and glass exploded against the wall.

"Calm down? You have kept me here for days with no access to the outside world. I haven't spoken to my friends. My boss has called and left emails, threatening that if I don't come in, I'll be fired. You have screwed with my life." Valentina yelled as she shoved her clothes into her suitcase.

"I know. I'm sorry for that. What are you doing?" John asked trying to get Valentina to stop.

"It's because of you that I'm in danger. Being with you is why this psycho wants me dead, and now my career is in jeopardy. I'm leaving," Valentina replied as she went into the bathroom and packed her toiletries and makeup.

"Valentina, I'll speak with your boss. He and I go way back, he'll understand. Just come back here and sit for a second," John said. He walked towards her to stop her, but the exhaustion hit him. He felt dizzy and faint.

"To hell with you," Valentina returned. She was mixing Spanish with her English as she cursed angrily. She stomped through the apartment gathered what she needed, "you don't need me anymore. I've served my purpose, run back to your ex-wife asshole."

"Valentina," John called out. He tried to stop her, but the dizziness overcame him as if he had been drugged. He fell back to the bed and watched Valentina exit the apartment as his vision went blurry until he could no longer keep his eyes open. His head was thumping in pain and John fell into a deep sleep and returned to his dream of the hallway. He returned to the claustrophobic, blood-red walls closing in and left him desperately trying to escape.

* * *

The third day of Detective Selena Lopez's investigation in this dreamy little town found her enjoying breakfast on the balcony of her room. The handsome officer who had taken an interest in her had brought her fresh-baked muffins and coffee. She was reluctant to allow such behaviour, not wanting to lead him on and give him the wrong impression, but who could resist the smell of a fresh blueberry muffin and a cup of hot coffee first thing in the morning.

They sat on the balcony, enjoying the view of the valley and chatting about the town and Selena opened-up more about the truth of why she was there and what she was looking for. The officer read the reports she had taken from the station the day earlier. The reports and history of both Lucas Durante and Nathaniel Whitaker's pasts. She explained how the information had been delivered to her, that Lucas Durante had given her the clue of Nathaniel Whitaker on his death bed.

It wasn't easy for her to share, but Selena told the officer of her daughter's murder. She explained her belief that this killer, Lucas Durante, Nathaniel Whitaker, and this recent string of murders back in her city Lugar De Paz were all connected somehow. All the roads of her investigation had led her to this point and her next stop was Mother Mary's Home for boys. Uncovering the connection of these two men was the only way to bring her daughter's killer to justice and bring Selena some much-needed peace.

The officer explained the forest fire that had destroyed the boy's home over twenty years before. He had been in high school when it happened and recalled being pleased that he and his classmates could miss school after being evacuated for several days. Unfortunately for the students, their school was untouched as the fire was brought under control and stopped before reaching the heart of the town. The fire was certainly before his time as a policeman, and he couldn't remember if they had ever found out the fire's origin.

After breakfast, Selena and her new-found friend, the handsome officer, set out to the site of where Mother Mary's had been located. From her interviews around town, Selena had found out that the mansion had been rebuilt and repurposed as a retirement home for the elderly equipped with a full nursing unit. As they drove out of the small town, Selena only hoped they had kept records of some kind. There had to be something, more pieces to finish the puzzle.

The property was surrounded by a large brick wall that was overgrown with thick brush. The large entranceway had someone manning the gate. A quick flash of their badges allowed for Selena and her new partner to pass through without incident. The drive up to the mansion was beautiful. There were massive trees that hung over the roadway, creating an evergreen canopy. The lawns were well-tended with residents walking around and enjoying various activities. It certainly was a peaceful property.

The driveway ended at a roundabout with a massive fountain at its center. The figures of a man and woman embracing with water cascading down all around them. The building itself was large and bore the appearance of an old-time, Victorian-style mansion. It reminded Selena of a dollhouse she once had when she was a little girl. The memory of her childhood forced a smile as she entered the building.

Inside, the lobby welcomed its guests with an impressive curved staircase. Antique furniture and fixtures made up the interior's décor throughout. The lobby boasted a massive, low-hanging, chandelier that reflected the natural light that shone down through a large skylight. This could have been an elegant hotel and make a fortune with its comfortable extravagance.

The front desk had a polite receptionist who was eager to help with Selena's request to speak with the proprietor of the retirement home. The helpful woman was quick to offer tea, coffee, or snacks, which Selena and the officer politely refused. They were directed into an office located off the main lobby where they were met with an exquisitely dressed woman in her early forties who offered them a seat at her desk next to the large bay windows that looked out into the lawn.

Selena wasted no time and explained she was looking for any, and all information on the building which stood on this very spot. Unfortunately, the director of the retirement home didn't have any information to give. She had taken this job only five years earlier when she moved her mother in from Seattle. She was, at one time, a hospital administrator and moved to get her family out of the big city as well as help her mother in her twilight years.

The director went on to explain all she knew of the current building's history. It was built twelve years before, with the land being purchased by an internet tycoon with political aspirations, who was looking to clean up his corporate image as well as providing care for his grandmother. He invested in the prestigious retirement home and nursing unit to be a haven for seniors to enjoy their remaining years with plenty of activities to occupy their time in the fresh mountain air.

There was seemingly nothing suspicious or clandestine about the director or the facility and its past. This was the first of several retirement communities built around the state that had begun with the initial investments of a wealthy governor hopeful. Providing such care for seniors was certainly a clean way to show potential voters how one cares. Selena feared that this might be the end of her search.

As Selena directed the conversation towards its end and thanked the director for her time. She was about to leave when the receptionist interrupted, saying that she had overheard the request for information on the boy's home that used to be on this site. The receptionist mentioned that she was a local who lived in town her whole life, and that there was a resident at the retirement home who used to work at the former boy's home. She suggested that she might recall some helpful information.

The director thanked her receptionist for her help and asked only that Selena and her partner not disrupt any of the activities of the residents as they went to question the former nurse of Mother Mary's. The receptionist went to her laptop and found the room number where Selena could find the former nurse. The nurse's name was Wynn Weatherby and her schedule placed her as being in the gardens behind the mansion.

With a new and only potential lead, Selena set out to the grounds with a description of the lady who hopefully could help her. She followed the directions given to her by the receptionist and made her way into the backyard of the facility. The yards were tremendous. It looked like a golf course resort. The residents were all friendly and helpful, telling Selena where she could find Ms. Weatherby, who was directing a yoga class for her fellow residents.

There was a gazebo a short walk from the main house where a small gathering of seniors wrapped up their class and were starting to roll up their yoga mats. Selena saw the instructor and the description she was given matched her perfectly. A very short woman with curly, snow-white hair, wearing a bright pink and orange yoga outfit. She was very cheerful as she ended her class and encouraged her members as they exited.

"Excuse me, Ms. Weatherby?" Selena asked as she stepped onto the floor of the gazebo.

"Yes dear, that's me. And you are?" The exuberant old lady responded.

"My name is Detective Selena Lopez, from Lugar De Paz California. I'm investigating a murderer's past who lived at Mother Mary's Home for Boy's before it burned down," Selena answered, sitting down next to the woman. "I was told you worked there; would it be alright if I asked you some questions?"

"Of course, dear. Such a beautiful face, you two make a very cute couple," the pleasant woman said patting Selena's cheek.

"Thank you, ma'am," Selena said with a chuckle, feeling her face turning red. "We're not a couple, he is a local police officer showing me around. So, can you tell me about what happened to Mother Mary's? What kind of place it was, how long you worked there, how it burned down?"

"My apologies," Wynn said with a laugh. "I worked at Mother Mary's for seventeen years. I started when I was twenty-eight. It wasn't always a pleasant place. We took in troubled boys with no families. Boys who had gotten themselves into a great deal of trouble. Some of them angry with such terrible pasts. Others were just kids with nowhere to go."

"Do you remember the names, Lucas Durante? Or perhaps, Nathaniel Whitaker?" Selena asked eagerly. The woman's eyes shot open in recognition and welled with tears. She knew these names.

"Yes, they were here," Wynn replied. "They both had come from horrible homes. Just horrific situations and wound up at Mother Mary's. Both were so angry when they were brought here."

"I've read the file the police had on their pasts and yes it was horrible. What I need to know was if they knew each other," Selena said, trying to stifle her excitement.

"They were inseparable," Wynn replied. "They idolized this young hiker. He was a transient who would always stop by for a free meal and warm bed when the weather was bad. I can't recall his name, very polite young man though. Nathaniel and Lucas befriended this hiker and though the boy was older than them, Lucas and this hiker seemed to look-up to Nathaniel."

"Why was that?" Selena inquired.

"Nathaniel was very manipulative and sneaky," Wynn explained, "he was tested at near genius level intelligence but was very devious. He would act one way around the workers, and another way around the other kids. He had this way about him, that he would convince Lucas and the others to do things at his request and they would. Like some sort of alpha wolf."

"What happened to Nathaniel?" Selena asked.

"One night, the boys had been placed under disciplinary lock-down for being caught stealing cigarettes. Nathaniel always smoked like a chimney. The hiker had told the staff of Nathaniel's smoking and sneaking out and attempts to purchase alcohol. He was a good lad," Wynn said.

"And then what happened?" Selena asked urgently.

"The hiker, who was always seen with his backpack and belongings, left. He ventured off outside and said he would be right back. It was a very dry spring that year and there were campgrounds not far from the house, not far from here. Anyway, we believe that was the young hiker's camp. The next evening the forest fire forced everyone out of the home. I remember, as we started the evacuation, seeing that hiker's large backpack in Nathaniel's room," Wynn recalled.

"What happened to Nathaniel?" Selena asked.

"The fire started so quickly. We had just made the children go to bed and most of them had fallen asleep by the time we heard the sirens. The police and firefighters told us all we had five minutes to take only what we needed and leave. We completed the evacuation and Nathaniel was nowhere to be found. Lucas mentioned he was in their bedroom when they went to sleep and when he woke up, Nathaniel wasn't there," Wynn explained.

"They never found Nathaniel's body?" Selena asked.

"It was never positively identified. There were bodies of children in the upper floors, so badly burnt that no I.D. could be made. There were also two bodies found down at the campground," Wynn said, wiping away a tear.

"I'm sorry for making you relive this Ms. Weatherby," Selena said, offering a tissue. "But I wouldn't be here if it weren't important. What do you think happened to Nathaniel?"

"I believe," Wynn said, "Nathaniel was mad at that young hiker for telling us about what he was doing. I think he snuck out of the house that night to confront that boy at his campsite. Something must've happened between them and the fire started and quickly got away from them, killing them both."

Selena and Wynn carried on their conversation and Wynn described how Nathaniel was the only boy who had ever frightened her in all her time working with troubled youths. She said it was like he had a mask on for the world where he appeared sweet and innocent but underneath there was something terrifying. When Nathaniel had first been brought to the home, he lashed out at the staff members, he would bite, kick and punch. As soon as he figured out the way the staff worked, he changed.

Suddenly, Nathaniel went from being a problem case to a poster child almost overnight. Wynn explained that Nathaniel's mean streak continued the entire time he was in the home but none of the incidents could ever be linked to him. Things would be stolen, fights would break out, things would get vandalized and people hurt, and nothing would ever point to Nathaniel being involved. But Wynn knew there was something about him that was all wrong.

It was a long conversation, but at its end, Selena was convinced that whoever Nathaniel Whitaker was, he didn't die that day of the fire. She thanked Wynn for her time and everything she had told her. She had a new destination to visit thanks to the former nurse. The building had mostly burned to the ground, however, before the final demolition the workers went through the ruins and the basement was still intact. It was filled with the records and belongings of the boys who lived there. There might be something within that collection.

As Selena and the officer drove away, her mind was abuzz with more unanswered questions. Who was this hiker? Was he Nathaniel Whitaker's first victim? Did Nathaniel set the fire to fake his death? Or was this all the work of Lucas Durante sending her up here to take credit for another kill? Her head hurt as she drove away. It was already early evening when they returned to town. And there wasn't much that could be done for the case that evening.

It was frustrating to Selena how early everything closed for the day in small towns. She wanted nothing more than to continue searching for clues. It was imperative that she locate those missing things from Mother Mary's basement and hoped they weren't simply destroyed after the fire. She didn't want to admit the likelihood of this and tried to remain positive. The curiosity was driving her mad. She could feel she was getting close to something huge.

The officer tried again to make a move on Selena, leaning in for a kiss at the end of the night. As politely as she could, she refused and let him down easy. With her reformed ways she couldn't get into another situation like this. Being around the handsome officer was calming and relaxing. She was certainly attracted to him. He was very attractive, and she had gawked at his muscular form imagining them in various sexual positions with their bodies intertwined. But she knew she had to keep things professional between them with her attentions focused on the case.

* * *

The police were taking down their equipment and moving their vehicles. Black body bags had been placed into the coroner's van and transported away. The heavy crowd had lightened, and everyone was beginning to the leave the building. The news reporters had left hours ago since the police refused to release a statement. The killer stood among the crowd admiring his latest completed work.

It was such a rush of adrenaline for this killer to stand next to the police. To stand within the crowd right near reporters just outside his own crime scene. He enjoyed watching the police work. Men and women following orders. The amount of people all working on something he had done. All these people were here for him and they had no idea the one responsible was standing right there among them watching. Just another onlooker.

Finally, the man the killer wanted to see emerged from the building. Detective John Davis. The detective looked exhausted and distraught. He seemed to be struggling. Was the crime scene too much for him to handle? Was the pressure too great for him to overcome? The killer thought of him as the worm, squirming in his grip right before skewering him on the hook and casting him out into the water.

Detective Davis left the scene with the killer close behind. As he had been for weeks, the killer remained a safe distance away, so the detective couldn't see. The police cruiser went down a series of streets and travelled in the opposite direction of police headquarters. This was out of character for the detective. After working a crime scene, he would always return to the station to write his reports. Now, after travelling to one of the wealthier parts of town, he was parked outside an elegantly decorated house, staring out like a prowler. Like a stalker. Like the killer who had been watching him.

After a long hesitation, John emerged from his car and walked up to the house where he had been staring. There were several times where he stopped and turned away to head back to his car, then turned around and went back to the door. The detective clearly did not want to make this visit. Perhaps it was a victim's family. The door opened, and John went inside. The killer put out the cigarette he had just lit and crept up for a closer look.

It was a large home. From the look of the perfectly tended lawn, the neighbourhood, and overall size and style of this house, it belonged to someone of great wealth. Using his well-crafted stalking skill, the killer positioned himself perfectly to see inside the house and remain invisible. John was enjoying a cup of coffee and looked incredibly uncomfortable. He did not want to be there.

A beautiful woman entered the kitchen with the man who had answered the door to let John in walking behind her. She looked familiar. The killer studied her closely as she talked with John. Was she the mother of a victim? Was she the wife of another cop? The killer knew he had seen her before. Then it became clear. She was a little older and her hair had changed but the killer recognized her. She was John's ex-wife. John had now revealed another of his weaknesses and had left it exposed.

It wasn't long before John exited the house and returned to his car. The killer remained close behind. John's car was swaying back and forth in his lane, it was clear he was struggling. His efforts to lose the killer were normally difficult to follow. On this morning, it was easy. John was not on his game at all. The detective parked in a vacant lot and walked into an alleyway. This could be an ambush. The killer continued his pursuit cautiously.

The killer followed John like a shadow down one alley, then another. John kept looking over his shoulder and the killer was quick to avoid being seen. John proceeded into the backyards of some houses, then crossed the street. He was going through a lot of trouble to get to where he intended to go. John continuously had to stop to catch his breath and brace himself. He walked as if he were dizzy or drunk. Something was wrong with the detective.

Finally, John entered a building and the killer moved in close. There was a commotion and muffled arguing. There was a crash of furniture and broken glass. The killer could hear John's voice and the voice of a woman. The windows had been covered, and the argument had gone from the front room into the back. The argument finished abruptly, and everything went silent. The killer motioned towards the front of the building but was too late to catch a glimpse of the woman leaving. Was it Valentina? Was this the place John had been keeping her?

The front door wasn't closed completely. The killer moved inside. He slithered his way through the relatively empty apartment. He went from room to room as carefully and quietly as he could. He could see the table and chairs had been overturned. There were broken dishes on the countertops and kitchen floor. The windows were mostly covered, allowing only a small amount of sunlight to peek through around the edges. The smell of cheap women's perfume lingered heavily in the air.

In the back of the apartment, the killer found John had fallen asleep on the bed. There was a moment where he had taken John's pistol and aimed at his left temple. The killer had his finger on the trigger and wanted to pull. He could end this right now and be rid of him, but it wasn't quite time yet. The killer searched the apartment for any sign of where Valentina might have gone but found nothing.

The killer decided the message he wanted to send John, the evidence taken from the crime scene, would make a more poignant message if left here rather than the station. The killer left the apartment briefly and returned with the box containing his message. He placed John's pistol in front of the box on the table and moved the table into the bedroom directly in front of John. It would be the first thing he would see when he woke up.

CHAPTER TWELVE

Indistinct chattering and muffled voices could be heard yelling and echoing in the distance. Blood soaked walls lined the hallway and the floor shrank. The blackness had formed from behind and was moving closer and closer. The sound of a heartbeat thumping became so loud. He ran towards the exit door seemed no use. The door seemed to move further and further away. There was no air in the room. The simple act of breathing was impossible. The darkness was right behind, right there. The walls were collapsing.

Gasping for air and soaked in sweat, John jolted from his bed and crashed into a table. He fell onto his back with his chest heaving. His lungs were burning from the effort. He choked and coughed as he struggled to breathe. He laid on the cool floor until the room stopped spinning. Until his breath had slowed along with his pulse. His thoughts recalled the last thing he could remember before the nightmare. The image of Valentina as she left the apartment.

John struggled to stand calling out for Valentina. There was no answer. As he rose to his feet, he wondered why the kitchen table was suddenly in the bedroom near the bed. He hadn't put it there. There was a wooden box in the shape of an old-fashioned coffin on the floor and his pistol beside it. There was also an envelope with his name written on its surface. John immediately recognized the writing. It belonged to the killer.

Fear surged throughout his entire body. All drowsiness and confusion had immediately been removed and John was fully alert. He quickly searched his pockets for his cell phone. It was gone. He ran to the kitchen cabinet and removed some latex gloves and grabbed a plastic, sealable bag, then returned to the letter. He carefully opened the envelope and removed the parchment to read the killer's latest taunt.

The letter was a poem in the killer's writing that read,

I am all around you, yet you cannot see.

I am closer than breath, yet you cannot feel.

I am in the wind.

I am on the ground.

You'll never catch me.

I'll see you around.

Yours truly, Shadow.

Using tweezers, John carefully placed the letter into the bag. Inside the envelope there was a bundle of more polaroid photographs. They were of the victims inside the penthouse in various stages of their torture. Each picture was more horrifying than the last. John placed them into another bag and closed it. He braced himself as he opened the box, unsure what he was about to see. He swallowed hard, then carefully opened the creaking lid.

Laid on top was a single polaroid of John's face as he slept. The killer must have taken it while he was knocked out. Under the photo was the missing clothes that were covered in blood. A three-piece suit that belonged to the slain lawyer from the penthouse. There was the lawyer's wallet, left open to his identification. There were more photos in the bottom of the box that showed the lawyers torture and death. Then, John opened the small plastic bag that was tucked inside the box.

John only peered inside the bag for a second and immediately closed it up. It was the lawyers severed penis and genitals. Panic returned as John stared down at the killer's delivery. The killer had found the safehouse where he had kept Valentina. He managed to sneak in and leave this demented message while John slept soundly. John knew how close he had just come to death and the thought of soon being called to Valentina's crime scene took over his thoughts. He knew he had to find her.

Moments later, John had the evidence repackaged and he was running in full sprint to his car. He didn't care if Valentina hated him or not. He had to find her. He would arrest her if he had to. The engine of his squad car came to life, John slipped the transmission into gear and pushed his foot to the floor. The engine roared and the tires screamed as the car was propelled forward. It was a race for Valentina's life, and John had to win.

The unmarked car raced through the streets. The flashing lights alerting motorists and pedestrians. The siren's scream echoed far into the distance. John slid the car around tight corners, sped up narrow paths, ran stop signs and red lights. He had to make up as much lost time as he could. He reached the police headquarters building in mere minutes and parked at the curbside out front. He grabbed the evidence and ran as fast his legs could carry him into the building.

There was no one in the laboratory in the basement of the building. John picked the lock and placed the box, the bag of pictures, and the letter on the desk and wrote a quick note to the technician he most trusted. He placed the bag containing the bloody, severed appendage and sealed it into a container with another note and put it with the sensitive evidence kept in the refrigerated storage space. He was confident his friend in the laboratory would follow his instructions to the letter.

The homicide unit was empty. Captain McGee wasn't in his office and most of the other detectives were gone. John went to his desk and removed his personal cell phone. He had deactivated it when he put Valentina into hiding after her attack and hadn't used it since. The battery was completely dead, and he had no time to wait for it to charge. He would have to charge it in the car. He knew where he had to go.

Back in the car, John plugged in his phone then raced toward his next destination. He sped across the bridge that would take him to Valentina's apartment. He armed himself with his pistol and stormed inside. As he ran up the stairs, he missed several steps and stumbled as he pushed himself to go faster. He reached the top floor and ran up to Valentina's apartment. He pounded his fist on the door but there was no response.

The newly repaired door-jam exploded into fragments as John used all his force and kicked it into the apartment as he had the day Valentina was attacked. He entered the apartment behind the protection of his aimed pistol. There was nobody there. It appeared as though Valentina had been there recently. He could see she had collected more of her clothes and costumes. She mentioned that her boss from Night Moves, Salvatore Di Sano, John's old-time friend had been hassling her to get back to work. That would be John's next stop.

As he made his way to leave the apartment, John noticed a small note left on the counter. The hot-pink paper caught his eye. He picked it up and it read simply, "I know you will try to find me John. Please don't. You make life too difficult. Take care of yourself and enjoy the memories we made. Goodbye. V."

John crumpled the paper. Valentina's foolishness was going to get her killed. Her childish jealousy of John's ex-wife was putting her in danger. If she only knew how dangerous this killer was. The killer could have her right now. The killer could be preparing his next torture room. He could be hurting her, raping her, or ending her life. John sprinted out of the apartment, down the hall, down the stairs, and outside to his car.

The sun was in its final stages of setting and patrons were driving up to the club Night Moves for an evening of pleasures from the city's most exotic dancers. As the crowd was making its way to the front door, a speeding, unmarked, police car hopped the sidewalk, and came barreling towards them. Everyone ran out of the way to avoid being struck as the car skidded to a stop. Nearest the front door, the speeding car slammed into the brass pillars that held up the red-velvet rope causing them to strike the side of the building.

The bouncers had to jump out of the way as John made his dramatic entrance. The massive men were still on the ground when John stomped his way into the club. He called out for Valentina and his frantic behaviour terrified the staff who were busy preparing to open for the evening. John left the main room and walked to the back where the dancers prepared themselves for their performances, where he first met Valentina weeks earlier.

The collection of beautiful women jumped out of their seats as John forced his way into their dressing room, desperately calling out Valentina's name. A few women were entirely unclothed, with only a towel to cover them. Several were in various stages of undress. The women screamed and yelled at John to get out as he furiously searched the room and adjoining locker room and shower stalls. Valentina was nowhere to be found.

John stood in the doorway trying to catch his breath again. He apologized to the dancers and was about to ask them if they had seen Valentina when he was grabbed from behind by one of the bouncers. The heavily muscled man tossed John onto the floor at the feet of his partner, an equally muscled man who stood John up in front of him. The massive men were pushing John out the door and ignored his demands to let him go and his threats of the penalty for manhandling a police officer.

The panic that coursed through John's mind was replaced with anger and rage. He saw red and his jaw tightened. His extensive self defense training took over and he swiftly broke free of the bouncers' tight grasp. The first man lunged forward and was brought to the floor, his face was slammed into the hard floor's surface with incredible force. Blood and teeth shot out from the injured bouncer's mouth.

The second bouncer tried to grapple John's shoulders and was flipped onto his back. John straddled him on the floor, and repeatedly pounded his fists into the man's face. John stood up as both bouncers remained on the floor in pain from John's attack. John unsheathed his pistol and wedged its muzzle into the flesh of the first bouncer's head. His thumb lowered the safety lever readying the pistol to fire. He chambered a bullet and was about to pull the trigger.

"John," a familiar voice shouted from the second-floor office. It drew John's attention away from the bouncer, "what the hell are you doing? Stop."

John holstered his pistol and raised up from the floor staring down at what he had done. He looked up to find his old friend Salvatore, the club's owner, who was running down the stairs towards him. He had his pistol removed from inside his suit and aimed at John as he approached. John's breathing was settling, and he felt himself calming down.

"I'm sorry," John said, realizing the gravity of the situation, "look Sal, these guys forced my hand. They wouldn't listen. I'm just here looking for Valentina, she's in danger from a killer. I have to protect her."

"What are you talking about?" Salvatore said lowering his pistol and stepping closer. "I don't care what's going on. You don't come in here and knock my guys around. You forget who exactly I am? Who my family is? You're goddamn lucky my father doesn't want us tussling with pigs. Now get your ass out of here before I break his rule."

Outside the club, a crowd had formed after seeing a police cruiser, slam into the velvet rope. John stepped out of the club. He had nowhere to turn. Nowhere to look for Valentina. She could be anywhere, and he had no idea where to start looking. If she wasn't at her apartment and she wasn't at the club, where could she be? John had potentially made a dangerous enemy of his old friend who was a member of a powerful organized crime family. He didn't care. The only thing John knew, was that Valentina's life was in grave danger.

* * *

Heavy raindrops cascaded down the windshield as the wipers did their best to keep the water clear. The sound of the rain as it hit the metal of the car was almost soothing. As she drove, passing milestone after milestone, Selena thought of her conversation with Wynn Weatherby. The former nurse at Mother Mary's had given her an insight of who she might be looking for. She was running out of time and had to find some more clues to go on.

Selena had been up early making phone calls to various towns in the surrounding area in her search for where she might find the paperwork and personal belongings of the residents of the Mother Mary's Home for Boys. Wynn had mentioned that the basement storeroom of the building had survived the fire but wasn't sure where all the unclaimed items ended up. Most likely they were destroyed. After several disappointing phone calls, Selena finally received a ray of hope.

One of the calls Selena had made was to a fire chief from a town a few hours north of where the old boy's home had stood. His crew had been called in to fight the fire to prevent it from spreading to the neighbouring towns. The chief recalled having taken part in the salvage of an old school, or what he thought was a school. His crew had been ordered to transport the unclaimed property and paperwork to a storage facility, which they had. He wasn't sure what happened to them after that.

With this new information, Selena telephoned another community where the fire chief had mentioned transporting the items. After being placed on hold several times and being directed to different departments, a clerk answered the phone and gave Selena an address of a warehouse. All unclaimed property and outdated paperwork and files resulting from a fire from that time would have been brought there, especially after such a confusing emergency evacuation.

The warehouse was a few hours drive north of Pine Valley, where Selena had begun her investigation several days before. She sped into the rain, chasing after the one clue that might help her solve Lucas Durante's riddle. She had the image of the note he had written to her the night he died. It was terribly confusing but with everything she had since learned, the tumblers were falling into place. All she needed was some more clarity before returning home to California.

It was nearly noon when Selena arrived at the warehouse. It was a massive building in a thickly forested area, well-hidden from sight. Luckily, the directions given by the clerk were so precise or the building would have been extremely difficult to find. Selena entered the front office where she was met by a security guard. She showed her identification and mentioned the clerk's name who said she would call ahead to allow Selena to enter the building.

The security guard was not very subtle in his flirtations with Selena. His eager eyes scanned her body up and down, pretending it was part of his job. Selena responded in kind, arching her back and removing her jacket to provide amble view of her tight jeans. It was easy to control these types of fools. Selena didn't mind playful flirting, especially if it helped her achieve her goal.

Selena was allowed through the secure gate and the guard was all too eager to help her locate the items she sought after. As they walked the isles of so many various collected items, Selena smirked at the idiocy of the mindless guard who had turned to putty at the thought she might be interested in him. Her attention returned to the search of her missing items.

The guard had mentioned that items collected before the year, two-thousand-nine were not entered into the computer system. He had scanned through the filing system and found a potential location where the items might be stored. The building was lined up in rows of chain-link cages which held a wide array of various materials. Magnetic placards were hung on the front of each storage cage with location labels, corresponding to the guard's simple filing system.

Finally, Selena and the guard reached the cage he was searching for. He quickly opened the locked door and helped Selena pull boxes out from the shadows into the isle where there was better light. Selena dove in and scanned through anything she could, looking for anything that mentioned Mother Mary's, or Nathaniel Whitaker, or Lucas Durante. It was yet another stack of hay for Selena to search through to find a needle that may not exist.

The guard returned to his duties and left Selena to rummage through the boxes. He returned with a cup of coffee for her after she had been searching for quite some time. Selena was laser focused. There had to be something. She took a break and sipped the surprisingly good coffee offered by the over-friendly guard. They were chatting briefly when something in the cage caught Selena's eye.

Leaning against the back corner of the cage was a hiker's backpack. Selena recalled her conversation with Wynn the day before where she mentioned Nathaniel Whitaker befriending a hiker who had such a pack. A pack Nathaniel had taken from the hiker before he went missing, before the mysterious fire had started at the camp site. Selena pulled the backpack from the cage.

There was nothing spectacular within the pack. There was a thermos, water bottle, various other containers. Some novels and magazines. There was a harmonica, an old pack of cigarettes. A half-empty flask. There was some men's clothing, spare boots and shoes tied to its base. There was a collection of polaroid pictures of the scenery, the mountains, rivers, waterfalls. There was a picture of three teenage boys that was quite faded. Could this old photo be of the missing hiker, Nathaniel Whitaker, and Lucas Durante?

Selena returned the items to the pack and went back into the cage to keep searching. She found several boxes with the Mother Mary's logo that contained receipts and ledgers. Nothing of consequence to Selena's investigation. She then found several boxes with the same logo belonging to a Dr. Warren Evans, a psychiatrist who worked with the boys at the home. The boxes had files with many names and inside were the doctor's notes and audio tapes.

There was file after file on various boys until finally Selena found an additional box solely dedicated to Nathaniel Whitaker. Written within the notes, the doctor confirmed the fear that Wynn had felt when dealing with the troubled boy. Dr Evans's notes speculated the boy's capacity for violence and described his repressed rage. There were more detailed police reports from the abuse sustained before Nathaniel's arrival to the home.

Within the box of Dr Evans's notes on Nathaniel was a small tape recorder and several audio tapes labelled with session numbers. Selena would have to get batteries to hear those sessions. She set aside the box and kept searching until she found the file for Lucas Durante. Dr Evans seemed to believe that he was more of a follower. He too, like Nathaniel, was angry and certainly acted out, but didn't possess the intelligence that Nathaniel had. Dr Evans noted how he had observed Nathaniel's easy manipulation of young Lucas.

Selena went back into the cage and found Lucas Durante's personal items. Typical for a teenage boy. Nothing out of the ordinary. She placed it with the other items she had found and returned to the cage. There was more Mother Mary's paperwork. More boxes labelled with other boys' names. Selena had nearly gone through every item until she uncovered one last box under all the rest. Reading the label nearly made her heart skip a beat. It read, "Property of Nathaniel Whitaker".

Under the light of the isle, Selena brought the box out with the others and opened it up. There were journals and diaries filled with handwritten entries. There were several pornographic videotapes that simulated rape. There were magazines and cigarettes. Then Selena found an old polaroid camera with faded initials engraved on its surface. There was an old lockbox underneath that had "Private" handwritten in felt pen on its lid.

It took several minutes but Selena managed to get inside the box. There were polaroid pictures of dead animals. Then there were more pictures of women showering. Some pictures of prostitutes standing on a street corner and some of strippers performing on stage. Then there were pictures of teenage boys sleeping with a knife in the frame hovering near their faces. The last several pictures in the lockbox were of a campsite, a young man who had been ferociously stabbed, then lit on fire.

Selena quickly returned to the backpack, she assumed belonged to the hiker. She found the last polaroid picture taken and left inside the backpack. The picture which had the three teenage boys. Selena held that photograph next to the picture of the dead body at the camp site. It was hard to tell for sure due to the fading, but it looked like a match for one of the boys. The background matched the camp shown in the photo of the dead teen.

As she went through the remaining items in the box, something dawned on Selena. She could see the connection. She remembered that third name Lucas Durante had written in his last note alongside Nathaniel Whitaker's. It didn't make sense at the time but now it was crystal clear. The last thing she found in Nathaniel's collection was a high school yearbook. There was a page that had the top edge folded down, *dogeared* to keep its place.

The high school was listed as being in Tacoma, Washington. Selena looked at all the young, hopeful faces. The smiles, the playfulness. She read through the achievements of the kids both academically and athletically. She couldn't help but think of her daughter, Anna-Maria and looking through her yearbook. Selena flipped through each page until she reached the one that had been marked. There was a picture circled in pen. It was the hiker, the dead body at the campsite. Selena read the name and nearly became sick.

The guard could see a look of sheer terror and disgust come over Selena and offered to help. Selena only asked if he wouldn't mind helping her load the items into her car. With everything loaded, Selena sped away from the warehouse to the nearest gas station. She had to purchase the particular batteries that would fit the recorder so she could hear what was on those audio tapes. She had to hear what this Dr Evans had recorded of his sessions with Nathaniel. She had to hear Nathaniel's voice.

The entire drive back to Pine Valley, Selena listened to Dr Evans ask Nathaniel question after question. The boy presented himself as polite and courteous. He had a strong vocabulary and spoke with a slight English accent. The doctor's private notes, and recorded thoughts in the post-sessions told a different story. He believed the boy to be playing a role, acting the innocent. It was clear the doctor believed that Nathaniel Whitaker was dangerous as a teenager and measures had to be taken to contain his inevitable violent nature.

Selena finally made it to her motel room in Pine Valley and opened her laptop. She ran a search on the name, Dr. Warren Evans. She found an old newspaper article, stating that he had been accused of sexually assaulting female patients under his care at his private practice in Seattle. Facing the accusations, the unmarried doctor committed suicide before the police could build their case against him. Was this the work of Nathaniel?

Reluctantly, Selena punched in the numbers of Captain McGee's private cell phone number. It was time to inform the captain of what she knew. The captain answered in his usual manner, he seemed unusually curt.

"Good evening sir, sorry to bother you like this. It's Selena," she said nervously.

"Selena?" the captain asked with surprise in his voice. "Where the hell are you? I know you're not in Nevada. There have been some interesting developments in your absence, and we need to talk."

"Yes, we do," Selena returned, "I am on my way home tomorrow, I'll let you know when I get there. Please meet me tomorrow evening. Just you. Don't tell anyone else. What I've found, I can only share this with you."

"So, tell me now," the captain demanded.

"No, this can't be over the phone. Please say you'll meet me," Selena begged.

"Call me tomorrow when you arrive, let me know when and where and I'll be there. You had better have some good goddamn answers detective. Things do not look so good for you right now," the captain said, expressing his frustration and concern

"I know, and yes, I have answers. Make sure you are alone tomorrow. I'm sorry for all this sir. Goodnight," Selena said quickly then hung up. She could only hope Captain McGee would hear what she had to say. She could hardly believe it herself. It would not be an easy task convincing the captain of what she had just discovered.

* * *

It was another long day in the homicide department. Captain McGee sat alone in his office. His cigar lit, filling the small room with smoke. The bottle of scotch, and the glass in his hand had returned his mind to painful memories as he tried to numb his thoughts, even if only for a short while. He stared out through his window as dusk was bringing out the lights of the city.

It had been nearly twelve hours since Captain McGee had left the crime scene at the lawyer's penthouse downtown and he hadn't slept since the night before. Detective John Davis's words had been troubling him with difficult thoughts all day with such terrible suspicions being brought against Selena Lopez. How could he have been so wrong about her? How could he not have known she had fallen so from the light of who she used to be and descend into such blackness?

The bottom of the glass tilted upward towards the ceiling and Captain McGee finished his second shot of scotch and pondered pouring a third. He glared out his window wondering where Selena had gone. What was she up to? Could she possibly have anything to do with these murders? The captain hoped John was wrong, but that would be a first for the star detective.

Ultimately, he decided against pouring that third shot and Captain McGee returned his bottle and glass to his bottom desk drawer and stood to leave. He wanted a good night's sleep before opening an investigation into the woman he had considered as his stand-in daughter for such a long time. He loved her like his own and cared a great deal for her. He didn't want to admit she might be capable of such atrocities. The thought of arresting her brought tears to his eyes. As he motioned for the door his sorrows were interrupted by the phone ringing.

"Hello?" He answered, clearing his throat, "this is Captain McGee, Metro Homicide, how can I help you?"

"Captain McGee, hello, my name is Clara Stephenson over at St. Paul's Memorial Hospital," the voice said.

"Yes, what can I do for you Ms. Stephenson?" Captain McGee asked.

"There is something here you need to see, I can't quite get into it over the phone, and thought it best to call you directly," Clara responded.

Confused, the captain agreed to meet with her and said he would be right over. He left the building and drove towards the hospital. Frustration was boiling his blood as he drove. All he wanted to do was return home to further drown his problems. Fall into slumber and forget that he suspected someone he cared for, of murder. His curiosity had been heightened, but it was probably nothing. Or so he thought.

The hospital was dark, much like the night Captain McGee had to save Lucas Durante from Selena's attack. As he entered the darkness of the building, he thought of all the times he had to bail her out without thought or question. He thought of all the help he had provided and how he had potentially enabled her to commit these violent crimes. Though it was difficult to do, the captain managed to silence his troubled mind and focus on the present task at hand.

The woman who had called Captain McGee into the hospital, Clara Stephenson, was pleasant and pretty woman who certainly was pleased to meet the captain. Women had always taken a liking to him, even in his advanced years. He was eager to get this out of the way, his anguish about Selena had made him flustered and he wasn't aware of the woman's flirtations. He asked her what this was about as politely as he could manage.

"Well, we had moved one of our beds into the basement after the incident with one of our patients, one you might be familiar with, Mr. Lucas Durante?" Ms. Stephenson said.

"Okay, but what does this have to do with me Ms. Stephenson?" The Captain replied.

"The bed had been damaged that evening and was removed to be repaired. When our maintenance crew went to break it down to repair it, they brought this to my attention," Clara said, directing Captain McGee to follow her into her office. She had the side rail of one of her hospital beds wrapped in plastic and handed it to the captain.

It was unclear why this warranted bringing the captain of homicide to the hospital in the late evening hours. Captain McGee took hold of the bag and pulled away the plastic. He could feel himself getting warm with anger as he continued to open the tangled bag. This was a waste of his time. He had better things to tend to and more difficult things on his mind. He finally pulled the plastic rail from the bag and turned it over. There was writing on the surface. Captain McGee adjusted his glasses to read what was scribbled on the rough surface.

As the words came into focus, Captain McGee nearly dropped the rail to the floor. He stood there in the dark office completely stunned. He didn't know what to think. His eyes remained affixed on the scarred plastic. Lucas Durante had written a name. He wrote the name of the person who attacked him. He had identified his own killer in his final moments.

The captain thanked Ms. Stephenson and asked her for her continued discretion regarding this discovery. He left the hospital and placed the new evidence into the trunk of his car then slid into the driver's seat. What he had just discovered had opened his eyes. The devastation he felt was immeasurable. He wished he had taken that third and maybe a fourth shot of scotch.

The silence was eventually broken by the buzzing of Captain McGee's cell phone. It was an unknown number. He answered it trying to clear the fog in his mind, it was Selena. She had something dire to tell him and demanded they meet in secret when she returned to Lugar De Paz the following night.

Now, more than ever, the captain had something to discuss with her.

CHAPTER THIRTEEN

With his pulse pounding, his jaw clenched, John sat in his car parked outside one of the well-known drug houses of the city. He had checked Valentina's apartment, he went and looked for her at Night Moves and found himself without a single lead to go on. He couldn't track her cell phone or credit cards after making her deactivate the phone and stick to using cash while keeping her in the safe house. It was as if she no longer existed, but there was one avenue to travel that he hadn't tried.

There was an old confidential informant John used to employ as his snitch when he worked in narcotics. This was the same informant who told John where to find Lucas Durante and had since vanished. The man, who called himself, Tricks, would only appear when he needed a new supplier to score junk. He might have been a street-dwelling junkie, but John knew his information was most often correct.

The informant lived on the street and in various drug dens, making it difficult to track him down. John was desperate. He knew he would have to rattle the man's usual drug suppliers to scare him out into the open. John picked, for his first stop, a dealer who lived near a high school whose clientele consisted largely of teenagers. He was running out of time and patience and as soon as the dealer got home, John's interrogation would begin.

Finally, a black sport utility vehicle pulled up and parked in the driveway. John knew this was the suspect's vehicle from the licence plate number. He got out of the car and put on his flack jacket. With his pistol on his hip and his taser and steel baton attached to his utility belt, John loaded his twelve-gage combat shotgun and walked towards the house. There were at least three suspects that had entered the small building that John would have to subdue.

Before one of the suspects could close the front door, John crept in close and kicked the door's hard wood against the suspect's back, knocking him to the floor. The other suspects didn't have a chance to react, John jumped inside the door and fired the taser prongs into the throat of the second suspect. Fifty-thousand volts coursed through the man's entire body completely incapacitating him. The first suspect had nearly risen from off the floor, but John rendered him unconscious slamming the stock of his shotgun into the back of his head.

The third suspect, the dealer John intended to question, ran towards the back bedroom of his house. John fired several warning blasts of the shotgun eviscerating the ceiling tiles. The dealer kept running and slammed the bedroom door closed. John fired at the edge of the door where the hinges were bolted. Two massive holes shot the damaged hinges into the room allowing the door to freefall to the floor.

John entered the room with his shotgun ready to fire again. The suspect was struggling to climb through the rear window. John was quick to pull him back into the room and force him to the floor, face-down. The zip-tie restraint bound his wrists then John rolled him over. His expression showed the full range of his anger as he glared down at his suspect. John picked him up off the floor and sat him onto the single chair he found in the room.

"Alright shithead, I'm looking for a junkie you supply. I don't care about you or your boys, I'm only looking for him. I'm looking for the guy who calls himself, 'Tricks'. Where is he?" John demanded.

"Fuck you," the suspect shouted then lunged toward John with a failed attempt to headbutt him.

"Ok. You want it rough? I can oblige," John said. He placed his powerful grip of his right hand around the suspects throat and held him against the back of the chair. His free hand gripped the handle of his telescopic baton and fully extended its reach. He slammed the metal rod against the shins of the seated suspect.

Time and time again the hard steel hit the flesh of the man's exposed legs. John didn't stop until he heard the bones crack and could see the that he had broken both of the man's legs, "where is Tricks? Where is he?"

"You, sick bastard, I don't know anyone named, Tricks," the man cried out in pain.

John tossed the man onto the floor and watched him struggle to crawl away. The man was screaming for help when John walked closer. He had lost all sense of duty, honor, and responsibility. He didn't care what this could do to his career. The only thought in his mind was saving Valentina from a depraved killer. John removed his pistol and fired one shot into the back of each of the man's thighs.

"Stop. Please. I don't know who you're looking for man. Stop," the man screamed.

The anger had reached its boiling point. John's right hand automatically raised up and aimed his pistol's muzzle to the back of the man's head. His finger covered the trigger and he squeezed. Who would really care if this drug dealer was killed? He sold drugs to children and made money from destroying lives. He was too smart to get caught by the law. John prepared himself to kill.

A silhouette blocked the light coming from another room and caught John's attention. As he left the room, John kicked the suspect's head, knocking him out cold. He raised his pistol and went to search for the figure who blacked out the light. The two other suspects were still asleep on the floor in the front room. There was no one else in the house. John moved from room to room until he heard a familiar voice.

"John?" the voice called from outside the house.

John looked out the nearest window to find his informant, Tricks, standing beside the black SUV in the driveway. John grabbed his weapons and left the house to meet his informant. Tricks could see the anger in John's dark blue eyes, he saw the weapons armed and the flack jacket strapped to John's chest. John didn't realize he was covered in the suspect's blood. Tricks took one look at John's frightening appearance and ran down the street.

The junkie ran at a surprisingly quick pace to get away from John. There was no option. John quickly got to his car to give chase and catch up to his informant. Tricks seemed to have disappeared by the time John had spun the vehicle around and sped down the dark street. He turned on the car's search light and shone it into the yards of the surrounding houses. A neighbour must've called in the gunshots, since sirens could be heard in the distance and were getting closer.

It would be difficult to explain what had happened at the dealer's house without a warrant or probable cause. John couldn't be seen by his fellow officers. The sirens were getting closer. John had to get out of there to remain unseen. He slammed his foot to the floor and sped away. As he turned the final corner to flee the neighbourhood, a dark figure suddenly appeared in front of the car. John couldn't avoid hitting it driving at that speed. The body of a man rolled onto the hood of the car then was thrown onto the pavement.

John quickly brought the car to a stop and emerged to check on who he had struck with his car and see if they were okay. As John approached the lifeless man on the street to check for signs of injury, he could see the man appeared to be hurt but still breathing. He didn't appear conscious as he laid sprawled out on the street. John moved in for a closer look. The man's body rolled onto its back and his face came into the car's headlight beam. It was Tricks.

The sirens were mere blocks away. John had to move fast. He dragged Tricks towards the back of the car and opened the trunk. With his informant secured inside John fled the scene as responding officers surrounded the dealer's house. John managed to get out of the area undetected. He needed to find somewhere that no one could interfere. If Tricks refused to answer his questions John would have to apply the same methods as he had with the dealer. This little snitch was a wealth of information, he had to know something.

For his interrogation room, John chose where this turn of events had all begun. The abandoned tenements near the industrial district where he found Lucas Durante weeks earlier. John set up in the exact apartment he had been directed to locate Durante. He secured Tricks to a chair and placed his bare feet in a metal water basin. He had the room lit with flashlights and brought in car batteries and jumper cables. It was time for Tricks to talk.

John opened some smelling salts and woke the sleeping junkie up. Tricks was confused and terrified but seemed to recognize where he was. John had removed Tricks' clothes and could see where the pavement had scraped away flesh from being hit by his car. John thought it best to get Tricks' attention early by hurting before asking any questions. He poured a large amount of salt in his hand and pressed it firmly onto the gaping wound on Tricks' back.

Screams of pain echoed out into the emptiness of the building. There was no one around for miles in any direction. Those that lived there were hiding from someone or had nowhere else to go and wouldn't dare seek out the source of the screaming. John found another gushing wound and again applied more salt. Tricks begged for answers asking John why he was doing this, but John didn't respond right away. He wanted the fear to build.

"You led me here a few weeks ago remember Tricksy?" John asked finally.

"Yes, I helped you catch that killer. I made you a hero again. So, why the hell are you doing this to me?" Tricks cried between deep breaths.

"Because Lucas Durante was never guilty, was he? He had no idea why he was here. I chased him, and he fought me and took a shot at me out of fear, but he didn't have the look of a man who had just been caught. He had the look you have right now. Fear. Confusion. He was as surprised to be in this room as I was to find him in it," John said in a slow and ominous voice.

"So, what does that have to do with me?" Tricks asked.

"Someone put you up to bringing me in to arrest Lucas, didn't they?" John asked.

"What are you talking about. I recognized him, I knew he was up to no good, so I called you. End of story. What does it matter now? He's dead, isn't he?" Tricks shot back.

"Yes, he is," John said, taking hold of the handles of the jumper cables. Touching the positive and negative terminals together to make them spark in Tricks' face. He lowered the close to the water where Trick's feet were resting. "He's dead because whoever put you up to having him arrested, wanted him dead. Who put you up to it?"

Tricks refused to answer. John's anger overboiled. He kept picturing beautiful Valentina sprawled across some mattress somewhere. Tied down, being beaten and raped. Her perfect flesh being bruised and broken. Her soft voice turning to blood-curdling screams. He didn't have anymore time for scare tactics. He shocked the water and electrocuting Tricks to make him answer. Tricks refused to speak.

John resorted to breaking bones and cutting flesh. He stopped the bleeding with wads of salt then started again. Tricks finally gave in and admitted that John was set up but was too afraid to give the name. John continued. Tricks' fear was far more powerful than his willingness to end the pain. John was running out of ways to hurt this junkie, and soon he would die from the effort. Then, John removed the sledgehammer.

"I'm gonna use this on you Tricks, you understand? You know what this'll do to you?" John said, breathing heavily from the effort.

"He'll kill me. You don't understand this guy is the devil. He's Satan incarnate. Please just stop," Tricks said, sobbing in the chair as blood dripped onto the floor.

"I'm going to kill you Tricksy, tell me his name and I'll do it quick. Keep stalling, I will hurt you worse and worse until you're dead. Save yourself the pain. I'll end you with a heavy load of morphine if you tell me. Come on," John said. He felt sick to his stomach realizing how far he had taken the torture. This wasn't him. How could he hurt someone so terribly?

"He calls himself," Tricks answered. He spat out thick gushes of clotting blood, "the Shadow. I don't know his real name, I swear. He has a helper too."

"A woman?" John asked with his back turned, not wanting to look at the maim he had inflicted.

"Y-yeah," Tricks stuttered, confused. "How'd you know?"

"Is her name Selena Lopez?" John asked, not really wanting to hear the answer.

"What? The cop? Your partner?" Tricks responded surprised, "no, some Spanish chick her name started with a V. Veronica, Valentia…"

"Valentina?" John asked as he spun around to face Tricks.

"Yeah, Valentina. That's her," Tricks said. "She used to be a dancer or something, why? Who is she to you?"

John didn't answer. He left the room to try and compose himself. Outside the building, John took deep breaths attempting to calm down. He had been played like a fool this entire time. Valentina was in on it. She wasn't a victim. John went into the trunk and loaded a syringe with a lethal dose of morphine from a vile that he had taken from the drug dealer's house. He would have to make Tricks disappear if he wanted to protect his job.

It surprised John how easy he found it to end Tricks' life. He cleaned the room and removed the tools used in his terrible interrogation. He knew where to get rid of the body. It had taken several hours, but he was confident he left no trace evidence at the abandoned tenement. John loaded the body and drove to a crematorium owned and used by the Di Sano crime family. He placed the body, his tools, and every other piece of blood-soaked evidence from Tricks' torture inside, then switched on the intense flames.

The orange light of the flames through the small opening lit up the room. John stared at the door thinking of what he had just done. He had gone against everything he believed in to save a woman who was now out to kill him. A woman who played on his emotions to get close to him and report back to her murderous partner. John fell to his knees at the thought. He was in utter disbelief. He knelt on the floor considering giving up when a troubling thought occurred to him. If Valentina's life wasn't the one in danger, then Selena's was.

* * *

A long day's drive was starting to effect Selena as she made her way back to Lugar De Paz, back to her home. She had her new-found information in the trunk of her rental car and was listening to Dr Evans's therapy sessions with Nathaniel Whitaker all day. As she sped home, she thought of how she would tell Captain McGee of everything she had discovered. What if he didn't believe her? The last conversations the captain had with Selena he expressed nothing but disappointment and resentment towards her. This might make matters worse.

Before she left Pine Valley, Selena searched the name of the hiker, that Nathaniel had circled in the high school yearbook from Tacoma. She phoned the high school which didn't exist anymore. The only information the Tacoma police could offer was that the young hiker had been reported missing by his boss where he worked as a line cook in a pizzeria. The young man was an orphan with no relatives. The hiker lived with friends who had left the state long ago.

The entire drive back Selena went over every detail repeatedly. She remembered the look on Lucas Durante's face as he scribbled his private note to her. That note had been stuck at the forefront of her mind ever since. All three of the names written in that note kept dominating in her thoughts. It was still unclear how her daughter fit into this situation.

Somehow all these crimes, the murders of these prostitutes and strippers. Lucas Durante, Nathaniel Whitaker, the hiker, they all had to be connected. Captain McGee would have to help her find out how.

As Selena entered the city of Lugar De Paz, she thought about visiting her motel first and dropping off her rental. This secret meeting, she had previously arranged with Captain McGee, was far more important. This investigation had to switch directions if they were to prevent more death and stop a killer who had gotten away with his crimes for decades. Selena pulled off the highway and drove up to a small diner. She borrowed their phone and dialed the captain's number.

It was a brief conversation. Selena told the captain to meet her at the top of a parking structure located in the downtown business district that supplied parking for the workers for the surrounding skyscrapers. It was after business hours and would be vacant at this time of night. A perfect place to meet in secret and remain unseen.

Selena was the first to arrive and waited exactly where she told Captain McGee she would. She had met with the captain on many occasions but never had she felt nervous or scared. On this night, she was terrified. It was clear that the captain had lost his trust and faith in her and looked upon her as if she were unstable or some deranged lunatic. Bringing this information could inflame this belief and he might try to have her committed or arrested. Selena was preparing for the worst-case scenario.

The sound of a car approaching alerted Selena. She immediately armed her pistol as she got out of her car. The car drove up and stopped in the middle of the roadway as if to prevent Selena from escape. The headlights were left on, and after a moment's hesitation, the driver's door opened, and the captain stepped out. He had his hand resting on the butt of his pistol as he walked towards Selena slowly. He intentionally left the headlights shining in her direction to obstruct her vision.

Once she saw Captain McGee's face, Selena's fear subsided. She took her pistol and tossed it inside her car on the driver's seat and closed the door to put the captain more at ease. He removed his hand from his hip and came to stand next to Selena. There was an awkward silence with each of them not knowing what to say first. Selena didn't know how to begin. It was obvious the captain was afraid of her or he wouldn't have been preparing to draw his pistol.

"Thank you for meeting me like this sir," Selena said finally.

"What is this big thing you found Detective?" Captain McGee said, still cautiously guarded.

Moving slowly to avoid causing an alert, Selena motioned to her trunk and opened it. She removed the boxes and let the captain see the material for himself. He looked through each box. He saw the photographs, the yearbook, the backpack. Selena told him about the nurse she had spoken to, Wynn Weatherby, and all the woman had to say about Nathaniel Whitaker and Lucas Durante. She took her time and explained her entire trip in full detail.

After pausing for a long time to consider her information. Captain McGee looked puzzled, "what made you decide to go up to Washington in the first place?"

"This," Selena answered, and went into the glove compartment and removed the note Lucas Durante had written to her on the night he died.

"Who gave you this? Who wrote it?" Captain McGee asked. His voice tight with concern.

"Lucas Durante," Selena said, watching Captain McGee's reaction intently. "That night you were called to the hospital. I confronted him with my daughter's picture. This was his response to me. My search for his background aimed me north."

"Oh my god," Captain McGee said through a long sigh. He stood, frozen in his confusion staring down at the three names on the paper. He looked at everything in the trunk and could only shake his head. He couldn't respond. He told Selena to wait at her car and walked back to his. He returned with the defaced bedrail he had been given. "This was from Lucas Durante's bed. It was brought to my attention just last night."

Selena took the piece of plastic from the captain. She compared the writing style from the bedrail to her note and they looked spookily similar. She tried to stifle her amazement and asked finally, "what are we going to do Captain?"

"I have no idea Selena," the captain replied, still in utter shock at what had just been uncovered.

"Where is John? I have to find him, now," Selena interrupted.

"I don't know where he is. I haven't seen him since we left the extremely gruesome crime scene that we had yesterday," the captain replied, finally removing his eyes from the paper.

"I'll find him tomorrow. I have a pretty good idea where to look," Selena returned.

"John suspects you of being involved. He brought me his suspicions and allegations. If you go out to find him alone it could end up putting you in a bad situation," Captain McGee warned.

"I've been his partner for years. He trained me. I know him better than anyone. I'll find him, and we'll get this case solved once and for all sir," Selena said proudly.

"Be careful. I'll keep trying to locate him on my end and let you know the moment I've found him. You do the same," the captain ordered, pulling her in tight for a hug. He seemed like he was relieved.

A sense of calm had returned. Selena had revealed all she had found, and the captain believed her. She closed her trunk and drove away from the parking structure. The streets were relatively empty as she drove to the rental agency. The car was empty, since she gave the boxes to the captain to take for safe keeping. She paid her fee to the clerk who mentioned there were people in the store asking about her, but the clerk couldn't remember a name. He just said it was an average looking man. It must have been John looking for his partner.

The cab pulled up to the small motel, Selena handed her driver the required fee in cash, then removed her bags from the trunk. The motel was so cheap, the light outside her room had burnt out and hadn't been changed. She wheeled her bags up to her door and unlocked it. She pushed her bags in first and kicked the door closed behind her. She reached out and flipped on the light switch, but the lights didn't turn on.

An intense surge of sheer panic shot through Selena's body. It was an ambush. She immediately dropped her bags and drew her pistol. The room was pitch-black, and she lost her footing and stumbled over the luggage she had dropped at her feet. Her outstretched hand found the doorknob and she quickly opened it and walked outside backwards, keeping her pistol aimed into the blackness of her room.

Selena stood aiming her gun, ordering anyone inside her room to come out. But nothing happened. She soon felt foolish. The stress of what she had discovered and the exhaustion from her days of travelling must have finally taken their toll. She must be paranoid and in need of rest. She returned her gun to its holster and rubbed her eyes as she laughed at her extreme reaction to what was obviously a blown fuse or light bulb. She never even heard the footsteps of her attacker approaching her from behind.

* * *

Everything was lost. The killer had intended to regain control of the game by leaving John in the small apartment with his message. Instead of the message breaking him, John seemed to have vanished off the face of the earth. The killer couldn't find him anywhere. He didn't return to work, or his ex-wife's place. He simply disappeared.

With John nowhere to be found, the killer attempted again to find Detective Lopez who was still missing. The moment of brief victory was replaced by more fear and vulnerability. Had the detectives uncovered the truth? Were they closing in on him? Had his horrible reign finally come to an end? Had he been defeated at his own game? He had never felt this exposed ever before.

A search of police headquarters turned up nothing. John and Selena's desks had been piled up with papers and hadn't been utilized for days. There was one person the killer had neglected to pursue. Perhaps it would be foolhardy, but this one person might lead him to John and possibly Selena. The person was Captain Thomas McGee.

The killer remained in the dark as the office staff left for the day. The cleaning crew came in and tidied up. All the while, the killer remained in the shadows silently watching. Captain McGee remained in his office drinking his scotch and smoking his cigar. He looked exhausted, as John had the last time, he had seen him. Maybe the captain would fall asleep in the same way and allow for another message to be delivered.

The captain received a phone call on his cell phone. He jotted down a quick note before hanging up. The killer watched his actions anxiously. What was he up to? The captain removed his shirt and applied his bullet-proof vest then put on a fresh shirt overtop, followed by his jacket. He checked the ammunition in his pistol and placed it in his holster. The captain poured one last shot of scotch and drank it quickly before exiting the office. The killer assumed he was preparing for something dangerous.

It was easier for the killer to tail the captain than it was to follow John. Perhaps being old had made the aged cop lose his edge. Maybe the threat of a loved one's life caused John to increase his skills. The captain drove along, completely unaware the killer was close behind him the entire way. He only hoped the captain was leading him to find his mice to return them to his maze. The game had since come to a halt, and the killer had a desperate need to play.

Captain McGee drove into a large parking structure, flashing his credentials to the security guard to get him through the gate. The killer parked up the street and would have to find a different way in. It wasn't difficult to slip by the overweight guard after causing a simple distraction. Now to find where the Captain had gone. The killer discerned that this was a meeting of some kind which at this time of night, would be best to take place at the very top floor.

The killer's guess was correct. Much to his surprise, the captain was meeting with what appeared to be a beautiful, younger woman. The killer moved in for a closer look. It was Selena. She had come back. The killer's heart thumped in his chest. He had to get closer, he had to find out what was being said. The two cops were squaring off and cautious. They looked like they were locked in an old western movie-like showdown. Both of them had their hands ready to draw their weapons. The killer had been successful in creating such distrust among long-time colleagues.

It would prove difficult and risky, but the killer moved closer. If he made a noise, he would have two angry, overly cautious, and heavily armed cops ready to open fire on him. He applied his skill of moving as silent as a phantom. As smooth as a snake and got as close as he could. He propped his head up to gain the best hearing advantage.

The long stare-down had ended, and the captain finally walked towards Selena. With the car's exhaust still throbbing, it blocked most of what was being said. The killer stepped out and moved even closer. He was leaning up against Selena's car and she had no idea. She was showing the captain something in the trunk of her car, and they were so intensely focused on what they were looking at, the killer felt safe being so close.

Suddenly, Selena mentioned a name. The killer's true name. She had uncovered the truth. She knew who he was. It was the first time he had heard his name spoken in years. Nathaniel Whitaker. The fear had returned and suddenly he felt like fleeing. How could she have found out? Had he not covered his bases perfectly? The killer strained to listen more intently to hear what else she had found out. She knew most of the truth, but not its entirety. It was still far too close for comfort.

The clandestine conversation between Captain McGee and Selena had ended and the killer escaped to the shadows. He watched the captain load all the boxes from Selena's trunk and place them into his own. Then he embraced Selena like a father would his daughter and drove away. Selena returned to her car and was preparing to leave. The killer had to descend the parking structure quickly and return to his own car to follow her when she exited.

Several moments later, Selena's car drove out of the structure and travelled up the street. The killer was close behind her. It was time to remove one of the mice from the game. This one would stop John for good. This kill would end this game. The killer found himself desiring Selena. He had wanted her since she had first come back to the force. He had wanted her since he killed Anna-Maria so long ago. Selena's death would be his crowning achievement, it would give him back the control he so longed for, and John Davis would be the fitting person for which to hang the blame.

CHAPTER FOURTEEN

The crowded waiting room watched nervously as John, dirtied and sweaty, paced back and forth. He couldn't calm himself after last night. There was no chance at finding sleep with the exhaustion fueling his inability to center his emotions. The guilt of torturing and killing his former informant, Tricks, hit John hard. He couldn't bare the thought of being used by Valentina. He believed he was falling in love with her and she was nothing but a pawn in this latest killer's twisted game, and John was the fool who fell for it.

It was time for John's weekly appointment with Dr Morrison. There wasn't any time to waste, he had to get back out and find this killer and Valentina before they hurt his partner, Detective Lopez. He couldn't sit still waiting for the doctor. He felt he had to constantly be moving to keep his mind free of imagining what he had done.

"John Davis?" the receptionist finally called out. "Dr Morrison will see you now."

John pushed through several more patients who had entered the waiting room and walked into the office. He was thinking of what he could tell the doctor in this session. He couldn't hide his behaviour she would pick up that something was wrong. He would have to tell her something. After all, she was his doctor and she was there to help him, right?

"Good morning John," Dr Morrison said in her soothing, whispery voice. "You've missed your last two appointments. How are things?"

It was difficult to manage but John settled into his usual chair in the office and tried to stop himself from fidgeting. The doctor was wearing a loose blouse with very low-cut neckline and a short skirt that had a slit travelling far up the side of her leg nearly exposing her right buttock. John stared at the doctor's long legs for a long while not hearing her repeat her question twice to get his attention.

"John?" Dr Morrison asked, "you don't look well, what's going on? What has happened?"

"You know, it's very distracting when you dress like that. I can't exactly talk about my problems when you're giving me a hard-on," John spurted out frustratedly.

"Excuse me?" Dr Morrison exclaimed. She had never heard John be so forward or rude. She was shocked. John's erratic behaviour was troubling. It was as if this were an entirely different person sitting before her. She took a seat behind her desk and switched tactics, "is this more comfortable for you?"

"I'm sorry," John couldn't believe he had said that to her. He felt so embarrassed. "I am just going through a tough time, I lashed out at you. It's not your fault. My attraction to you is not your fault."

"Why don't you tell me what's bothering you John," Dr Morrison said, studying John as he squirmed on the couch, looking like a drug addict going through withdrawals.

"My girlfriend, well she was a stripper. She was using me, playing me to get information for the killer who has been taunting me. They made me suspect my partner and now Selena's in danger, and I don't know where she is," John explained, nervously biting his fingernails.

"Oh my god. I'm so sorry. Is there anything I can…" Dr Morrison said, before she was abruptly interrupted.

"And I killed a man. Last night, I fucking killed a man. An informant of mine, I was desperate for information and he wouldn't talk. I tortured the poor bastard," John interrupted, he rose off the couch and hid the tears in his paling blue eyes from the doctor. He couldn't believe he told her what he had done.

"John, please sit down. Tell me more about this. I want to help you, but you need to calm down," Dr Morrison said trying to mask her fear. She had never seen this side of John before and didn't know what he might do.

In the panic of what he let come out of his mouth, John moved towards the doctor's desk and grabbed her recorder. He smashed it on the surface of the desk to destroy any record of what he had just confessed. "Never mind what I just said okay, I'm stressed and confused. That didn't happen, I don't know why I said it, just forget it okay doctor?"

Dr Morrison was trembling. She had removed her cell phone and had it in her lap. She dialed Captain McGee's number. John could see she was looking at something in her lap and darted around her desk. Quickly, he snatched the phone from her hand and could see the captain's number. He didn't know what to do. He could see the terror in Dr Morrison's face. He smashed the glass face of the phone on the corner of the desk and threw it out the window. He pulled the cord for her landline and tossed it in the trash.

"You're my doctor. I'm supposed to be able to trust you. You were going to turn me in? I told you nothing happened, I'm just stressed," John pleaded to make her understand.

"I believe you John. I'm sorry. Please sit down and we'll continue your session," Dr Morrison managed to hide the fear in her voice and try to calm John down.

"I'll pay for what I broke, I'm sorry. I have to go," John said as he fled for the office door and walked quickly down the hall.

It would only be a matter of minutes before the doctor called the captain and told him what John had said, what he had done in her office. John couldn't worry about that now. He could feel that Selena was in trouble. He needed to find somewhere quiet to clear his head and calm down. He couldn't go to his apartment, or the station. The captain already didn't trust John, after hearing what Dr Morrison would have to say would give him all the ammunition he needed. John knew he had to get his story straight to explain what just happened.

There was a park on the hillside that overlooked the cityscape and had an excellent view of the harbor. John used to bring his wife there when they had first started dating. No one would be looking for him there. It was quiet and peaceful, and he would be able to gather his thoughts and calm down. John had to center himself and get to his usual demeaner if he was to have any chance at saving Selena, his career, and his freedom.

It took over twenty minutes to reach the park and John parked in a thick gathering of shrubbery to hide the car. He disconnected the car battery just in case dispatch was ordered to activate the locator installed in each police issued vehicle. It was hot out, and John removed his jacket and grabbed a bottle of water from the trunk then walked up the hill and out of sight. There was a trail that he knew of, that led to the top of the hill where he had his first date with his wife. He hadn't been there in years, but it was easy to find.

John eventually made it to the clearing at the top of the hill and sat down staring down at the city. There were no other sounds except for the birds chirping and insects buzzing. John laid back and shut his eyes. If he could just sleep for a short while he could bring his old self back. If he could just rest, he could think of how to handle everything. His eyelids felt heavy and soon he drifted off to sleep. Until his cell phone's ring alerted him.

Quickly, John removed the phone from his jacket pocket. He thought he had switched it off. If Captain McGee was looking for him, the police could track him. John was once again sent into panic mode. He fumbled through his pocket to retrieve the phone. One ring, two rings, then three. John finally got hold of the phone. The number was coming from his ex-wife's house.

"Hey, what's going on? Is everything okay?" John asked, trying to sound like his usual self.

"For me? Yes. For others, not so much," a familiar voice answered. It wasn't John's ex-wife, but he recognized the sound.

"Who is this?" John demanded, "Valentina?"

"Aww, and I wanted you to have to guess longer," she said in a taunting tone.

"What are you doing at my wife's house?" John replied angrily.

"Spending some quality time with loved ones," she responded, her tone slow and creepy.

"What the hell do you want Valentina?" John barked.

"Its not what I want," Valentina said slowly, "it's what HE wants."

"What does that mean?" John asked.

"The game is almost over John. HE always wins. Goodbye," Valentina said tauntingly.

John tried to call his ex-wife on her cell phone. There was no answer. He tried calling the same number Valentina had just called from. No answer. John thought for a brief second of involving Captain McGee but knew Dr Morrison must've alerted him to John's behaviour at her office. He got up and ran back to his car as fast as he could. There was a sharp pain on the right side of his ribs, it must be a stitch, John ignored it and pushed himself to run faster.

The parking lot was still empty when John neared. A strange feeling warned him to stop and he slowed his running and stepped off the path and into the thick brush. He watched carefully and moved so he could get a view of where he parked his car. There were two uniformed, patrol officers walking around the hidden sedan. Captain McGee must have issued a search for his car.

It was difficult to manage but John made his way out of the park on foot. He found the closest parking lot, a gas station, and commandeered the fastest vehicle available. There was a young man fueling up his Ford Mustang. The man removed the nozzle and was about to get behind the wheel when John removed his badge from his belt and held it up to the man's face.

"Police emergency sir. I need this vehicle immediately," John said as he pushed the man aside.

Furious, the young man took hold of John's shirt and tried to remove him from the sportscar. John was the stronger opponent. He placed the man in a choke hold, wrapping his muscular arms around the poor man's throat and squeezing tightly until he managed to put him to sleep. John got into the car and brought the loud engine to life leaving two trails of smoking black rubber as he sped out of the parking lot and entered the freeway. He only hoped he would be fast enough to save his ex-wife.

* * *

The smell of bleach lingered heavily in the air. Selena awoke to the smell of chlorine that stung in her nostrils. She tried to focus and retain her memory, but her mind was foggy. The last image in her mind, before everything went black, was stepping out of her motel room afraid someone was waiting for her inside. She tried to move but she had been tied to a hard surface. It felt like a concrete floor.

It was impossible to move as Selena struggled to break free. Her wrists were bound behind her back. Her ankles were secured together and hogtied to the bounds on her wrists. The fear and panic had overshadowed the pain. She controlled her breathing, taking long, deep breaths to calm herself down and focus. The blindfold was too tight around her head for her to slide off by dragging it against the floor, but the force had exposed a small tear which allowed her the ability to see minimally through one eye.

There was a rag taped inside Selena's mouth. She had to control her breathing through her nose. The intensity of the scent of bleach made it difficult to maintain her deep breathing technique. Her struggling managed to open the tear a little wider in her blindfold and she could see that she was in a basement with concrete walls. There was a bed in the corner draped in plastic sheeting and a van parked not far from where she was laying on the floor.

The sound of voices caused Selena to stop struggling and listen. She tried as best she could to see through the small rip of the blindfold to see who had taken her. She couldn't make out what was being said clearly. The voices were too far away. But there was a man and a woman's voice. As they came closer, Selena heard that the man spoke with an English accent with a gravelly, strained voice that sounded like the growl of an animal. The female voice had a very strong Spanish accent. Neither of them ventured into Selena's limited view.

There was the sound of a generator being switched on and blinding work lights illuminated the area surrounding the bed. The male and female voices continued to argue. Selena could clearly hear the female pleading with male, saying she had done all he had asked of her and that the man had promised to spare her life and the life of the man she loved. The male argued back, telling her to help him with the, "bitch cop". Through the blindfold, Selena could see the black silhouette of a massive figure approaching.

Selena couldn't see his face, but the man picked her up and she could feel he had placed her on the bed. The smell of bleach was now combined with the strong scent of fresh cigarette smoke. The argument between the male and female was becoming more heated as the man was trying to reposition Selena on the bed. Selena tried to be patient and wait for an opportunity to escape. Through the small rip she could see a small table with knives. All she needed was for the man to cut the tie that secured her wrists to her ankles.

The loud argument continued and sounded as if it was turning violent. The female was yelling at the man and crying out that she wanted, "John", to live. Selena wondered if the woman was referring to her partner, John Davis. It sounded like the man had struck the woman, and the female voice went silent. The man's hands were on Selena again and she could feel him cut the tie behind her. His strength was incredible, and Selena knew she wouldn't be able to fight him off. He moved to Selena's ankles and cut the tie that bound them. Selena had to act.

A violent, and powerful kick struck the man in the side of the face and Selena could hear him fall to the floor and knock one of the light-stands over. She quickly brought her wrists, still bound together, under her buttocks, behind the back of her legs, then under her feet until they were in front of her. She could hear the man growling in pain, trying to get up. Selena removed her blindfold and her gag. She armed herself with a knife from the table just as the man grabbed at her shirt, tearing it nearly completely off her body.

Selena spun around with the knife in hand and sliced a deep gash into the right side of the man's ribcage. The bright lights had been broken when the man fell against them, preventing Selena from seeing his face. The man screamed in pain from the knife wound and Selena seized the opportunity and ran towards the van. Luckily, the door was unlocked, and the keys were in the ignition. She tossed the bloodied knife onto the passenger seat then started the engine and locked the doors. She turned on the headlights but before she could see who had abducted her, three quick gunshots struck the front of the van and the windshield.

The man kept firing at the van. Selena placed the gearshift in the reverse position and ducked down on the seat to avoid the barrage of bullets. She pushed her foot to the floor and the van's tires squealed as it propelled backwards through the empty building. The gunshots stopped; the man must've stopped to reload. Selena spun the van around in an impressive one-hundred-eighty degree turn and put the gear to drive. More gunshots struck the back of the van as Selena sped towards the massive doors at the end of the building.

Large projectiles of wood, nails, glass, and plastic exploded through the air as the van crashed through the locked warehouse doors. Selena kept driving as fast as she could. She drove out of the area until she could find the nearest telephone. There was a small coffee shop not far from where she had been held captive. Selena stopped the van and ran to the door hoping it was open.

Without any shoes or pants on, her shirt torn and barely covering her, Selena ran up to the door of the building. The owner of the small shop was preparing to open for the day when he saw Selena's troubled state and let her in to use the phone. He was a kindly old man who wanted to help. He brought Selena one of his large jackets to cover herself. She hadn't realized she was near completely nude. She graciously accepted the large coat and thanked the kind stranger for his help and concern.

In mere minutes, a team of officers sped by the small coffee shop and drove to where Selena had directed them over the phone. Search helicopters arrived quickly overhead, scanning the ground from the air searching for a suspect. An ambulance arrived shortly after the police with Captain McGee, fast behind them. The captain lifted Selena off the ground in a massive bear hug when he saw she was alright.

"Are you okay? How did you get out of there?" he asked excitedly.

"I'm fine," Selena said, making her way to the back of the ambulance. "He must have knabbed me at my motel, he ambushed me. I woke up tied to the floor. He had me blindfolded; I couldn't see anything."

"How did you get free?" the captain persisted.

"There was someone else with him. A woman. They were arguing about something, I couldn't make it out. She was begging him to spare the man she loved. She called him, 'John'. When he was distracted fighting with her, he left an opening. He cut me loose and was moving me into another position, so I fought him off," Selena explained.

"Good. I hope you hurt the son-of-a-bitch," the captain said sternly.

"I did. There was a knife on the table next to the bed. I was able to cut him, I cut him good on the right side of his ribs. His blood is on the knife. Its still in the van," she said and pointed to the shot-up and damaged van that aided in her escape.

The swarm of officers surrounded the area. Selena wanted to aid in the search saying she was fine, but Captain McGee refused. He ordered her to go to the hospital for observation. Selena hadn't realized the gravity of the situation. The adrenaline was starting to wear off and it dawned on her how close she had come to death. During her dark times, as she struggled with the grief of losing her daughter, she would have gladly sacrificed her live to be free of her pain. Coming face-to-face with it now, Selena knew she wanted to live. She sobbed as the ambulance sped away.

It wasn't until later into the evening when Selena woke up in the hospital. The doctor came in and told her she had some deep cuts on her wrists and ankles. Her left wrist had a pretty bad sprain that would require the wearing of a strong tensor bandage. But she was relatively fine physically. He offered the assistance of the resident psychologist should she have the need to talk about what happened. The doctor signed her release and said she had some people here to see her.

Still drowsy from the trauma and pain medication, Selena's vision was slightly blurred. As the doctor exited her room, she could see two more figures walking in. It looked like Captain McGee and beside him was an elderly woman. Selena blinked and forced her eyes to adjust. It was her therapist, certainly not someone she wanted to see. Selena knew that her shrink would've been told by the captain of the lie she had told for her secret trip to Washington, saying it was a break ordered by her therapist. She didn't want to hear the scolding.

The captain had brought Selena her clothes from her motel and waited outside the room for her to change out of her hospital gown. Selena strained to hear the conversation between Captain McGee and her therapist in the hall, but they were carefully whispering, and Selena couldn't hear anything. She changed into her comfortable tracksuit that the captain had brought for her. She struggled to slide socks over her cut up feet, injured from escaping without shoes.

Selena remained silent as she followed Captain McGee and her doctor. She didn't feel much like talking and was listening to what the two of them were talking about. The therapist was constructing a psychological profile of the killer, the man who had taken Selena. She had some interesting insights and continued to probe Selena for more information. Selena responded vaguely to show her discontent for the old woman. She didn't trust shrinks and never would.

The group left the hospital and stopped at the doctor's building to drop her off. Selena promised to reschedule her next appointment as soon as she felt up to it. She had no intention of speaking to her. The captain had arranged for Selena to stay with him until this situation had ended. Selena asked what happened at the warehouse after she had left for the hospital.

The captain told the tale of events. When the officers arrived at the warehouse, they found no one there. The table Selena had described with the collection of knives had been taken. All the team found in the warehouse was the mattress and broken work lights. The helicopters and ground search turned up nothing. It was as if no one was in the building with Selena. Whoever might have been there had vanished into thin air.

In the van, the only fingerprints found belonged to Selena. The team found the bloodied knife, with Selena's fingerprints on its hilt. It was sent away to analyze the blood left on its sharp blade. They were back to square one. There were no new leads to follow. The killer was still at large and now with a female accomplice. This investigation continued to get stranger and the captain thought it best to remove Selena from the case. He placed her on medical leave until her therapist could clear her once again for active duty.

Upon arriving at the captain's house, Selena was infuriated by the captain's decision. She stormed into the guest bedroom and slammed the door behind her. This was her case. She had found the killer's true identity on her own. The killer caught wind of how close she was and attacked her. In the struggle he left the only piece of physical evidence throughout the entire investigation. When the blood analysis came back, the captain would see her value and would have to reinstate her.

The next morning Selena woke early from having a nightmare of what had happened to her. She couldn't go back to sleep, with those images in her mind. She could hear the captain arguing on the phone and emerged from her room as the call ended. The captain was seated at his kitchen table with his morning coffee. He slammed the phone onto the surface of the table and placed his head in his hands. Whatever had happened on that phone call, wasn't good. Selena had never seen the captain so stressed.

"Oh, sorry if I woke you dear," Captain McGee said when he noticed Selena had taken a seat nearest him.

"That's okay. What's wrong?" Selena asked, concerned.

"It's John," The captain replied, his voice tight.

"What about him?" Selena asked intently, "what about John?".

* * *

Bang. The first gunshot hit the van's front bumper. Bang. The second shot exploded one of the headlights. Bang. The third shot smashed through the middle of the windshield. The killer kept firing and hit the grille and front bumper of the van. He tried to penetrate the radiator and disable the engine. The shots missed the target until the magazine was empty. The killer's left thumb released the empty magazine and dropped it to the floor. He quickly searched through Selena's things for more ammunition.

Armed with a fully loaded, fifteen-round magazine, the killer continued to fire upon the van. Selena had spun the large vehicle around with an impressive maneuver and was heading straight for the exit doors. The killer emptied the second magazine of bullets into the back of the van until it turned the corner and was out of sight. Selena had escaped.

The pain of the massive gash on his ribs made it difficult to move. The killer walked back to his duffel bag and grabbed the rags he used to clean up after he completed his work. He made a rudimentary bandage and tied it as tightly as he could to stem the bleeding. He knew with Selena's escape the police would come in full-force and storm the warehouse. He had to move quickly.

As he moved swiftly, he placed his remaining knives into his bag and rolled up his plastic sheeting. Valentina was waking up off the floor. She had been arguing with the killer while he prepared Selena for his next kill. He struck her with a massive blow to the head from a powerful punch from his left hand. The hit knocked Valentina out for over five minutes allowing Selena to get the drop on the killer and flee. Now, for the first time since he had begun to play his evil and twisted games, he was the closest he had ever been to being caught.

"Look what you've done. You let her get away," the killer screamed.

"I didn't mean to. I'm sorry," Valentina cried as she forced herself to stand, still stumbling from the injury to her head.

"You said you would bring her to me. You said you could deliver John and keep him distracted. That's why I let you live. That's why I made you," the killer shouted. He finished wiping down the floor with bleach where he had dropped his blood.

"I did as you asked. I helped you. I had John eating out of my hand, its not my fault. I underestimated his love for his wife. Please don't hurt me," Valentina begged.

With the area as clean as he could manage in such a short time. The killer placed his duffle bag on his back and used the thick strap's pressure to hold his bandage in place and stop the bleeding. He grew tired of listening to Valentina's pleas. He wanted to kill her before, but she had gotten away. She promised she could help bring control back to the game, and she failed. To allow her to live would be a grave mistake. He reloaded Selena's pistol with the last of her full magazines and aimed for Valentina's chest.

Bang. Bang. Bang. The killer fired three shots without warning. Valentina barely got out of the way. She had been to this warehouse before with her dark accomplice and knew a way out of the building. Bang. Bang. The killer shot at Valentina as she scrambled to get away. He clicked on his flashlight that revealed a small crack in the building's wall where Valentina must have slipped through. He forced himself through, intent on finally killing Valentina.

Outside the building, the killer searched desperately to find his prey. He stood silently and listened for any trace. Her heavy breathing, or her footsteps on the loose gravel. Everything was silent. There was no sound. A shadow against an adjacent building caught his eye. He had found her. He prepared the pistol and walked towards her. There she was with her back turned cowering against a fence.

The killer stepped forward. He was just about to fire when the sound of a helicopter in the distance forced him to remove his attention from her. The collective sound of multiple sets of sirens blared as they sped closer. The killer turned back to Valentina. She used the distraction to her advantage and was gone. The killer fled the area as fast as he could. In selecting this, one of many, locations to commit his crimes, he always left an escape route. This was the first time he had ever had to use it.

Within moments, the killer was in a clean, unknown car, driving calmly away from the area. The helicopter was searching the hills in the opposite direction and the cops were inside the abandoned structure and searching the surrounding property thinking their suspect was on foot. The killer was too smart for them. He knew how police responded. He knew their procedures and methods. It was always how he managed to stay a step ahead of them.

In a rest stop, on the other side of the city, the killer felt confident he was finally safe to stop. He had an intricately put together first aid kit in the trunk of his escape car. There was also clean clothes, cash, and keys to another hideout. The killer removed his shirt, then the soaked-through bandage and cleaned the wound. He removed the medical stapler from the kit and clamped together the separated skin to close the wound. He barely flinched. Pain was never a problem for him to ignore.

After painstakingly cleaning his blood from the sink and floor, the killer changed his clothes carefully to not leave any sign he had stopped there. He carefully dressed in clean clothes and wrapped his bloodied garments in the plastic sheeting he removed from the warehouse. He placed the bundle at the bottom of the dumpster under several heavy garbage bags and left the area. Now, more than ever, the killer knew he had to end this game. He would find John, Selena, and Valentina. He would kill them all, then leave California forever.

CHAPTER FIFTEEN

The loud growl of the muscle car's exhaust roared through the streets. John was pushing the nimble Mustang to its limits putting his extensive evasive driving training to use. The car shot through heavy traffic like a bullet through glass. Bobbing and weaving, dodging cars like a boxer avoiding combination punches. John had to get to his ex-wife's house, he had to save her. He couldn't lose another woman he cared about to the same killer.

The Mustang blew through several red lights like a blur activating the traffic cameras. It was a risk drawing so much attention, but John had no choice. He resigned to the fact that once this whole thing was over, once this case had been solved and the killer caught or killed, the misunderstanding could all be explained. Then everything would return to the way it was. He couldn't waste precious moments thinking about that now. He rounded the last corner on his ex-wife's street. Her house was located at the end of the block.

The neighbourhood was filled with quiet families and small children. It was a small community onto itself where everyone knew each other. There was rarely any need for police to be called onto the block unless someone violated the evening noise by-law. Life moved slower on this street where nothing out of the ordinary ever happened. That was until John and his stolen Mustang drifted around the final corner at top speed. Exhaust thundering, tires screaming, until John finally brought the four-wheeled rocket to a stop in front of his ex-wife's home.

There was John's ex-wife's car parked in the driveway and her husband's in the garage, with the heavy door left open. He armed himself and charged up to the front door which had been left ajar. John pushed through the doorway and called out for his wife. There was no answer. He called out for her husband. Still no answer. He stepped into the home cautiously. There was no sound at all in the house. This could have been a perfectly articulated ambush.

John searched the entirety of the first floor, basement, and garage. There was no sign of anyone. He quickly made his way up the stairs. He reached the top floor and had another flashback of his nightmares that nearly took him off his feet. The narrow hallway was the same one he had been stuck in for weeks in his nightmares. He shook it off and tried to stay in-the-moment as he checked each room carefully.

The first door led to a bathroom, empty. The next led to an office, also empty. There was a linen closet with no room for anyone to hide. Finally, John approached the room at the end of the hall. The door was left partially open. He stepped slowly and cautiously, unaware of what waited within. This was the last room of the house. He took a deep breath and gently pushed the door open with his foot. What he saw next brought him to his knees.

"No. Not her. Not her," John's cries of pain filled the empty house.

There was a chair at the foot of the bed. John's ex-wife's husband had been nailed into its seat. His hands had been nailed to the arms of the chair and his feet to the floor with several nails each. His eyelids appeared to be stapled open and forced to face the bed. His tongue had been removed and his face and neck had extensive bruising and lacerations. The man's chest and abdomen had been torn open with a fury of stab wounds, far too many to count.

On the bed lay John's ex-wife. She was stripped completely nude with her hands and ankles secured to the four corners of the bed with razor wire. She had a gag taped into her mouth. She was, in life, a fair-skinned woman. With the beating she had suffered from head-to-foot, her entire body was dark purple and covered in blood. Without taking the time to investigate, there was no obvious way of telling what ultimately caused her demise. Like the other victims, she had suffered greatly and died a horrible death.

The devastation was too much to bear. John crawled towards the bed. He climbed on top and took his ex-wife into his arms. He sobbed heavily and kept repeating, "I'm sorry baby. I'm so sorry". He eventually rose from the bed. He knew his stunt with the car outside would cause the nosey neighbours to call the cops. He turned to exit the room and noticed the video camera on a tripod still recording. At least the police would see this crime wasn't committed by him.

John was in a daze as he walked out of the house. He was unaware that the front of his clothes was covered in his ex-wife's blood from holding her body. The loud police sirens could be heard echoing in the distance. He had given up. He sat down on the front porch stairs he waited for his fellow officers to arrive. He would offer his explanation but didn't care if anyone believed him. What would it matter? His ex-wife died a horrible, brutal death and it was because of the sick game that a killer had chosen John to play against.

Memories and regrets flooded John's tormented mind as he waited for his colleagues. His blank stare gazing up the street as he waited for the flashing red and blue lights. He imagined his ex-wife on their first date. He remembered walking up to her door and seeing her all dressed up for the first time. She wore a flowered sundress with her hair hanging low on her shoulders. When she opened the door to greet him that long-ago day, he fell in love in that moment. He had never seen anything so beautiful in his life. His royal blue eyes turned pale as they filled with tears and poured down his cheeks as he replayed his cherished memories of his beautiful wife.

The ringtone of his cell phone brought John out of his haze. He looked around at the neighbours who stood around staring at him in horror. The cell phone rang again, then again. John looked down to see an unknown number calling him. He didn't want to answer it. He cocked back his right hand and prepared to throw his cell phone at the onlooking neighbours. He paused, then decided to answer.

"What?" John said, his voice hoarse from his sorrow.

"J-John is that you?" the frightened female voice stuttered.

John knew in an instant it was Valentina on the other line. "What the fuck do you want? You want to rub it in? What you've done? I'm outside my wife's house right now, you, crazy bitch," John growled.

"John it wasn't me," Valentina cried. Her voice sounded terrified, "I'm so sorry you have to believe me. It was this guy, he calls himself, 'The Shadow'. You have no idea how terrifying he is, he can make you do things."

"I don't want to hear it," John said. He wished he hadn't answered.

"Look, I betrayed him to save your partner Selena. He wants me dead now. He's coming for me John. Please. You have to stop him," Valentina begged.

There was a long pause. John's anger pushed aside his sorrow. He wanted blood. He wanted revenge for what had happened to his ex-wife and Alexis. This would be the end of his career as a police officer. He would go to wherever Valentina was and kill this "Shadow", then he would kill Valentina. They both had to pay for what they had done, and John was the one who was going to collect the debt.

"Alright Valentina," John said finally, "don't worry. I'm on my way. Text me your location."

John hung up the call and walked towards the waiting Mustang parked at the curb. The cell phone sang an alert of an incoming text message. John opened it and knew in an instant where Valentina was leading him. He didn't care if this was an ambush. If he had to die serving justice, he would do so gladly. John boarded the car and fired-up the engine. Blue smoke filled the air as the tires spun briefly in place, then gained traction. The powerful Mustang roared out of sight just before the police arrived on his ex-wife's street.

It was a short drive to connect with the freeway. All John hoped for was to not be stopped before he could flee the area. The last thing he needed was to be pulled over by some uniformed cop going by-the-book. He couldn't explain everything in time. John wanted to be the one to kill "The Shadow". He wanted to kill Valentina. The location wasn't far outside the city limits and John was confident that the freeway would be clear the whole way.

As his car sped onto the highway, John remembered Selena's daughter, Anna-Maria. Somehow this, "Shadow" was involved in her death too. By killing him, John would be able to avenge Anna's death as well. It pained him to have to take that from Selena. He knew how much she had struggled and how much she had lost since her daughter's death. It had angered John that he was foolish enough to entertain the thought that Selena could have been a killer. He had to make it right for her.

The thought occurred to John, that taking down these two killers might be his last act as a detective. He could very well die this day. There was too much left unexplained and he wanted to tell everything to his partner. If he was going to take away her right to avenge her daughter's death, she at least deserved to know why. Selena deserved a proper goodbye before losing her partner. John opened his cell phone, found Selena in his contact list, and dialed her number.

"This is Detective Lopez, hello?" Selena announced.

"Selena," John said after a long pause. He wasn't sure he could find the right words. "Selena it's John."

"John, where are you? You need to come in and explain some things," Selena said with tension in her voice.

"I know. Things look really bad, and I can explain them all, but not right now," John said, his voice cracking.

"John do you know where I am right now. I'm at your ex-wife's house. I think you know why and what I've found here. You need to come in," Selena returned.

"Tell me," John replied, "what would you do if you found the guy who raped and killed Ana-Maria?"

Selena didn't know what to say. She immediately cried and fought to hold her emotions back to find the words to answer, "I-I don't know," she said through tears. "I would take him down. I would want him dead."

"That's where I'm going now Selena," John said in hopes of easing her pain. "I'm going to get the man who hurt and killed your little girl, your Anna. I'm going to get that bastard who killed my wife and so many others. I'm going there now, and I'm not going as a cop."

"John, wait," Selena cried out.

"I'm sorry Selena. You were always the better cop. Always remember that. Goodbye," John said then quickly hung up. It was time to end this. It was time for revenge.

* * *

It was still early in the morning when Selena watched Captain McGee leave for work. They talked about their suspicions and their troubles. The captain told her what had bothered him so badly on the phone. John had gotten himself into some trouble and Selena knew she had to find him. The captain had always hated John. Selena knew if they needed to bring John in, it had to be her to do it regardless if she wasn't considered to be, "on-duty".

After showering, she managed to overcome the difficulty of dressing with her severely sprained wrist. Selena left the captain's house and set out to find her partner. It had been days since the captain had last seen him. They had worked an exceptionally brutal crime scene while Selena was away in Washington. Her first stop would be his apartment.

The landlord of the building was a short, angry, little man who could barely speak a word of English. He was going on about how John was irresponsible, and messy. The landlord said John was two months behind in rent and that he hadn't seen John in weeks. Selena wasn't sure what to make of what the landlord had told her. John always appeared to be responsible, clean, and very anal about such mundane details like paying bills. Selena promised to speak to John about it if he would let her into John's apartment.

After some hesitation, and some playful flirtation by Selena, the landlord unlocked the door and went back to his unit at the front of the building. Selena opened the door and had to cover her nose from the smell of rotten food. There was rotted fruit on the countertop. Piles of dirtied dishes in the sink had formed a mountain. Flies and insects were buzzing around making Selena's skin crawl. This did not seem like John she knew.

The rest of the apartment was much the same. Dirty clothes strewn about. There was a collection of women's underwear and lingerie in the closet. Selena knew John frequented the strip club, Night Moves and was very secretive when it came to his latest girlfriend. Now Selena knew why, she must have been one of the club's dancers. Selena felt better as she left the filthy apartment and breathed in the fresh morning air again. Something wasn't right with John.

The next stop on Selena's list was John's ex-wife. It was a longshot, but Selena thought maybe he had been in touch with her recently and perhaps she had noticed a change in his behaviour. As awkward and uncomfortable as the conversation might be, Selena knew she had to try. Dispatch called out the address over the radio as Selena had requested and she drove to the quieter side of the city where the wealthier of its citizens resided.

The people of the neighbourhood stopped whatever humdrum, suburban task they were doing and stared at the dark sedan as it drove by. It was obvious these people weren't too familiar with having police around. Selena laughed at the people's expressions as she drove by and smiled at the children playing safely in their yards. The street looked like a scene form a fifties television show. It was surprising quiet places like this still existed today, especially being a suburb of such a bustling city as Lugar De Paz. The peacefulness reminded Selena of her time in Washington.

After several knocks on the door had gone unanswered, Selena looked around the corner of the house towards the garage. There were two vehicles parked inside. Someone must be home and simply didn't want to answer. This time, Selena tried ringing the doorbell. She listened intently for any signs of activity from within the house. With no apparent noise or motion inside, she turned to leave.

"Excuse me, can I help you?" a voice called out from behind.

"Yes, hello, do you live here?" Selena asked, slightly startled from the sudden voice.

"Selena Lopez, right?" the woman asked.

"Detective Selena Lopez, yes," Selena replied.

"I'm John Davis's ex-wife Catherine. How are you?" she asked extending her hand.

"Oh, hi. Sorry, we've never met, have we?" Selena asked still unsure how this woman knew who she was.

"You're John's partner. He used to hang pictures of you guys all over the place. I actually suspected it was you he was sleeping with at the end of our marriage," Catherine said as she unlocked her front door and invited Selena inside.

"I assure you our partnership never included that," Selena said with a laugh and accepted the invitation to sit at the table and have a cup of coffee.

"Oh, I know," Catherine said, pouring two cups of coffee and handing a mug to Selena, "I followed him one night when he said he was working late. I know cops work crazy hours, but he was never at home. He always had this smell of perfume whenever he did show up. It smelled strong, something cheap. He would tell me it was yours and you two were working a case all day. He said it must've gotten on his clothes from being in the car with you."

"Go on," Selena said, offering her wrist to prove her perfume wasn't what Catherine had smelled on John.

"I followed him one night to this old, dilapidated building near the industrial district. I watched him park the car and get out with, I'm sorry to say, what could only be described as a hooker given the way she was dressed." Catherine continued as she sipped her coffee.

"Then what happened?" Selena inquired.

"I went to go inside the building. Before I could get there, he turned and spotted me. The girl must've been high or drunk because she could barely walk and was laughing hysterically. So, I ran to the car and left. When I confronted him later, he acted confused, like he had no recollection of seeing me that night. He denied ever seeing a girl or even being at that part of town, even with me confronting him there. Such a damn liar," Catherine said.

"John always said that things just fell apart. He never said what actually happened," Selena replied.

"In truth, things between me and him went downhill long before that. He had become so distant. He would never talk to me and when he did, half the time he was like an entirely different person. His voice would even change with his demeanor. It got to the point where I felt afraid around him all the time," Catherine admitted. "I don't think you came here to talk about my failed marriage to your partner though, did you?"

"No," Selena said, as she pondered what Catherine had just said about John. Was this the over exaggeration of a bitter ex-wife, or was John that much of an asshole? "I'm sorry to bring that up. I'm here because John has sort of retreated to the shadows, so-to-speak. Have you seen him recently? Maybe spoken to him?"

"Well, he is usually parked outside my house. All different hours of the night. He just sits out there staring sometimes. I hadn't had a conversation with him since the divorce but the other day he showed up out-of-the-blue and forced his way through the door. He nearly pushed my husband to the floor. He kept saying that I was in danger, that he had to protect me from a killer. He honestly seemed drunk or something, I've never seen him act like that before. He was quite upset." Catherine answered.

"Why didn't you call it in? How did you get him to leave?" Selena asked.

"He's a cop. He would just be protected if I called it in. The whole *'Brothers-In-Blue'* thing. Finally, my husband pushed him out of the door and John just gave up and drove off. I haven't seen him since," Catherine responded.

"I'm sorry that happened. If he happens to come back, or is parked outside or tries to come in, or if he calls, I would appreciate a call please." Selena offered her assistance and handed Catherine her business card.

The women spoke candidly about the home and the neighbourhood before Selena finally returned to her car. She had never been so confused. The John she knew loved his wife and would never cheat. He despised prostitutes and men who admitted to cheating on their wives. He was also obsessively neat and tidy, always criticizing Selena for her messiness. The image she had of John had certainly changed. She needed more answers.

Selena then decided to stop by the club, Night Moves. She knew John was a close friend of the club's owner. It was possible he had seen John and could point Selena in the right direction. The club appeared closed when Selena drove up but after knocking at the door and showing her badge to the camera, the door locks buzzed, and she was allowed in. There was no one inside the building and the lights were off as she walked through.

A voice called out from the second floor and directed Selena upstairs to the office. She found the staircase and followed the long stairs to the top. The door was left open, and she walked inside. Selena knew the club's owner only from the reports from the police station and what she had read about him and his family in the news. His picture showed him as being as handsome as a movie star. The reality was quite different.

The man sat behind the desk with one of his eyes completely swollen shut. The other eye had been heavily bruised. The man's jaw appeared to be broken and wired shut and he was wearing his left arm in a sling. Whoever this man had tangled with had most certainly gotten the better of him.

"I'm Detective Lopez, Mr. Di Sano," Selena announced.

"I know who you are," Salvatore Di Sano interjected. He was struggling to speak through his wired-shut, clenched teeth. "You're John Davis's partner, right? Believe me I have files on all of you. What do you want?"

"Well," Selena said, taken by surprise by Salvatore's candid response, "I'm not here for you or whatever you have going on here. I'm only here looking for John. He has gotten himself into trouble and…"

"You're damn right he's in trouble. He came in here the other night in a blind rage. The crazy bastard put me and two of my men in the hospital looking for some woman he thought I was hiding from him. The man is insane," Salvatore explained angrily, still struggling to speak through the pain of his wired jaw.

"John did this, are you sure? Who was he looking for? Did he give a name?" Selena asked, even more confused.

"I don't know, he said 'Valentina' I think. He said she was one of my dancers. I've never had a Valentina work here before. And yes, I'm certain it was him who did this. He's lucky my father and grandfather don't want any trouble with you cops. If I find this psycho before you, I'm putting him down," Salvatore warned.

"I'm sorry this happened. Like I said, he's gotten himself into some trouble. So, you have no idea who this Valentina is?" Selena insisted.

"No. John said she danced here; he scared the shit out of my girls then attacked my men when they tried to stop him. This guy is off the chain. How can the city have a guy like this as a cop?" Salvatore said scornfully.

Salvatore was becoming more agitated as they continued to speak, and Selena took that as her cue to leave. The more she looked for her partner the more confusing his life became. He never showed excessive violence on the job. He was always mild-mannered and used extreme restraint when handling suspects. Selena felt somewhat guarded with what Salvatore had told her about John. This was an accusation against a cop coming from a known criminal.

The last stop on Selena's list was Dr Morrison's office. John was scheduled to have an appointment with her that morning. It was unlikely, but hopefully John showed up and maybe the doctor could provide some more insights. Selena's dislike for shrinks was nagging her but the need for answers gave her no other choice. She left the company of the known mob figure and his house of ill repute and returned to the hustle of the concrete jungle.

"I didn't think you had an appointment today Ms. Lopez," the perky receptionist called out.

"Detective Lopez," Selena corrected, "and I'm just here to speak with the doctor and ask a few questions."

The intercom buzzed, and Dr Morrison told her receptionist to let Selena in. Selena hated coming into this office. She hated having to talk about herself and about her problems. This office was just a reminder of her pain. The elderly doctor was seated behind her desk. Her frail form cowering behind her computer monitor. She appeared to be terrified.

The annoyed patient persona switched to the concerned detective and Selena probed into why the doctor was so scared. Dr Morrison told her about the incident that happened earlier that morning. John had come in for his appointment in a very agitated state. He threatened the doctor and smashed her recorder and cell phone before leaving the office. The phone call Captain McGee received that morning, the call that made him so upset came from Dr Morrison telling him what John had done.

Selena left the office and returned to the captain's house. Something terrible was going on with John. She had nowhere else to turn for answers, nowhere else to search for him. John was going through something and needed to be brought in before he got hurt, or before he hurt someone else. He was in no shape to be investigating a killer, he was too vulnerable. Selena called into the police dispatch to put out a *"stake-and -notify"* order, to be on the lookout for John's vehicle and call her or Captain McGee immediately when he was located.

Trying to relax that evening was next to impossible. There were far too many unanswered questions. The captain had returned to his house with the latest news of John's activities. It was surreal. How could someone appear one way and be completely different on the inside. Selena refused to believe the stories and accusations of John being corrupt. She had known John for a long time. He had shown her the ropes when she first joined homicide. There was a kindness and an honor about John that most people don't possess.

Over a pepperoni pizza and a case of beer, Selena and Captain McGee dissected the rumors and speculation with what they knew. Together, they discussed the facts and tried to figure what was going on. It was as if there was a large piece missing from the puzzle they were trying to solve. No amount of talking and speculating could prepare them for what was about to happen next.

Captain McGee's cell phone interrupted the intense discussion. Selena cleared the plates from the table when she heard the captain repeat the address over the phone. It was John's ex-wife's address. Quickly, she put the plates down and joined the captain near the door trying to hear what was being said. Finally, the captain ended the call. The look on his face was as if he had been shot. He stood silent and still, unable to move.

"Get in the car," Captain McGee said finally.

"Why? Captain, what's wrong? What the hell just happened?" Selena asked to get any other response from the devastated captain.

"I'll tell you in the car. Let's go," He ordered.

Inside the car, the captain told Selena what was said on the phone call. Patrol officers had been alerted to a domestic disturbance call of someone driving erratically in the neighbourhood. There was also a report phoned in that the driver of the speeding car had entered a house, John's ex-wife's house, and emerged moments later covered in blood. Before the police arrived, the driver got into the car a drove away.

Selena admitted to the captain that she had left his house that morning. She told him that she spoke with John's ex-wife that morning and she was fine. There was nothing afoot in the neighbourhood when she left. They remained silent as they pulled up to the house. The yellow tape surrounded the yard. The mobile lab was parked in the driveway. Police cruisers were parked up and down the small street.

Inside the house, the coroner had just confirmed that there were, in fact, two dead bodies upstairs. Selena put on her latex gloves and walked upstairs. The small hallway was cramped with officers, she had to ask several to move out of her way. She stopped before entering the master bedroom. She didn't want to see the scene beyond the door. She centered herself and walked through the doorway just as the captain walked up behind her.

The brutality of the scene was indescribable. Catherine and her husband suffered terribly before meeting their deaths. There was blood covering the walls and pooling in various places on the floor. It was hard to step inside the room and not step on evidence. The site was too much for Selena. She could feel she was losing her breath and she felt overcome with nausea. She had to get out of the room. She had to get out of that house. She needed air.

Out on the lawn, Selena brought up the pizza and beer she had just shared with the captain. She had never seen anything so brutal. In a strange way she felt responsible. Maybe if she hadn't spoke to Catherine, maybe if she hadn't gone to this house, Catherine would still be alive. With everything out of her stomach, Selena grabbed a bottle of water and opened a pack of gum found in the mobile lab. She couldn't go back in that house.

As she sat blaming herself for what had happened to Catherine, Selena's cell phone rang. She didn't want to answer it. She felt terrible and was in no mood to talk to anyone. Though it was difficult, she ignored the annoying ringtone alerting her of the call and walked back to the captain's car. Before she could reach the car, her phone rang again. This time she answered it simply to stop from hearing the annoying sound of its ring. It was John.

Selena finished the phone call and hung up after John said, goodbye. She had to confront him. She had to look him in the eye and get some answers. Inside the captain's car, Selena used the radio and ordered an immediate trace on

John's personal cell phone. She provided the number and waited. The captain was standing in the front doorway of the house looking for Selena. The radio buzzed and gave Selena a location. It was time to meet John face-to-face.

* * *

Staring down at the bloodied bodies of his latest kill, the killer smiled. He wanted to end the game in dramatic fashion. To end with a kill no one would expect. This would have to make up for the failure to kill Selena and Valentina and letting them both get away. This kill would irreparably destroy John's spirit and leave him a broken-down mess. This would make John seek him out for a kill not for an arrest. This would turn John into the very thing he dedicated his career to stop. This kill would turn John to seek vengeance and become a murderer.

The killer decided it would be an added touch to use a video camera to film what he had done then leave it behind for the cops to find. He made sure not to show anything he didn't want, namely his identity. His actions were executed as swiftly and silently as possible. With such nosey neighbours close by, desperate to be involved in something noteworthy, any sign of something being awry would have them knocking on the door and interrupting or involving the police too early.

The end of the game was near. The killer could sense it. He had now set the stage for John's final destruction and he would use Valentina to do it. After his escape at the warehouse where he intended to kill Selena, the killer fled and returned to the shadows. Valentina was too weak to stay out on her own. He knew that she would try to reconnect with John somehow for protection. When she went to contact John, he captured her and brought her to the final arena of his demented game.

There were many abandoned properties around the city of Lugar De Paz and its surrounding areas. Over the past two decades the killer used many to conduct his affairs. There were many condemned tenements that had been forgotten by the city's development committee. With a troubled economy, there were massive warehouses and structures left unused in the industrial district. With so many buildings to use, the killer moved around for each kill, never leaving a body where he had committed the deed. Unless using it to frame someone, or send a message, as he did with John's ex-wife.

This cycle of games had been played many times, with many good detectives. None of them had ever come so close to catching him. The killer changed his methods with each cycle. He would mimic other crime scenes and copy other killer's methods to remain hidden. In all the years he kept up this dark routine, he never made a mistake. He had spent years perfecting his skills and now it was all coming to an end.

There was a grown-over dirt road off the highway that was a twenty-minute drive south of the city. Several years before, the killer had used this very spot as one of his hideouts to commit several kills. At the end of the forgotten road was a fenced-off private airstrip. The fence was rusted and had weeds that had grown nearly as tall as the fence itself that covered the many faded and half-broken, "No Trespassing" signs hanging along the chain-link barricade.

There was a small office attached to a single hangar. The dirt runway had all but disappeared. The building was built in the fifties and used to warehouse small planes used for crop-dusting. As the farming industry collapsed in the area, the airstrip changed to a tourist destination and flight school. In the early years of the new millennium, the last owner was arrested after it had been discovered he used the airstrip to transport drugs and weapons for various criminal enterprises using the clean image of a flight school as a front.

The building had been seized by the ATF, *Alcohol, Tobacco, & Firearms,* agency when they had finished building their case against the owner. It yielded some major arrests and drug seizures at the time and made worldwide news. Now, the area was quiet and secluded with no one around for miles in any direction. The killer found it a fitting place to end the game since John was part of the team to close this place down when he was a narcotics officer.

The killer hid in the shadows, lying in wait for the end to begin. He released Valentina with specific instructions of what to say and handed her a phone. She was terrified and played the part perfectly. She dialed John's number and managed to lure him. It was only a matter of time. The game would either finally come to an end with John standing victorious. Or simply, this cycle of kills would end with John's corpse at The Shadow's feet. It was all too exciting for the killer. The game had never been so much fun.

CHAPTER SIXTEEN

Dusk had fallen over the horizon as John approached the dirt road. The text message he received from Valentina, that provided him her location, was well-known to him. He turned the Mustang off the highway and sped up the road creating a cloud of kicked-up dust as he drove. John hadn't been to this area in over fifteen years back when he worked in the narcotics division. He was part of the task force that raided this place with the ATF.

Fifteen years earlier, John had gone to visit his old friend, Salvatore Di Sano. The Di Sano crime family had been using the owner of the small flight school to transport drugs and weapons from their suppliers. John had already been brought under Salvatore's thumb. He was collecting large payoffs to warn of any entanglements with the law. John also provided protection and acted as muscle in some instances for extra money. Being a public servant didn't pay well, and at the time, he wanted to make enough money for his new wife.

As the car sped up the darkening road, he thought of his entire career. He had always considered himself a good cop. It was true, he had taken money from a known criminal. He had looked the other way on certain cases and cracked down harder on ones he shouldn't have. But for all the bad things he had done, for all the compromises he had made, he tried his best to uphold the law where it counted. Salvatore Di Sano and his organization were criminals, murderers even, but they would never target or harm the innocent. John now saw himself as a hypocrite.

John thought to himself, if he had only been an honest cop. If he had only played by-the-book and not placed himself in such precarious positions to get ahead and become a star detective, he might never have lost his wife Catherine. Maybe he would have made Lieutenant, or even Captain by now, and they could have moved into a nicer place. They could've had children like Catherine always wanted. That was all gone now. Catherine was dead and soon John's career, and possibly his life, would be over.

As the Mustang approached the clearing nearest the airfield, John turned off the headlights. He stopped the car and switched off the engine. There was no doubt that whoever was waiting for him would have heard the car's rumbling exhaust driving up, but at least John could sneak up to the building on foot. He checked his pistol and made sure he had spare magazines at the ready. John climbed the fence and made his way towards the dark hangar.

As he approached the building shrouded in blackness, John couldn't hear any noise. There was no sign of anyone.

There were no voices from inside, or commotion. Was this a clever ruse? Had Valentina played him one last time? John entered the building and took cover against some old crates. Slowly, he moved along the wall. All was silent. He was growing tired of this game and wanted blood.

"Valentina," John shouted as he remained hidden, "come out with your hands up. It's John," there was no response.

John waited several seconds and called out for Valentina again. Still there was nothing. He called out for "The Shadow". There was still no sound. There was no sign of anyone there. Why would Valentina lead him here and not show up? Had "The Shadow" already killed her? Where was he hiding? John exited his hiding place and walked to the center of the room where there was a mattress wrapped in plastic sheeting. This must have been the setting for one of "The Shadow's" kills.

Fed up, John shouted out loud for "The Shadow" to show himself. He challenged him and called him a coward. The hangar remained silent. There was no sign that anyone was there. John turned to leave. Soon, Selena would have figured out where he was, and he would have to answer some difficult questions. As he neared the door, Valentina cried out for him.

He turned around slowly and John saw Valentina standing near the mattress. She appeared to be hurt. She was stripped half-nude and appeared to be bleeding. John didn't care if she was hurt. She helped this "Shadow" kill Catherine. She lied and deceived him and made him look like a fool. This twisted couple had ruined John's career and nearly drove him mad and he wanted revenge. He wanted them to pay. He wanted them dead.

* * *

The voice of the dispatcher came over the radio and echoed in the car. The distorted voice gave Selena an address and a location of where John's cell phone had been tracked. The signal had pinged off a cell tower at a location south of the city. It was the site of a shut-down airstrip. Selena locked eyes with Captain McGee as she started his car. He motioned to stop her, but she had already reversed the car. The captain called out for her to stop but she sped away from the crime scene. She had to speak to John herself.

"Selena. Answer," the captain's voice came over the radio.

"John called me sir. I have his location. I'm going to see what he has to say," Selena responded, dodging traffic at top speed with the red and blue lights flashing a warning, and the siren waling.

"Where is the location Selena? Don't go out there alone. Do you hear me?" the captain's voice raged over the radio, "respond."

"Dispatch has the location sir. I'm sorry. He trusts me, he called me. I'm going to see what the hell is going on. I have to," Selena responded curtly, turning the volume knob of the radio all the way to the left switching it off.

Dusk was giving way to night as Selena sped through the busy city. She made it to the freeway, then switched onto the highway. As she drove, she hoped she would make it to John first. Captain McGee might not want to hear the answers, he might shoot first and ask questions later. John deserved the benefit of the doubt. He was a fellow officer, a brother-in-arms, he was Selena's trainer. Selena knew there had to be more to the situation and wanted to hear John's response.

The adrenaline was coursing through Selena's entire body. Travelling at such high speed, she nearly missed the highway's exit. She brought the car under control and sped up the dirt road. It was unknown what she was about to encounter. Selena switched off the siren and the lights as she pulled up behind the Mustang. The car had been reported stolen that morning from a motorist at a gas station. It was the same car reported fleeing the scene where Catherine and her husband had been found slaughtered.

The car was turned off and Selena drew her pistol. Her wrapped-up wrist was throbbing from the tension of her high-speed dash through town. The thought occurred to her, if John put up a struggle, she would be no match for him. She hoped it wouldn't come to that. With her flashlight on, her pistol armed, Selena moved in closer. She placed her hand on the hood of the Mustang to check if it was warm. It felt hot. John hadn't been here for too long.

There was no sign of any other vehicles. Selena moved closer. There was a hole torn into the fencing that was big enough for her to slip through. The small office and hangar were still quite a distance away. Selena quickened her pace, keeping her senses sharp to pick up any sign of an ambush. She neared the building. The small office was completely empty and dark. There was no sign of John.

As she exited the small office, Selena could hear John's angered voice shouting from inside the hangar. He was screaming and yelling at someone. He must have caught the killer. That's why he brought Selena out here in the middle of nowhere. He caught the killer and wanted Selena as a witness and to participate in the arrest. She quickly entered the building to help John. He sounded enraged and if she didn't hurry, he might kill their suspect.

At the center of the large, ominous hangar, there was a mattress wrapped in plastic. Selena could see John standing with his back to her. She couldn't quite see who or what he was yelling at. John was still unaware she had arrived, and she quickly shone her flashlight into the corners behind her to make sure there was no one waiting to attack. John's wild and angered screams echoed throughout the empty space of the building. Selena knew she had to be careful not to startle him.

"John," Selena called out finally, "it's Selena. I'm here. What's going on?"

The screaming stopped, and John stood straight up. He was breathing heavily from the effort and slowly turned to face Selena. It was still unclear why he was yelling. John was standing in front of something, but his position was blocking it from Selena's view as she slowly walked towards him. The situation was terrifying and confusing, Selena kept searching the corners and ceiling for signs of anyone else in the room. There was no one.

"Selena," John said as he turned to face her, he was sobbing, his voice seemed relieved she was there, "I got her, it's her. She was helping him all along. It was her."

"Who?" Selena asked. John was pointing behind himself trying to make Selena see, "who are you talking about John?"

"It was her. Valentina," John cried out. He turned his back to Selena and started shouting again, "you tell Selena you bitch. You fucking tell her what you did."

Still unable to see behind John, Selena was frozen. She couldn't see what he was yelling at. She tried to see around him but could only make out the frame of an old chair. She couldn't see who was sitting there. She moved closer for a better look but was halted by the sound of a familiar voice. It was the voice of the woman with a heavy Spanish accent in the room when Selena was attacked.

"I'm sorry John. Please. He made me do it," Valentina's voice cried out in sheer terror, "Selena. Stop him. Please."

"Shut the fuck up," John growled as he moved to strike whoever sat in the chair.

Selena had moved in closer and walked to the side for a better view. There was no one else in the room. The chair in front of John was empty. John was screaming and trying to hit nothing but air. As he yelled and fought, Selena witnessed both John's and Valentina's voice coming from John himself. Selena covered her mouth in horror at the scene before her eyes. John was thrashing around, fighting and beating on an invisible person.

"John," Selena cried out to make him stop. "What's going on? Who the hell are you yelling at?"

"Valentina god damnit," John shouted, still on his knees and pounded his fists against the broken pieces of the empty chair. "I can get her to talk, just give me a few more minutes. She admitted everything right before you got here."

"Where is she John?" Selena asked, her voice trembled in fear. "Where is Valentina?"

"Are you blind. She's right here. Don't tell me to stop Selena. This bitch deserves everything she's about to get," John growled angrily. He was still beating an invisible Valentina.

Confusion and terror filled Selena's entire body. She couldn't believe what she was seeing. The detective in her knew she had to record evidence. While John was distracted, fighting an imaginary Valentina, Selena switched on her cell phone's camera and recorded a video. There was a crate directly behind her where she propped the camera against an old beer bottle. She made sure the camera captured the view of where John was kneeling, then she turned to face her old partner.

"John. Stop," Selena called out finally. John paused. He stopped his screaming and thrashing on the floor to listen to her, "there is no Valentina."

"Are you fucking crazy? She's right…" John looked back to the floor. He seemed confused. He tore away at the floorboards in a desperate search for her.

"John listen to me. You need to stop what you're doing and talk to me," Selena said in a slow calming tone. She placed her pistol back in its holster to try and calm John down.

The screaming and thrashing started again. Selena jumped back to avoid being struck by the debris of John's destruction. He was terrified and confused, screaming for Valentina to show herself. Yelling for "The Shadow" to appear. John smashed into the floor, threw the mattress across the room. He was like a wild animal, out of control. Selena watched in horror. She had never been so terrified.

"John. John. John," Selena cried out, each time she yelled louder and louder. It was no use. John continued his horrific episode. As John struggled and fought, his shirt had gotten caught between the wood of the broken floorboards, tearing the fabric open wide and exposing John's ribs. Selena could see a large, stapled, gash in the same place she had cut her attacker from the warehouse when she fled for her life. Suddenly a thought popped into Selena's mind. Something clicked, and she could see everything so clearly. She knew what would make John stop.

"Nathaniel," Selena shouted finally, "Nathaniel Whitaker."

In an instant John stopped and stood straight up. His back was facing Selena. The empty building had fallen silent, deathly silent. John stood in place, perfectly still, not moving a muscle, just breathing. He made no sound other than the air pumping in and out of his mouth. Selena watched from a careful distance. She was too afraid to approach him.

"So, you figured it out, eh?" an evil, deep, and growling voice finally said. It was the same voice Selena had heard when she was tied-up and blindfolded. The same evil voice with an English accent. "You're smarter than I gave you credit for. I underestimated you."

"J-John?" Selena stuttered, arming herself with her pistol again.

"John isn't here anymore, dearie. And won't be coming back," the evil voice croaked, echoing its terrible tone into the darkness. John's body turned to face Selena. John's handsome face had somehow contorted into an evil expression. His usually brilliant blue eyes had gone completely black. "Don't you know who I am Selena?"

"No," Selena responded, "who exactly are you?"

"You don't know me?" the voice said through John's mouth. "Don't you remember me from the other day? You got away before we could have some fun."

Outside the building, unbeknownst to Selena, Captain McGee and a small force of officers had formed a perimeter around the building. The captain had crept inside the building during John's battle with his imagined Valentina. He ordered the other officers to remain outside and cover all the exits. He remained silent as he watched John transition to a completely different person right in front of Selena.

"You sure you don't know me detective?" the evil voice from within John asked.

"No, but I would like to speak to John," Selena demanded, trying to stay calm.

"You don't know me," the voice repeated, "but your daughter sure did."

"What did you say?" Selena asked angrily, her hands trembled around the grip of her pistol.

"Anna-Maria, such a sweet girl. Didn't you ever wonder why John never solved her murder?" the voice taunted.

"I-I don't know what you're talking about," Selena said, quivering with anger. She slowly raised her pistol.

"She was so innocent. Oh, how I enjoyed her touch, how she tasted," the voice continued.

"Shut-up," Selena shouted. She took aim with her pistol in her shaking hand.

"I came as the light went out of her eyes. She kept calling for her mommy to save her. I had my way with her for days and you never showed up. She died knowing you didn't care," the seething voice said, trying to push Selena to murder.

"Selena," Captain McGee shouted. He stepped out from the shadows, "lower your weapon Detective Lopez. That's an order."

"He deserves to die," Selena cried out, heavy tears poured from her eyes as she sobbed. Her finger was on the trigger. She could feel the tension as she squeezed.

"That's what he wants. He wants you to be like him. Don't you do it," Captain McGee ordered as he stepped closer.

"Your daughter was tighter than anyone I've ever had. She was my favourite," the voice kept taunting. He could see the look of a killer in Selena's eyes.

The torment was too much to handle. Selena had been searching for her daughter's killer for over two years and it was the man she had trusted as her partner. A man who acted like an uncle towards the poor girl. As the evil voice kept sputtering his vile deeds and what he had done to poor Anna-

Maria, all Selena wanted to do was squeeze the trigger all the way back and end John's life for what he had done to her daughter.

The evil voice kept prompting her and listed the horrific details of what he enjoyed doing to Anna-Maria. Captain McGee was trying to get her to drop her weapon and see to reason. Selena had made up her mind. She tightened her index finger and prepared to fire. A brilliant bright light suddenly appeared behind John's body. The image of Anna-Maria in a white gown stood with the light behind her. She was smiling at her mother and mouthed the words, "don't do it mom. I love you".

Captain McGee inched his way closer as the evil voice inside John tempted Selena to commit murder. He was certain Selena would fire and knew he had to act fast. As he neared Selena, her face suddenly changed. She was staring behind John at something and her expression went from anguish and rage to peace. Shockingly, she lowered her weapon and backed away.

"Get down on the ground," Captain McGee ordered then stepped in front of Selena to face John himself.

It was over. John obeyed the captain and knelt down. He placed his hands above his head. The captain stepped forward, reading the Miranda Rights as he moved in close to apply restraints. John was too quick. He knocked the gun free from the captain's hands and tackled him to the ground. Selena was making her way out of the building when she heard the scuffle. Immediately, she spun around and dove behind a crate for cover as John fired several shots with the captain's gun.

Crouching and crawling behind the crate, Selena snuck towards John. He continued firing the pistol, then turned and ran towards the rear of the building. Selena returned fire, but John jumped behind more crates avoiding the bullets. John fired more shots and from the shadows, Selena couldn't see where he was. She fired blindly in the direction she had last saw him running.

John fired the last remaining rounds in the magazine and dropped the empty pistol. He was near the rear exit and decided to chance being shot and ran through. Selena fired warning shots into the heavy door, but it didn't stop him. John pushed the heavy doors open and escaped the building. Selena checked the captain. He was knocked unconscious, but still alive. Selena reloaded her pistol and gave chase.

The rear door was still open, and Selena could see John's back as she ran towards him. She couldn't allow him to escape. Her daughter's killer had finally revealed himself and she couldn't let him get away. She pushed herself to run faster.

The opening was large enough for Selena to run straight-through. John was so close, Selena prepared to tackle him.

Suddenly, one of the captain's officer who had been ordered to cover the exits stepped-out of the dark and shot John in the back with a beanbag round. John fell, face-down in the dirt. Seconds later, John rose to his feet and was about to continue fleeing. A second officer, who had since run up closer to where John fell, fired his taser. The wires shot out of the weapon and attached the metal prongs to the flesh of John's back. The fifty-thousand volts that shocked his body had finally brought John to a stop. It was finally over.

An ambulance and a swarm of more officers arrived at the airfield. Captain McGee sat on the back bumper of the ambulance while the paramedic stitched the wound on his forehead where John had struck him. Selena stood by herself away from the hangar. She had to take a moment to compose herself. The events of that evening had traumatized her. The sound of that evil voice describing what he had done to her daughter was still in her ears. She knew she had made the right decision, but she was struggling with the fact she didn't pull the trigger.

The officers had taken John into custody. His wrists had been double bound as well has his ankles. He had since recovered from the taser and was placed in the back of a patrol car. He sat in the backseat staring out of the window directly at Selena. A crooked smile formed on his face as if he had beaten them in some way. Selena stared right back. Though it was John's face, one she had seen and known for years, it now looked like a completely different person. In place of John's kind and handsome face was now the face of evil with the black eyes of the devil staring back at her.

"Get him the hell out of here." Selena ordered the officers as she turned to tend the captain.

CHAPTER SEVENTEEN

Six Months Later

The heavenly aroma of rich, Columbian coffee filled the morning air. The sound of the toaster oven's timer chimed aloud alerting it had finished baking whatever delicious treats had been placed inside. Selena had finished preparing herself for the day and sat at the table to enjoy a quick breakfast. As she enjoyed her coffee and bagel, she opened the news on her tablet and scrolled through the latest articles. She had been hailed a hero by the press for catching one of history's most notorious serial killers.

In the six moths since the events at the airfield, Selena received a promotion and an award from the mayor's office. The F.B.I. had taken over John's case, and Captain McGee was forced to retire. It bothered Selena, that a man as great as Captain Thomas McGee, who had dedicated decades of his life to cleaning up the streets of Lugar De Paz and stopping killers had been hung out to dry. The press held Captain McGee responsible for not seeing the monster John Davis really was the entire time he was under the captain's command. How could he, or anyone, have known.

This would be Selena's first official day as Sergeant-Detective Lopez, and she had mixed feelings about taking the job. If Captain McGee was considered responsible for not being aware of John's actions, Selena felt she should have been too. She worked alongside the man for years without seeing his true nature. It felt wrong receiving praise, promotions and awards while the Captain McGee was publicly shamed.

At the police headquarters, there was a small celebration in Selena's honor. She brought her box of things from her old desk and moved them into her new office. This was going to take some getting used to. She set up her new computer, telephone, and file folders and organizers the way she liked and was prepared to start the day. Before she could take on any new cases, however, she was scheduled to meet with the F.B.I. agent in charge of John Davis's, also known as Nathaniel Whitaker's, case.

The meeting had been set for several weeks. Selena had already given her statements many times over the past six months and really didn't want to have to go back to that night in her mind. She wanted to move forward with her life, finally, and put everything behind her. She resigned to the thought that as soon as she could appease the F.B.I. and their requests, she could be done with all of it.

The F.B.I. agent was a tall, clean-cut, slender man. He seemed the type of person more comfortable behind a computer screen than out in the field. He was quite young for an agent and had a difficult time making eye-contact with Selena. He tried not to make his attraction towards her obvious but failed tremendously. Selena broke the ice with a polite smile and handshake, adjusting herself behind the desk to not draw the young agent's attention to her exposed legs.

The meeting started, and Selena answered the agent's questions as best she could. They were the same questions she had been answering for months. The agent wanted to know about John's (Nathaniel's) cases. The F.B.I. had to go through each of John's cases throughout his entire career to find out which murders were truly committed by the men and women sent to prison for the deed, and which ones John did himself and had covered up. This would be no easy task and could take years if not longer.

The interview lasted several hours until the young agent felt he had all his questions answered. Selena knew this wouldn't be the last time she would have to answer these questions, or be involved in John's case, but hopefully this interview would satisfy the F.B.I.'s need for clarity for a while. She closed her files and prepared to leave the conference room. She was unprepared for what the agent was about to ask.

"Before I leave," the agent said as he collected his files, "do you remember Dr Morrison? I recall her mentioning you are a former patient."

"Yes, that's true. Why do ask?" Selena said as she started for the door.

"Well she was also John Davis's doctor prior to the discovery of his true identity as Nathaniel Whitaker," the agent explained. "The doctor was brought in to help with Mr. Whitaker's profile. Our own therapists weren't getting anywhere with him and she had previously built a rapport."

"Get to your question," Selena interrupted.

"Okay, Dr Morrison asked if you might consider coming in to help get Mr. Whitaker to talk," the agent answered.

"I have no interest in seeing that man ever again, I'm sorry," Selena said, opening the door wanting to leave the room.

"I understand Ms. Lopez. I saw the footage you captured that night. I know what happened to your daughter and cannot imagine the pain you have had to overcome. But consider the families. How many other daughters has this man tortured and killed? How many deaths have gone unavenged or with wrongful conviction? If there's a chance you can get those answers, couldn't you at least consider trying?" the agent said, switching from an authoritative federal agent to a more compassionate tone.

"I'll think about it," Selena said finally, leaving the room and closing the door behind her.

That evening, Selena sat at her laptop waiting for her new boyfriend to answer an impending chat session. She had started a relationship with the young officer she met while in Washington looking for answers. After the events at the airfield, she had gone back to Pine Valley for a few weeks to recover. There was an attraction between them during her first visit and the first place she could think of visiting was the peaceful small town where she met the handsome cop.

As the couple chatted, Selena explained to her new boyfriend what the F.B.I. requested of her. She told him she wanted to refuse and that she didn't know if she could face her former partner after everything that had been revealed. Her boyfriend understood her viewpoint and why she wanted to refuse. His passion for justice and his belief in helping the families gain closure made her think of possibly changing her mind.

The conversation ended, and Selena settled into bed. As she slept, she dreamt of her daughter. The night of John's admission, her daughter appeared to her in a vision. She hadn't mentioned it to anyone, not even her boyfriend. Over the past few months she tried to recapture that vision. She tried meditations and prayers, and nothing worked. That night, out of the blue, Anna-Maria came back to her in a dream.

The dream had begun with Selena back inside the hangar. In the dream she was surrounded by the bodies of John's victims. The corpses stood against the wall staring down at Selena. Stamped into their foreheads was the word, *Unsolved*. Selena walked among the bodies trying to apologize, begging for their forgiveness. Anna-Maria appeared in the light much like she had in the previous vision and repeatedly told Selena she had to help them.

With her sheets soaked in sweat, Selena woke up crying. She took what her daughter said in the dream as an omen. If there was any way she could help, she had to face her fear and go see John. This would be only way to truly get beyond what had happened and allow her daughter to finally rest peacefully. The decision was made, she would contact Dr Morrison and arrange a meeting.

In the days following her dream, Selena had arranged with the F.B.I. and Dr Morrison to meet. She drove several hours to the state mental health facility for the criminally insane. There was an extensive screening process with security, but the agent and Dr Morrison left word to give Selena a security pass. Selena surrendered her weapon and all other metal objects and followed the directions to where she was to meet Dr Morrison.

The elderly doctor waited in the interview room and was eager to greet Selena. They hadn't spoken with each other since before John's arrest. Selena switched therapists after she got back from her stress break in Washington. It was difficult to speak with her knowing she was treating the man who murdered her daughter. Selena ignored her impulse to be rude and dismiss the woman and maintained her calm façade.

"Hello Ms. Lopez," Dr Morrison greeted, shaking Selena's hand and inviting her to take a seat. "I understand this must be difficult for you, but I feel that with your help, we can get John, or Nathaniel, to open up and provide us the intel we need to solve his crimes."

"You're the doctor. I don't see how my being here is going change anything. You are supposed to be the mental health professional, how am I supposed to help?" Selena asked, frustratedly.

"Let me explain what has happened," Dr Morrison said, "with the information you uncovered in Washington, and the footage of his dramatic transformation six months ago, I have come to the conclusion that John, or rather, Nathaniel suffers from D.I.D. Dissociative Identity Disorder. Commonly referred to as, Multiple Personality Disorder."

Dr Morrison took her time to explain her findings. She explained that when Nathaniel was a little boy, his mother physically and sexually abused him. Being too young to deal with such trauma, Nathaniel's psyche became fragmented. He created a personality, a strong, powerful, figure who called himself, *The Shadow*. This dark figure was Nathaniel's protector. The Shadow would take the abuse and fight back as needed, allowing for young Nathaniel to retreat into his own mind to a peaceful place where all was well.

As Nathaniel grew older and more developed, the abuse increased. Nathaniel's mother allowed her clients to abuse her son and would take pictures and movies to later sell to anyone who would purchase them. All the while, young Nathaniel's persona remained safely hidden and guarded by The Shadow's protection. This abusive cycle continued for years, with young Nathaniel forever kept hidden away from the world, and The Shadow becoming the dominant personality dwelling within Nathaniel Whitaker's body.

Nathaniel Whitaker's intelligence was beyond measure for his age allowing him to beguile and fool anyone he wanted. After being detained and sent to the Mother Mary's Home for Boys, The Shadow learned he would have to get better at hiding his violent outbursts. He wanted to remain free in the outside world and impose his rage and hatred of women

on others simultaneously. To do both and survive, The
Shadow knew he needed a cover life.

During his time at Mother Mary's, Nathaniel
befriended a hiker from Tacoma named, Jonathan Davis. He
was a handsome young man who had been orphaned and was
somewhat of a loner. The boy enjoyed hiking and the outdoors
and his only aspiration in life was to remain a free spirit, a
wanderer of the wild with no ties to any place or anyone.
Nathaniel saw this as the perfect cover identity for his devious
acts. It was then, Nathaniel, The Shadow, took his first victim.

One afternoon, after overhearing the young hiker,
Jonathan Davis, telling the staff at the boy's home that
Nathaniel was breaking the house rules, The Shadow knew it
was time to act. He snuck away, unseen, to Jonathan's camp
and murdered him with the boy's switchblade. He took
polaroid pictures of the event to remember it by, but was
interrupted by his friend, Lucas Durante, a fellow resident at
the boy's home.

The Shadow was unable to cover up what he had done,
and he wasn't sure how much Lucas had seen. That night, The
Shadow returned to the campsite and made the death look like
an accident. There was a camper close by who tried to stop the
blaze and The Shadow added to his growing body count,
causing two victims at the campsite, making it look like they

were friends camping together caught in an unfortunate incident.

The dry vegetation made the fire spread easily; The Shadow aided its path up towards the where the boy's home stood. It was the perfect cover and escape. The residents of the house remained asleep as the building caught fire. In the confusion, The Shadow managed to subdue several of his bunkmates and leave them to the flames to allow him to fake Nathaniel Whitaker's demise. His only mistake was leaving Lucas Durante alive.

As the years passed, the newly created Jonathan Davis took shape. The Shadow had to tie one loose end before leaving the Pacific Northwest. He located the therapist, Dr. Warren Evans, assigned to care for the boys at Mother Mary's. He managed to get a hold of the doctor's patient list and targeted several young women. The Shadow drugged them and sexually assaulted them.

When the young women awoke, they were unaware of what had happened except for photographs of them taken inside the doctor's office. The Shadow managed to break-in to Dr Evans's office after hours to commit the assaults and took the pictures to leave as evidence for the women to find. With the good doctor's image and credibility disgraced, The Shadow returned to kill the doctor and make it look like a suicide. The last tie of his past had been cut, so The Shadow thought.

From there Jonathan Davis moved to Lugar De Paz, California. With The Shadow's incredible intellect, he was able to cleverly fabricate a past for his character that was believable. Over time, the false character created by The Shadow took hold and formed another personality within Nathaniel Whitaker's body. The new personality, John Davis, was completely unaware of the existence of The Shadow, or young Nathaniel, still protected in his own world. Jonathan Davis believed his fake past as his own reality, when all the while it was the lie The Shadow created as the fake cover life to protect himself.

As the Jonathan Davis personality progressed, he became a stronger personality that could overpower The Shadow and remain in control of Nathaniel's body for extended periods of time. Just as The Shadow was formed from all the anger and rage from Nathaniel's abused past, John's strength came from the best parts of Nathaniel's personality. John joined the police force, started dating, and eventually got married to his love, Catherine. He moved from patrol and was promoted to narcotics. He managed to maintain his job and become one of the most successful officers in the division. As his career got stronger, he made the rank of detective and joined homicide.

As John strengthened the reality of the cover life, The Shadow was able to watch from the sidelines. He discovered how to take control of the body and quench his thirst for violence and causing pain, then return to the background without John ever being aware that anything had happened. It wasn't until John had developed such strength, that The Shadow knew he had to defeat John. The only way to defeat him was to destroy all John had built in his life and take away all he had gained. The Shadow had to weaken John, to defeat him.

Selena had to remove herself for a moment. Hearing the description of Nathaniel's life, hearing that John, the personality she knew and respected, was not responsible for her daughter's death. That in fact, "The Shadow" was the actual one who killed her daughter and John was an innocent victim. The thought of everything she had learned was tormenting. She had hated John for the last six months after hearing the confession come from his very mouth. The vile description and joy of what he had done. She wasn't sure she believed the doctor.

"So, John or *'The Shadow'* as you call it, told this little tale?" Selena asked when she returned to the room.

"Partially," Dr Morrison responded, "your findings, plus the F.B.I. managed to get any and all information they could on the names involved, helped piece it all together. John has been locked away, and unable to speak since the incident at the airfield."

"What do you mean, 'locked away'?" Selena asked.

"During our sessions, before the airfield, John kept having a recurring nightmare. In the dream, he had the image of a hallway. A narrow hallway with slender doors on either side and an exit at the end. He always saw the walls as closing in on him, a terrible blackness would be behind him chasing him, he couldn't breathe, and he would have to reach the exit to wake up," Dr Morrison answered.

"And this means, what?" Selena asked, trying to make sense of it all.

"The hallway represents what is going on in Nathaniel's mind. You see, the personalities that exist within this body, live in their own rooms. They must exit the hallway to control the body. John believed himself to be in control of the body without any knowledge of the existence of the other personalities. When John thought he was having this nightmare, in actuality, it was The Shadow who had forced him into the hallway to take control." Dr Morrison explained.

"So, how did you learn about how this hallway system inside Nathaniel's mind works?" Selena inquired.

"At first, the only personality who I could speak with was The Shadow. He is mean, vile, and disgusting. That is who you captured on video, who taunted you about your daughter six month's ago. Eventually, a personality who calls himself, Nate emerged. Nate is a six-year-old boy. He is the original personality. He is who Nathaniel Whitaker was before the abuse, before creating The Shadow. He still believes he's a little boy," Dr Morrison continued.

"This Nate has told you everything. So, why do you need me?" Selena asked.

"Nate can only sneak through in small increments. He is terrified of The Shadow. But he knows which room John's is. With your help, you can bring John back, and we can solve these crimes. He trusts you. He knows you. You're considered safe to him," Dr Morrison said.

"What if The Shadow interferes, then all is lost," Selena said.

"We have to try," Dr Morrison said.

After coming this far, Selena wasn't about to turn back. She agreed she would do this. This wouldn't be for John, Dr Morrison, or the F.B.I. This wouldn't be for the victims. This wouldn't be for her boyfriend or herself. Selena did this for her daughter. She would face John, or this Shadow and get the answers she needed.

In the room next to where Selena and Dr Morrison had been talking. There was another interview room. John's body was in the room, curled on the floor, scribbling lines on a coloring book. As Selena entered, a small, soft, voice was singing a child's song. The voice was that of a child's. Selena took a seat at the table and observed. John, or the little boy, acted shy and wouldn't meet her gaze.

"Hello. Do you know who I am?" Selena asked finally.

"Hi. My name is Nathaniel Whitaker, but everybody calls me Nate," The little boy's voice exclaimed.

"Nice to meet you Nate. Can I talk with you?" Selena asked, motioning for him to sit at the table. He nodded and sat across from her.

"I'm not supposed to talk to you," Nate whispered.

"Of course, you can talk to me, who told you you're not supposed to?" Selena asked.

"Shadow says, you're bad like mommy. You want to hurt me," Nate said, his head focused on his drawing.

"Nate, I am not your mommy. I am a police officer. I am a good guy. I put bad guys in jail. You can talk to me," Selena said softly, reaching out and touching his arm.

"Dr M says I have to help get John out," Nate said.

"Can you do that?" Selena asked.

Nate didn't respond. An expression of fear came across his face and he retreated to the corner of the room. Selena took the papers off the table and looked through them. They were the scribbled drawings of a kindergarten student. There were countless pictures of a little boy with a larger, dark figure next to him. Each new drawing depicted scenes that Dr Morrison had described, including the red hallway.

To bring the boy, Nate, back to conversation, Selena asked him to tell her about his drawings. He became interested and sat next to her. He described each picture in detail. He described The Shadow as being scary, but only when Nate doesn't listen to the rules. There was a picture of a woman in a dress, which Nate described as a woman named, V who talked funny but wore sparkly dresses and played toys with him.

With each new picture Nate painted a vivid picture of how shattered John's, or Nathaniel Whitaker's, mind really was. The boy named several different names of people in the hallway he often saw there. There was a man with the name "Tricks" who wore his hat backwards and used bad language, there were several others that Nate wasn't allowed to meet because The Shadow ordered him not too.

Nate described his room within the hallway. He mentioned he wasn't allowed in The Shadow's room but had spent time with the woman he named, V in hers. Selena wondered if he was describing Valentina as the woman in sparkling dresses. The boy then pointed at his drawing of the hallway, saying John's room was at the end, in the dark, where he was too scared to go. The boy said The Shadow threatened to hurt him if he went too far down the hallway. He refused to go.

"Nate, do you like superheroes?" Selena asked while the boy kept showing his drawings.

"Yep. My favourite is Superman," the boy said proudly.

"Good. I like Superman too. I need you to be like Superman now. Superman isn't scared of anyone. He certainly isn't scared of The Shadow. I need you to be like Superman and go unlock John from his room. Help him come here so that I can speak to him okay?" Selena asked. She was trying to build the boy's courage.

The boy kept arguing and saying how scared he was to disobey The Shadow. Selena kept telling tales of how strong the boy's hero was and that The Shadow couldn't hurt him. She told Nate about how strong John was and that if he helped get John out of his room, John would protect him from The Shadow's wrath. It took some convincing, but the boy finally agreed. Selena sat back in her chair and watched John's body slump forward in his chair. Nate had entered the hallway and left control of the body.

There was a long delay as John's body sat, slumped forward against the table. Selena waved her hand in front of his face and snapped her fingers near his ears to see if this was a ploy. There was no movement. There was no one in control of the body. Suddenly, John's body jolted back in the chair. John's eyes opened wide and he gasped for air. He was struggling to catch his breath.

The guards swarmed into the room to protect Selena, but she told them to stand back. John regulated his breath and seemed happy to see Selena. She remained guarded. This was still the body that killed her daughter, it was still those hands that tortured her and broke her. This was still the face who spoke such vile things of what he had done. Selena tried to put that to the back of her mind and maintain a clear view of her mission and of what she knew had to be done. She focused on John's eyes as the black had turned back to the intense royal blue she was used to seeing when she looked at her old partner.

"John?" Selena asked, "it's me Selena."

"Where am I?" he asked, looking around the room confused.

"It is way too complicated to explain and I don't know how much time we have John. You need to focus, and you need to help me," Selena explained.

John tried to speak but Selena stopped him. She told him a very vague story of what had happened and why he had been detained in a mental institution. It was difficult to make him see, but Selena told John everything Dr Morrison had told her. She explained the meaning of the hallway nightmare and that there were different personalities living within his mind. John sat in disbelief of what was being told to him.

Eventually, John mentioned where he had been for the past six months. He couldn't remember what happened at the airfield that night. The last thing he remembered was screaming at Valentina as she sat in a chair then he woke up in a small motel room with no windows. The door was locked, and he couldn't escape. He could hear voices all around him, but no one could hear his screams for help. There was no sense of time and he was unaware how long he was locked in the room.

John mentioned that right before he woke up, a little boy opened his door and had taken him by the hand, walking him up the hallway that he had seen in his dreams many times. As they walked, he read the names posted on the doors as they neared the exit. He recognized, "Duke", the door directly across from John's, "Tricks", was his old confidential informant, "Valentina" was his exotic dancer girlfriend, "Nate", the little boy who was helping him, "The Shadow", whose door was nearest the exit.

As John described his experience to Selena, Dr Morrison entered the room. John didn't recognize the older woman who sat down to talk with him. He recalled his sessions with Dr Morrison and described her being very young, beautiful, and voluptuous. Dr Morrison explained this was one of his many delusions. They were running out of time. They didn't know how long The Shadow would allow John to control the body. He was now the stronger personality since breaking John's spirit.

Dr Morrison told John what he had to do. She told him that John had to name all The Shadow's victims to set things right. John could still be the hero detective he set out to be. He could end many families' sufferings. All he had to do was enter the hallway and confront The Shadow. It wouldn't be easy, but Dr Morrison stressed upon him the importance of solving these crimes. She reaffirmed his sense of duty and justice until he was ready. Selena told him she believed in him, that if anyone could do it, he could. John closed his eyes and prepared to face, The Shadow.

***

There was blackness all around and with absolutely no sound. John felt around with his hands until he found a light switch. The light came on to reveal he had successfully returned to the small motel room. There were no windows, and everything was a different shade of red. He always hated the color and now it was all around him. John had Selena's and Dr Morrison's encouraging words in his thoughts, and he knew what he needed to do.

The door to the room was locked. John had tried to open this door before, but it was too strong, and it wouldn't budge. The only way it had opened was with the help of the little boy, Nate. It seemed weaker somehow, John felt it giving way to his force. He placed his foot on the side of the wall and pulled. The door cracked; it was breaking loose. John pulled with everything he had. The door popped open and John fell back from the force.

Outside the room, the hallway was exactly as John remembered from his nightmares. This time, however, he didn't feel afraid. He could breathe easier, and he felt he could walk freely. He walked towards the end of the hall towards the exit door. The doors were all labelled with names. John walked by Duke's and Tricks' room, then Valentina's. He kept going. He saw Nate's room then finally, The Shadow's. The crippling fear was starting to return as he opened the door and ventured inside.

The walls of the room were obsidian. They looked wet as if they were dripping tar. There was no sign of the dark figure. John looked around the room, displayed on the walls were polaroid pictures of women and men's faces and underneath there were names written in blood. These were trophies. Mental pictures The Shadow had collected of his victims at the time of their death.

The faces all shared the same petrified expression. John was overcome with sorrow looking at all the lives The Shadow had destroyed. He read the many names until he came to Anna-Maria's. He continued reading until he came to the second last picture of the gruesome collage. It was his wife Catherine. The last picture on the wall, at the end of this list, was a picture of John.

Back in the interview room of the mental institution, Dr Morrison and Selena watched John's body intently for any sign of him. He jarred and mumbled until finally his hand mimicked the motion of writing. Selena quickly placed a pen in his hand and a paper beneath its tip. Immediately, John's hand responded by writing line after line. He was listing the names of The Shadow's many victims.

Inside The Shadow's room, John could feel The Shadow returning. He could hear him coming up the hallway. John had found a piece of paper and pen on the desk in The Shadow's room and was writing down the names underneath each polaroid picture. He was writing as fast as he could. The bass of The Shadow's thunderous footsteps vibrated through the floor under John's feet. The Shadow was almost at the door.

John was so close. He had the last few names to write down. The pounding footsteps drew closer and closer. John did his best to ignore his rising fear. He had to complete this mission. He knew somehow, someway, his writing was getting through to Selena and Dr Morrison. He managed to get to the last name. As he finished writing the name "Catherine Davis", the dark figure, The Shadow burst into the room. The battle was about to begin.

The paper on top of the interview room's table was filled with names. Dr Morrison collected the paper and read. Selena could recognize many of the names listed on the paper. John's body had stopped moving after writing Catherine's name. Suddenly, John's body went into a full-blown seizure. His body slammed against the surface of the table, then rolled onto the floor. His muscles twisted and contorted as he thrashed, writhed, and kicked on the floor.

Dr Morrison directed everyone to get back and let him ride the seizure out. It lasted several minutes until John went completely limp and stopped struggling. He was placed on a stretcher and rushed to the medical unit. Whatever happened within John's mind was a terrible struggle. An epic battle. Only time would tell which personalities survived and which ones perished. At least John had succeeded in listing The Shadow's victims. He had fulfilled his promise and accomplished his mission, though it may have cost him his life.

* * *

Outside the institution, Selena was wiping tears from her eyes as she walked back to her car with Dr Morrison beside her. The doctor thanked her for showing the courage and fortitude to come and face John. Selena hoped that now with the list of the victim's names this case could finally be closed. She hugged the doctor before getting into her car. It was a trying day, and all she wanted was a tall drink, and to speak with her boyfriend.

As she drove away from the institution, Selena felt better about going. She promised her daughter she would confront John and help Dr Morrison retrieve the names of all the people John had killed. As difficult as it was to do and as terrifying as it was to witness, Selena had kept her promise. A sense of peace and clarity came over her, and she could see clearly what she wanted from her life now. It was time to make a change. It was time to take a different path.

CHAPTER EIGHTEEN

In the year that followed the interview at the mental institution back in California, Selena had quit her job as sergeant and moved away from Lugar De Paz, the only city she had ever lived. It was far too difficult to return to her old home. She had lost too much in that place. Everywhere she looked she was haunted by her partner's evil deeds. Fearing she would return to her path of self-destruction, Selena decided to move to Washington.

The small town of Pine Valley had a lasting effect on Selena. She enjoyed the sense of community and peace. Her boyfriend, the young officer who had helped her with her investigation, had been promoted to Sherriff, since his predecessor had since retired. Selena's boyfriend was well-known and liked among the community. It was an easy election for him to win.

With the proceeds of the sale of her house in California, and her limited savings, Selena purchased a popular, local pub in town. She no longer wanted the stress of police work. She had her fill of corpses and chasing bad guys. She wanted to enjoy her life. Her partner, co-owner and manager, was her old friend, former Captain Thomas McGee. He had taken Selena's suggestion to move to Pine Valley,

Washington when he was forced to retire from the police force.

Life had become simpler and Selena finally felt what happiness could be again. As she was planning her upcoming, first year anniversary of moving to Pine Valley, Selena was sitting in her kitchen jotting down ideas for the celebration at the bar. The phone rang, and Selena answered it in her polite manner, thinking it was one of her waitresses or bartenders calling in sick for their shift. She wasn't expecting who would be on the other line.

The call was from Dr Morrison. She was calling to tell Selena that John had shown great progress in his treatments over the past year and the decision was being made to move him to a minimum-security hospital in hopes of completing his treatment and eventually releasing him. Selena was appalled. She understood that the personality of John wasn't responsible for the lives he had taken, but he was sick. There was no treatment that could remove that evil that dwelled within him.

After the interview at the institution the year before, after John's massive seizure. He had fallen into a catatonic state for nearly two months. When he woke up, he awoke as the personality of Nate. Eventually Dr Morrison brought back John's personality who told her he had destroyed The Shadow that day when he wrote down the victim's names. Since then he appeared to be the dominant personality, with no sign of The Shadow.

The hearing for the decision to eventually release John, which Dr Morrison had mentioned, was being based on the past year's treatments and John's positive response to them. The doctor seemed confident that it was the right thing and John was ready to start reintegrating into the world. Selena knew this had to be stopped. Though John's personality was not responsible, his body had to remain locked-away from the public. He could never be released. If he was ever let free, there was no guarantee The Shadow wouldn't reappear to kill again.

Selena arranged for Captain McGee to take care of the bar. She kissed her boyfriend, the Sherriff, and explained her reasoning for returning to California. He gave her his full support and offered to accompany her. This was something she had to do alone. She had to go back to California and stop the release of a potentially dangerous killer. She left as soon as she could to prevent this from happening.

After explaining herself to Dr Morrison and why she had to come down, Selena was granted access to speak with John. Dr Morrison didn't appreciate having her judgement questioned but thought once Selena spoke to her patient, she could see for herself the progress that had been made. Once

John proved to Selena face-to-face that he was in control, Dr Morrison felt confident that Selena would support her decision of helping John.

The interview room had been set up. The cameras and microphones were switched on to record everything. Selena walked in and sat down. She purposefully dressed in her most revealing clothing to resemble the prostitutes and strippers that made up The Shadow's list of victims. The real John had always seen her as a little sister and would never comment on or notice Selena's sexuality. The Shadow was a devious pervert who preyed upon and targeted women dressed in this way. She knew, being dressed in this attire would be the best way to provoke a reaction.

The guards opened the door and walked John in. His restraints had been removed and the guards stepped outside. They assured Selena that they were right outside the door should she need them. John snuck a quick glimpse at Selena's bulging cleavage, and her exposed legs covered in fishnet stockings protruding from her extremely short skirt as he was brought in. It was subtle. Perhaps too subtle for the cameras or Dr Morrison, but Selena noticed the look immediately.

"Selena. It's so good to see you. You look well. How are things?" John said, his voice seemed hoarse.

"Fine," Selena answered, adjusting her bra to further draw John's attention towards her near fully exposed breasts, "how is John?"

"I'm good," John responded, "getting better and better everyday."

"No Shadow," Selena challenged. She glared back into the black holes where she once saw John's brilliant blue eyes. After a long pause, she returned, "I don't care how you're doing. I want to speak to John."

"Selena, I am John, okay, It's me," John replied urgently with the undertone of a slight, nervous laugh.

"You know a thought that always makes me smile?" Selena asked rhetorically, "kicking your face back in that warehouse. Slicing you with your own knife. As strong as you are and as many women as you forced yourself upon, you could never have me."

"Selena," John said, his voice cracked. Anger had made his face red and his hands clench. The impersonation of John's voice was slipping. "This is unnecessary, I'm John. It's me, your old partner."

"I was the only one who escaped wasn't I? I was the only one you couldn't dominate, and you never will. How does that make you feel Shadow?" Selena said.

She stood up from her chair and leaned on the cold steel of the interview table so John could view her entire body. She tugged at the opening of her shirt slightly and pulled her bra down and revealed more skin. She leaned her backside against the side of the table and slowly raised the front of her already short skirt with her free hand. He appeared to shudder. He glared back at her with a seething expression of hatred.

"I'm sorry, Selena," he said, removing a cigarette from his pocket with his left hand and lighting it. His voice was starting to change to that evil, hoarse tone. He sat back in his chair and casually puffed at the cigarette, drawing each drag away with the smoldering tube of tobacco held daintily in between the knuckles of his left index and middle fingers. "I don't know why you're acting like this, or why you don't believe me. I'm not going to say it again. I am John."

"No, you're not," Selena said. She bent over the table to get closer to his face and stare him directly in his eyes one last time, "but thanks for proving that to me. You see, John's eyes are a strikingly, beautiful blue, not empty and back like yours."

Selena stood and slowly sauntered towards the door. As she walked, she could feel The Shadow's eyes upon her body, the one woman he could never defile. She neared the door then turned her head and added, "By the way, Shadow,

John is right-handed, not a lefty. He despised cigarettes with a passion and would never smoke. Thanks for the demonstration. It was a nice try. Good luck to you, Shadow."

Selena had a proud smile as she slowly walked out of the door. She could see in an instant that it wasn't John she had seen in those eyes. The brilliant blue color of the real John Davis's eyes had once again disappeared and in its place was the empty blackness of evil. The devil's eyes. It was the same evil she had seen back in the hangar at that airfield. Whatever happened to John after he managed to get the victim's names was unclear. But the man seated at the interview table. The man proudly enjoying his cigarette was certainly not John. It was most definitely The Shadow.

"You're far too clever for me my dear," the Shadow said, his evil, graveled voice reverberating off the walls of the small room. The sound made Selena cringe as she exited the door and entered the hallway. "Let's hope these wankers are as clever as you. I'll see you soon sweetheart. I know how much you've missed sweet Anna-Maria. You'll join her soon bitch. I promise you."

"Have a nice life," Selena said with her back turned. She was struggling to maintain her composed defiance of the Shadow's taunts.

"You think you've won whore? You think I won't have you?" the vile, hoarse voice shouted like some demonic presence. "You won't get far. I may not have gotten you before, but I will. You'll see honey. Oh, you'll see. I'll have you. You'll be nothing but a picture on my wall like the rest of them."

The door opened, and Selena exited. As she walked down the corridor by Dr Morrison, the beleaguered doctor stared at her in utter disbelief. The Shadow's voice could be heard in the hallway as he threatened and screamed. He called out to Selena, vowing that he would finish what he had started. That she would never be safe from him. Selena ignored every word. She had her new life waiting for her. She walked down the narrow hallway to the exit door at its end, towards the bright light of day. Towards her freedom.

THE END

ACKNOWLEDGEMENTS

I would like to thank my beautiful girlfriend for her love and support while I achieved my dream of being a published author.

Love and thanks to my wonderful mother who not only brought me into this world, has saved my life many times over. Her love and wisdom have formed the man I am today.

Many thanks to my friends and family for their encouragement in pursing this dream.

Finally, to my teacher who was the first to recognize my talent in writing and was the first person to put me on the path to become an author.

Made in the USA
Middletown, DE
31 January 2023

23626728R00229